# THE HIGH FLYER

# THE HIGH FLYER

*A Ben Norton Aviation Mystery*

## Elizabeth Darrell

This first world edition published 2016
in Great Britain and the USA by
SEVERN HOUSE PUBLISHERS LTD of
19 Cedar Road, Sutton, Surrey, England, SM2 5DA.
Trade paperback edition first published
in Great Britain and the USA 2016 by
SEVERN HOUSE PUBLISHERS LTD

British Library Cataloguing in Publication Data

Darrell, Elizabeth author.
  The high flyer.
  1. Test pilots–Fiction. 2. Suspense fiction.
  I. Title
  823.9'14-dc23

ISBN-13: 978-0-7278-8573-9 (cased)
ISBN-13: 978-1-84751-681-7 (trade paper)
ISBN-13: 978-1-78010-299-3 (e-book)

*All Severn House titles are printed on acid-free paper.*

Severn House Publishers support the Forest Stewardship Council™ [FSC™],
the leading international forest certification organisation.
All our titles that are printed on FSC certified paper carry the FSC logo.

MIX
Paper from
responsible sources
FSC
www.fsc.org   FSC® C013056

Typeset by Palimpsest Book Production Ltd.,
Falkirk, Stirlingshire, Scotland.
Printed and bound in Great Britain by
TJ International, Padstow, Cornwall.

# ONE

He was there when it happened. Not by invitation. He had simply waved a piece of card resembling an official pass and entered the small enclosure with a bunch of newspapermen. Nobody questioned his right to be there.

Chris Peterson had taken off and flown over Pitman Hill in preparation for his display of aerobatics designed to impress the company directors, government ministers and several high-ranking RAF officers who clustered on the balcony with the principal shareholders of Marshfield Aviation. Peterson would have been told to fly his heart out during the next twenty minutes.

Binoculars were raised to capture the first glimpse of the silver aircraft's reappearance over the hill. It approached and flashed past causing heads to swing from left to right before tilting back to follow the steep climb out over the sea.

As he watched the dazzling display his heartbeat quickened and his senses fizzed with remembered elation. He was mentally in a cockpit with icy gusts buffeting his face. He smelled the hot fuel, felt the throb of the engine, heard the stutter of his guns and shivered with that unique mix of fear and excitement on sighting the enemy. It was the height of living . . . and possibly dying.

Peterson was nearing the end of his thrilling demonstration when he flew fast and breathtakingly low over the airfield before executing a high-climbing roll which was impressive enough to round off the display. However, always a show-off, Peterson came again out of the sun in a daring high-speed dive which would surely have everyone holding their breath.

As he watched in reluctant admiration his blood began to freeze. Peterson was not pulling out of the downward plunge. 'Come on! Come on!' he breathed urgently, although he knew it was too late.

He was lost in past horror as the vaunted new fighter spiralled into the ground at a speed that caused the earth to tremble under his feet. A fearsome explosion of sound heralded the destruction of man and machine, and he was instantly back to that time when ending their lives in such a way was their greatest dread. A time when he and Chris Peterson had been as close as brothers. A time when that bond had been tested to the limit and irrevocably broken.

The newsmen around him were excitedly photographing the wreckage filling a crater, but shock rooted him to the spot. He had come here intending to blackmail Peterson into giving him what he badly wanted. Now he could just walk in and take it. As his staring eyes watched the *Lance* fighter disintegrate around the mangled body of the pilot, he realized it would be an empty victory.

The funeral attracted a large crowd. Peterson had been a war hero; a pilot of great skill and daring who had shot down eighteen of the enemy including the German ace Gustav Blomfeld, for which deed he had received a medal and promotion. Sir Edwin Lance would almost certainly have wanted a quiet service, but the British public revered their heroes even twelve years after the devastating war had ended. They turned out in their hundreds, wearing their Sunday best, to throw flowers on the horse-drawn hearse during its slow progress from Clanford House to the village church.

He bided his time, making no attempt to mingle with the Lance family and their close friends who filled the pews. No sign, of course, of those important men who had witnessed the tragic end to a superb display designed to persuade them into investing in mass production of Marshfield's prototype aircraft.

He had no difficulty in identifying the widow. Barely a few months passed without pictures in newspapers or magazines of Julia Peterson, née Lance, doing what socialites like her did to fill their days. She was playing her role to perfection for the benefit of the Press, as well as for the uninvited hoi polloi trampling the flowers on the graves in their determination to see and hear everything, but rumour had it the marriage had been a rocky one.

The mourners were dispersing, treading carefully between ancient and modern gravestones to reach their cars filling the lane outside the small churchyard when he finally approached and offered formal condolences.

Julia's stony stare raked him from head to foot. 'Journalist? Marshfield employee? Village worthy?' she queried tonelessly.

He put out his hand and held it steady. 'Ben Norton. Chris and I flew together during the war, often on dawn patrol. We were a highly successful pair.'

When she could no longer ignore his hand she briefly shook it. 'My husband never talked about the war, I'm afraid, or about his colleagues during those years.'

He nodded, saying easily, 'Most of us tended to put those experiences behind us. I went as far as Egypt in a bid to forget people I'd known and things I'd done, but when I read of Chris's tragic death I knew I had to say a personal farewell to a man who had shared so many perilous hours in the air with me.' He produced a sad smile. 'It's impossible to completely erase those memories, you see.'

His moment was instantly ruined by a blonde in a black dress and a heavily veiled hat who pushed between them crying, 'Dahling, so yearn to stay and comfort you, but Simon has to get back to the bloody House for a vital debate. Divine service. I cried right through it. You're being so wonderfully stoic. I'd utterly dissolve if it was Simon going from my life forever.' She made kissing sounds beside each of Julia's cheeks. 'Must fly, dahling. Call me any time! Don't try to bear it alone.'

She went off to join a balding man shaking the hand of Sir Edwin Lance while gripping the man's shoulder in commiseration. For what? The loss of his son-in-law, his test pilot or the aircraft designed to put Marshfield up with the aviation giants and revive grossly flagging company profits, wondered Ben as he watched them.

'So shallow!'

Ben turned back to see Julia's mouth twisted cynically as she observed the scene he had found so interesting. 'Lord Murchison?'

Still eyeing the group, she gave a slight shake of her head. 'Simon's a harmless enough fool, but Cynthia can cause serious trouble with her heedless blabbing.' Focusing again on Ben, there was now a hint of curiosity in her manner. 'You'll come back to the house, Captain Norton.'

It was a statement, not an invitation. He guessed she liked to be in command, but her peremptory manner washed over him. He had intended going back to the house, anyway. She had simply made it easy for him. As he walked the short distance to Clanford House with other black-clad mourners he decided to retain the rank Julia had instinctively bestowed on him. In this status-conscious set it would serve him well, particularly when he encountered Sir Edwin's heir.

The gravelled drive widened to a half moon, the straight side of which abutted the pale stone facade of the three storey house. It had been the home of the Lance family since 1862, having been gifted to Sir Godfrey Lance for his distinguished service in India. And, if rumour could be believed, for another more delicate service concerning one of Her Majesty's erring offspring.

Ben studied the manor with great interest. Chris had certainly done well for himself by marrying into this family. How much would he have been prepared to do in order to hold on to it? Ben would now never find out. The interior matched up to the photographs in glossy magazines taken during important social occasions, including Chris and Julia's wedding. Ben had bought copies when they reached Alexandria and raged inwardly. He could have put pressure on his former friend then but there had been nothing he had wanted from Chris at that stage. As soon as he had read about the radical warplane he had known his time had come.

They gathered in a long salon richly decorated in blue and gold with Chinese figured brocade curtains. Footmen moved among the grave-faced guests offering drinks, while a butler supervised an array of cocktail fare arranged on a long table near two sets of French windows giving views of lawns, trees and statuary. These were deeply recessed with long cushioned seats from which to enjoy sight of the perfectly tended grounds when it was impossible to wander there. Ben stationed himself in one of these alcoves with a plate of canapés and a glass of red wine, hoping that wherever Chris was now he could see Flight Sergeant Jack Norton lording it up as if to the manner born.

Many of the guests were strangers but Ben's scrapbook collection of pictures and articles about Marshfield Aviation and the Lance family now made it easy enough for him to identify the major players. Ray Povey, chief engineer, was standing with a group of men Ben guessed were heads of the various departments in the extensive workshops. All were expressionless, tight-lipped, clearly anxious for enough time to elapse to allow them to leave. Near them a quartet of women in black costumes which could be their normal working clothes, spoke in hushed tones and kept looking at the ornate clock on the wall. Secretaries? Housekeeper? Ben had no interest in these people.

By the other recessed French windows Freddie Lance, playboy, womanizer, prince of motor racing circuits all over Europe was entertaining several girls and young men who were emptying the trays of full glasses each time the footmen passed. Before long they would all be irresponsibly drunk enough to create a scene. Ben had met shallow, egotistical characters like Freddie during the war, but they had at least gone bravely into battle when the time came. This one unfortunately would never face the test. Ben had no interest in Sir Edwin's younger son, either.

In the centre of the room the widow was flanked by her father and elder brother in a demonstration of family support, but their drawn expressions were almost certainly prompted by the disastrous failure of their hope for the future more than the moving eulogy for Chris. Pilots were two a penny. Flying machines were monstrously expensive to develop.

Sir Edwin Lance was first and foremost a businessman; an entrepreneur who had had the foresight to recognize that the future for warfare lay heavily with aerial weapons. In short, fighters with speed, manoeuvrability and quick-firing guns. He had supplied the capital, driving force and corporate know-how to produce the *Lance*, but had never flown through the sky, elated by the wonderful sense of freedom not possible on the ground. He had never had a love affair with aeroplanes.

Ben's gaze left the tall, grey-moustached knight, slid over Julia, and fastened on the heir. He had not seen Major Hugo Lance for thirteen years, but he had never forgotten that handsome, autocratic face with steely grey eyes that had looked right through him as if he was not standing there beside Chris. Major Lance had been blinded during the final months of the war, so he would be unable to repeat that insult when introduced to Captain Ben Norton. His mouth twisted in a wry smile. A small settlement of an old score perhaps, but a satisfying one to be getting on with, knowing the real payback was yet to come.

Time to make his move. Putting his empty plate on the cushioned seat, Ben crossed to where Roger Hall, Marshfield's chief designer, stood alone in the far corner he had occupied since entering after the funeral. The lean, round-shouldered man looked to be in a state of shock, as well he might. If Ben himself had designed an aircraft which had crashed during its commercial display, killing the pilot, he would be feeling suicidal.

Reaching Hall, Ben said conversationally, 'Impressive funeral, wasn't it? Indicative of how highly regarded by the British public Chris was.'

'Yes.'

Hall's curt reply suggested he wanted to be left to wallow in his misery but, feigning ignorance, Ben asked, 'Friend of the family?'

The other man's drawn features worked nervously. 'You could say that.'

'Tragedy seems to dog them, doesn't it? Lady Lance's lingering terminal illness, Hugo's legacy of the war, now Julia's tragic loss. One dreads Freddie completing the cycle on a racetrack one of these days.'

'Yes.'

It was hard going but Ben persisted. 'Of course, I only read about all that in newspapers. Never met them until today.' When Hall frowned, he added, 'Feel a bit awkward, really, but when I told Julia how close Chris and I had been she insisted I come here after the service.'

Hall's frown deepened.

'So I explained to her that I moved out to the Middle East at the end of the war. Flew over for the funeral. Although we'd lost touch over the years the bond was still strong enough for me to want to pay my last respects to a man who had shared four exacting years of my life.'

'Oh?'

A small spark of interest now, so Ben embarked on the speech he had worked on in his room in the pub last night. 'Chris and I were dubbed "The Skylarks" by the rest of the squadron because we did the dawn patrols so often. A perfect partnership from the word go. No need to signal our intentions because we instinctively knew what the other would do in an encounter with the Hun. In situations when half the squadron was up we still worked in tandem during any scrap.' He gave a faint smile. 'The boys straight from school with no more than a few hours of training could be a bloody nuisance, fouling up chances of downing the enemy.'

'Flew over from where?' came the sudden brusque question.

Ben knew Hall had played the right card. The rest should be easy.

'Alexandria. My base. I bummed around Cairo for the first two years after the war, taking any job that kept me from starving. When I'd driven the demons to the far recesses of my mind I moved up to Alex, found a sponsor, and set up an air freight company. In the past ten years I've repaid my sponsor, bought out a rival and expanded enough to warrant establishing several support centres along the Med.' He smiled. 'I refuelled there free of charge, of course, but the French demanded a king's ransom before they filled my tanks. Can't blame them. We made a dog's dinner of their country then skedaddled leaving them to it.'

Hall's interest was obvious now. 'You flew yourself here from Alex?'

'That's right. Two of my pilots are standing by to fly the kite back, if necessary.'

'If necessary?'

Oh, Roger Hall was saying exactly the right things! 'I might stay in England for a spell. Hadn't counted on the strength of nostalgia for my homeland. So many memories returning hot on the heels of each other.' He gave a faint sigh. 'Thinking of Chris being in on the birth of a machine as exciting as the *Lance* brought an urge to return to that brand of flying.' Another sigh filled the pause nicely. 'In spite of what happened.' Ben allowed silence to reign for some moments, before continuing. 'Christ, the designer must be feeling pretty bloody right now. Most unlikely to have been pilot error. Chris was far too experienced to make a mistake during a manoeuvre he'd done so many times. There has to be a flaw in the design.'

'No!' It was snapped out fiercely as Hall slapped a clenched fist into the palm of his other hand. 'We covered everything. Tested and retested. He was perfectly confident when he climbed into the cockpit. There's no flaw! He made no mistake! He tried to tell me over the radio, but his voice was so faint I . . .'

Loud shrieks of laughter caused all conversation to cease as every person in the room stared at the girls in the alcove with Freddie Lance, who were clinging drunkenly to him for support. The silence continued while Julia crossed to her brother and spoke in a furious undertone. To his credit, Freddie turned scarlet and shook the girls off as he made his quiet apology then opened the French windows and ushered his rowdy friends out to the terrace.

In turning away Julia caught sight of Ben and approached him, mastering her anger with well-bred social aplomb.

'Captain Norton, I'm sorry to have neglected you, but I see you've already made the acquaintance of our chief designer. Let me introduce you to my father and my other brother.'

She took his arm as he cursed her intervention, and led him to where the members of her family were saying goodbye to guests eager to be on their way. Waiting for the farewells to end, she edged Ben forward. 'Father, you haven't yet met Captain Norton who served with Chris during the war. He flew over from Egypt to attend the funeral.'

Sir Edwin gave a brief nod as he shook Ben's hand. 'Good of you, Captain. I'm sure you'll have a few things to talk over with my son, but you'll have to excuse me. Several important telephone calls to make.' With a vague wave of his hand towards his heir, which served as an introduction, he murmured a few words to Julia and walked off.

Hugo offered his hand. 'Yes, good of you to come, Captain Norton. Friendships forged during those dark days remain strong, don't they?' As Ben completed the handshake, he asked, 'Where were you based?'

Ben named a few areas where his squadron had set up temporary camps as the war had progressed, which inevitably led to the subject he wanted to avoid.

'Ah, before Chris transferred to my squadron.'

'That's right. He was badly missed.'

'Particularly by you, I imagine,' put in Julia, unconsciously adding to the tricky moment. 'You said you and Chris had been a very successful pair on dawn patrols.'

Hugo frowned, so Ben swiftly turned the conversation in another direction. He found it unnerving to look at those grey eyes even though he knew they could not see him.

'How different it would have been if we'd had an aircraft like the *Lance* in those days, eh sir?'

The man's face gave away the depth of the gravity which afflicted this family at present, but he managed to say, 'Well . . . yes. Yes, indeed.'

'I plan to spend a month or two checking the prospects for expansion of my air freight business here in England,' Ben said, moving on to the vital subject. 'Now's the time to be one jump ahead of competitors; seize the bull by the horns before some other chap does.' He smiled, hoping Hugo would hear it in his tone. 'Like Marshfield has done. Seen the need for an aircraft like the *Lance* before all those short-sighted stuffed shirts at the War Office wake up to the fact. We can't rest on our laurels while they're forging ahead with production of several new models in Germany.'

Hugo Lance took the bait. 'You fly freight in the Middle East?'

'And all along the Med. Built the company up from scratch in Alex, then gradually extended the routes as far as Gibraltar. Last year Norton Freight began operating from Lille. Brought back some memories, you bet.'

Realizing he was skirting dangerous ground again, Ben hurriedly broached the real reason for his projected stay in England.

'Before I move on I'd very much like to look over your workshops, departmental offices, hangars; get some idea of how difficult it might be to set up a full-scale aerial operation in this country.' Into the expected pause, he said, 'Of course, I know you'll be hard at it after the tragedy last week, although Roger Hall told me just now he was certain there was no design flaw. We all know Chris was a top rate pilot. He would certainly have picked up even the slightest fault before agreeing to undertake a proving flight.' He glanced at Julia. 'Has there been any evidence of a medical condition which could have caused Chris to lose consciousness?'

'You're taking great interest in what is a purely Marshfield affair,' she said speculatively.

'Forgive me, Mrs Peterson, but when a superb aircraft flown by a man at the top of his profession fails so disastrously, it's of vital interest to all pilots. I knew Chris the aviator, and so did you, sir,' he continued, turning instinctively to Hugo. 'When something like this occurs we're driven to find out why, aren't we? Surely we owe it to the man we've just said a final farewell to.' Allowing a reverent pause he added more forcefully, 'And to the team that created the *Lance*.'

During the subsequent silence it was perfectly clear to Ben, if not to Julia, that it was those final eight words that stirred Hugo Lance into a thoughtful response.

'You intend to spend a couple of months over here before returning to Alex, Captain Norton?' At Ben's affirmative, he continued. 'You're welcome to cast your eyes over the Marshfield establishment, talk to departmental managers and our work force to get some idea of whether to extend your business this far from your headquarters. It's an ambitious project. You'll find conditions vastly different from Egypt and places along the southern Med coast. Labour costs will be trebled if not more, and you'll be astounded by what you'd have to lay out for land compared with acres of semi-desert scrubland in Misratah, Tunis or Oran.'

Speaking like the avaricious businessman he was not, Ben interrupted him at that point with a smile that was wasted on Hugo. It was meant for his imperious sister.

'I've done some preliminary totting up based on what I've read in the British press, so I'm aware of the problems, sir. If I should decide to return to my homeland I'd sell off my acres of semi-desert scrubland and move my headquarters here. From what I've gleaned there's plenty of scope for air freight around the British Isles. Smaller loads, shorter flights, the chance to win long-term contracts. Steadier work, more reliable customers. I could enjoy far more flying instead of chasing slippery devils through the bazaars and brothels of filthy cities with romantic names to collect what they owe.'

'Dear me, you have been leading an exciting life,' Julia said smoothly. 'Stay to dinner and intrigue us further.'

'Not tonight,' snapped Hugo, a reminder that she had just witnessed what remained of her husband lowered into the ground.

'Of course not. When you come to inspect our workshops, Captain Norton.' She did not appear in the least chastened by her brother's admonition, and Ben was aware that her curiosity about his past was liable to cause difficulties once he was part of Marshfield Aviation. He had no interest in taking over Chris Peterson's wife. He was aiming higher than that.

'Where are you lodging?' Hugo asked.

'The local inn. Comfortable enough but rather noisy. It reminds me of trying to sleep when aircrew are determined on making a night of it. Thanks for permission to do a spot of research at Marshfield, sir. I'll make a start tomorrow, if that's all right with you.'

He turned to Julia. 'Goodbye, Mrs Peterson. I'm sorry to meet you under such tragic circumstances, but it has somehow made my memories of Chris more vivid.' He was tempted to quote the eternal *Time is a great healer*, but there did not appear to be a very deep loss to heal where this widow was concerned.

At the top of a flight of steps Ben halted to gaze at the pale sky dotted with clouds. Within a month, maybe six weeks, he would be filling the gap left by a man who had finally met the fate he had escaped several times during those years they had flown wingtip to wingtip in warm, loyal accord, putting their lives in each other's hands without hesitation.

Back at The Dancing Bear, Ben avoided the locals still in their Sunday best who were gossiping in the bar and used his charm to persuade the chambermaid to bring a pot of strong coffee to his room. Removing the hastily hired black suit, he pulled on a pair of tweed trousers and a fawn pullover, then sat before the dormer window mentally reviewing the two hours he had spent in Clanford House as Captain Ben Norton, close friend of the deceased and international aviation entrepreneur.

There was a vein of truth in all he had said if the Lances chose to follow it up, but they would not. Their sort only moved in the best social circles. If a man had a cultured voice, dressed correctly and spoke expansively they would never question the credibility of someone so clearly one of them, so much the officer and gentleman.

Ben sipped his coffee reflectively. He had worked damned hard, after his first encounter with Major Hugo Lance. The arrogant bastard had looked right through him. Even if the man were not now blind he would not have done so today. His sister had introduced Captain Norton, not Flight Sergeant Jack 'Farmer' Norton who spoke like a yokel and bought clothes off the peg. No monthly allowance from 'the Pater' for John Benjamin Norton, no elegant manor owned by his family, no titled godfather who had the ear of political and commercial giants.

That earlier meeting with the Lance heir, coming so soon after the affair that had caused the irreversible rift between two young men living dangerously side by side, had lit a fire inside Ben that was still burning. He now realized that fate had been slowly leading him to Marshfield Aviation and the family that owned the prestigious company.

When the war ended Jack Norton had worked his passage on a cargo boat heading eastwards. At the end of the voyage he had set about worming his way in to the shabby-genteel society in Cairo while boosting his finances by any available means. He was not ashamed of that period of his life. In the post war shambles everyone was doing it in order to survive. He had not gone through four years of hell to emerge loaded with scruples.

The level in the coffee pot lowered as Ben remembered the wealthy matrons he had charmed into lending him money to buy his first aircraft. And the eager young women who had willingly persuaded Daddy to invest in Norton's Fast Air Service – one beat up old biplane and he the sole pilot. He had nearly flown himself into the ground with exhaustion.

During those precarious years Ben had learned how to speak the way Chris and his ilk did. He had watched and listened and imitated until, by the time he moved to Alexandria to set up Norton Freight, he had outwardly become 'one of them'. He had then adopted his middle name, pulling the final curtain on Jack, the farmer's son who, no matter how courageous he was, could never apparently match up with those who considered themselves his betters.

His mouth twisted as he recalled Hugo that afternoon referring to 'acres of semi-desert scrubland' in supercilious tones. Dear

God, little did the Lance heir know Ben's bases all along the Med were no more than shacks manned by alcoholic layabouts who only survived because packs of pye-dogs defended the wire enclosures around their fuel dumps at ramshackle local airports. As for starting a British branch of Norton Freight, it was a load of tosh! However, his lies had given him entry to where he wanted to be.

Once he put foot inside the Marshfield establishment he would be no more than a step away from what he had intended to wrest from Chris by threat of exposure. No need for that now, but his death had revealed a stumbling block. A mammoth one. If the crash was not due to pilot error or a design fault (which Roger Hall had violently denied) or because Chris had a medical problem which the constant check-ups required of pilots had not discovered, there could be only one other explanation.

The chief designer had been on the verge of confessing that Chris had been shouting over the intercom in alarm just before he hit the ground, when Freddie's alcoholic friends had caused Julia to bear down on them in rage before leading Ben away. His first aim tomorrow was to track down Roger Hall. If someone had sabotaged the demonstration flight, that someone had to be a member of Marshfield's staff with intimate knowledge of and easy access to the prototype.

Staring from the window at the early evening sky, Ben told himself there were several options. The saboteur could be a pacifist crank driven to destroy weapons that could be used in another ghastly war. He could be a crank of another kind who had reason to hate Peterson enough to kill him and decided to do it in what he considered the most fitting way. Or he could be in the pay of a rival company with a pressing need to critically damage Marshfield Aviation.

He pursed his lips and frowned as he considered each of these options, almost immediately dismissing the first. A pacifist would surely not have allowed the aircraft to be completed before destroying it; he would have acted to prevent one ever being made. No, that premise had too many holes in it. So, to the second. Assuming the killer to be working for Marshfield, surely he would not take revenge on Chris by risking his own job and future. Destruction of the prototype would bring heavy financial loss to the company and certain staff reductions. There would have been any number of opportunities to murder Chris somewhere out of the way with no danger of being seen or of damage to his career. As Ben had himself discovered, but he had only once almost put an end to his former friend.

Dragging his thoughts back from that memory which still occasionally caused him to grow cold with shock at the depth of his malice, he reviewed the third and most likely option. Industrial sabotage. It made sense to allow the aircraft to be fully created – years of financial outlay hopefully to be recovered with the successful launch of the prototype followed by a flow of orders – and to destroy it before the eyes of all possible buyers. The malfunction could easily be created, but the resultant loss of all confidence in Marshfield's design would be catastrophic. This would allow a rival time to produce its own super fighter using many of the same design factors stolen by the saboteur, who would return to his masters by becoming one of the workers laid off due to the tragedy. He would doubtless earn lavish praise and financial reward for his actions. That a man had been destroyed along with the machine would be regarded as an unfortunate sacrifice to the greater object, but would he sleep untroubled by the knowledge that he had committed premeditated murder that day?

Ben got to his feet and stood for a long while studying the pink clouds hanging in the paling sky above the airstrip where Chris had met his horrific end. His death might have made it easy for Ben to replace him as Marshfield's test pilot, but he would certainly not climb up among the clouds in the next prototype until he had identified the cold-blooded bastard who had robbed a man of his life for commercial gain.

# TWO

Repressing his eagerness to have an early breakfast and visit the Marshfield establishment, Ben reminded himself he must live up to the image he had created. The Lance family would doubtless rise each morning, read the newspapers over scrambled eggs, devilled kidneys or kedgeree, then *saunter* to the huge workshops they owned.

That was too much to ask of a man filled with nervous energy who practically sizzled with excitement at being within reach of his goal. However, he did take his time over bacon and eggs, toast, marmalade and strong tea while gaining the innkeeper's opinion of Marshfield Aviation's next move.

Phil Bunyan was only too ready to gossip about both the company and the Lance family. What he revealed intrigued Ben no end. A thin, restless man, with thinning hair and a pencil moustache, Bunyan said he had driven an ambulance during the war which had claimed his two younger brothers. Their loss had turned his mother's mind and taken a heavy toll of Bunyan senior.

'He can't do much these days,' he confided, bringing Ben's tea and toast. 'Struggled on after Mother went back to her child-hood, but he'd lost all interest in the business when I came back from France, so me and Mary had no choice but to take it on. It was their living, see. I've got to keep going at least until I see them both out.'

Ben watched him walk back to the bar. 'That sounds as if you don't enjoy what you do here.'

'Oh, it's a good enough prospect, sir. The only licensed prem-ises in Clanford. Not a great deal of passing trade, mind you, but good steady business with the farming community and when the Lances hold the Easter and autumn point-to-point, we have to get in a couple of local girls. They, the Missus and me, we're run off our feet.'

He picked up a cloth and began polishing glasses. 'No, sir, I had my sights set on aircraft engineering as a lad and I won an apprenticeship at Marshfield. I'd just completed it when conscription began in 1916. They'd have taken me back after the armistice, no doubt about that.' He paused his polishing and sighed. 'Mebbe, it's all turned out for the best, eh? What happened last week puts the kibosh on any chance of the RAF or anyone else giving orders for the new fighter plane, so there's sure to be lay-offs now.' He shook his head. 'I always said it were a step too far, sir. I'd see Captain Peterson take it up – well, I'd hear the damned thing before I saw it – and I'd say to Mary, "That's a step too far, that is. They'd be past each other before they'd time to fire their guns". No, sir, men can't take on an enemy in that. Stands to reason it's too fast. Marshfield should've stuck to making craft to carry folk in comfort where they want to go. There's money enough in that. No shortage of orders now everyone wants to fly all over the world. I prefer the ground under my feet, don't you, sir?'

Without waiting for an answer he resumed his polishing. 'Of course, it were Major Hugo who persuaded Sir Edwin to start on the *Lance*. His war experience made him crazy for a machine to beat all comers. He can't see them, but he's attended every Schneider Trophy event to talk to pilots and manufacturers about their float planes that keep breaking speed records. But I see it this way. That race is one thing – it's no more than daredevil men risking their lives to do the impossible, like mountain climbers and Arctic explorers – but who wants an aeroplane that whizzes through the sky so fast a pilot hasn't time to work out his strategy before he's well past an enemy at the same disadvantage? Don't make sense!'

Ben refilled his cup from the brown earthenware pot while Bunyan rambled on.

'The Marshfield *Broadwing*, now there's a beautiful machine,' he enthused. 'See one of them going overhead it's lovely to watch. Glides, it does. Great white and blue bird.' He polished with extra zeal. 'I worked on them as an apprentice. There was plans to develop a larger one, but 1916 put a stop to that. Government made them switch to making spares for warplanes. With Major Hugo flying them, Sir Edwin offered no resistance, but they should've returned to the *Broadwing* and her like instead of taking a foolhardy decision like they did.

'Mind you,' he continued, 'they still produce the *Snowbird* to satisfy demand, and that isn't to be sniffed at, I hear. That's what I'd aim to work on if I went back there, but that's even less likely now. There's been rumours circulating for a long time that Marshfield has had a struggle to keep afloat and was relying on the *Lance* to get things up and running again.'

'Is that right?' asked Ben in mock surprise.

Bunyan tapped the side of his nose. 'You didn't hear that from me, Mr Norton, but anyone in the village will tell you the same. I suppose it's turned into something of a blessing to have The Dancing Bear to keep me and my family going when so many poor ex-soldiers are still begging on the streets.' His pale face lit in a smile. 'Mustn't grumble, eh?'

Ben smiled back; did not point out that grumble was all he'd been doing for the past ten minutes. 'You seem to be making a success of this place. Best keep at it for a while until you see how things at Marshfield develop.'

He got to his feet on seeing the hands of the clock over the bar showing nine fifteen. An acceptable time for an aviation entrepreneur to start his day. He returned to his room, swiftly brushed his teeth and hair, pulled on his raincoat and was ready to *saunter* to the village garage and take the taxi to Marshfield.

Down in the bar Phil Bunyan was still polishing glasses. He called out, 'If you'd like a meal this evening, Mr Norton, Mary'll be happy to give you something round about seven. If the bar's too busy you're welcome to have it in your room.'

'Thank you, but I could be dining elsewhere. However, in the event that that falls through I'll be glad of something in my room.' Ben stopped by the door and turned. 'If you'd completed an apprenticeship at Marshfield, why were you driving ambulances during the war?'

He lowered the glass to the counter and straightened up. 'Because I'm a conscientious objector, sir. I refused to fight, but I did my bit for mankind by helping those who did and suffered the consequences. I don't believe in war and those who cause them. Making warplanes is wrong. Same with any weapons. Make 'em and some bloody idiots will immediately create a situation to use 'em. Then it's a case of trying to make something bigger and better and nastier than anyone else. No. I saw things in France I never want to see again.' Bunyan came round the bar, cloth in hand. 'Don't get me wrong, Mr Norton, I deplore the loss of Captain Peterson's life but I can't help feeling what happened was a sign from the Almighty which the Lance family will do well to heed and act on.'

Ben walked to the end of the long road running through the village centre pondering on what he had just heard. Bunyan had worked at Marshfield for four years learning about the manufacture of aircraft. He would be familiar with the layout of the workshops and know his way around the vital aspects of any flying machine. He was vociferous against the production of the *Lance*.

At the garage the owner left the repair job he was working on, stripped off his protective overalls, cleaned oil from his hands, then donned a jacket to complete his other guise as a taxi driver. During that time Ben weighed up the pros and cons, eventually deciding Phil Bunyan was not cranky enough to have sabotaged the *Lance*. He was a pacifist. No way would he have deliberately caused a man's death. Yet someone with intimate knowledge of the new fighter surely had.

The man at Marshfield's gated entrance was warmly wrapped against the March wind which whipped across the airfield. He needed to be for there was a hint of ice in its blasts. Winter had not yet eased its grip on England. Ben's raincoat was too thin for a man fresh from Middle Eastern temperatures, yet excitement heated his body as the gate was opened to allow the taxi through.

'Doan bother shutting it, Tom,' said the driver. 'I'll be back in half a mo. The gent doan want me to wait.'

'Right y'are, Fred. I'll stay inside me little shed till you goes back through. It's too bloody cold to stand out here fer long.'

Ben had asked to be taken to the head office. He thought it politic to announce his presence, but he also wanted to find out who was on the premises. Ideally, he needed freedom to do whatever he wished without a constant guide to limit his movements. Hugo Lance could, and probably would, hamper his plans to get Roger Hall alone and glean from him what he had been prevented from saying by the antics of Freddie Lance's brainless friends yesterday.

It had been apparent to Ben that the chief designer had been alerted to some performance abnormality by Chris from the cockpit just before impact with the ground. From the violence of Hall's denial of a design flaw, Ben had deduced a suspicion of deliberate tampering before takeoff in the mind of the man whose skill was being doubted by everyone who had witnessed the crash.

During the war, Ben and his fellow pilots had tended to rely on their flight engineers and mechanics to ensure the aircraft were fully airworthy. Many of them, like Ben himself, had been given only the barest number of hours in which to learn how to take a machine off the ground and keep it in the air until ready to bring it down again. Add the complication of enemies intent on shooting them out of the sky and that was as much as they could handle.

When Ben had set up Norton's Fast Air Service, he had had to keep his one old biplane airworthy with just the help of a gruff ageing mechanic who had been put out to pasture and agreed to work for little more than food and a roof over his head. Back then Ben had acquainted himself fast with the essentials for keeping an aircraft in full working condition. Oh yes, Jack 'Farmer' Norton had learned engineering the hard way so he knew the variables that could give way under stress and cause failure to pullout from a dive.

Paying the taxi driver, he headed in to the impressive foyer where a young woman in a smart fawn costume was half-heartedly using a typewriter. She forgot to smile when she glanced up to ask listlessly if she could help him.

Umm, lassitude setting in already at the prospect of job losses, thought Ben. 'I've been invited by Major Lance to tour the establishment,' he said crisply.

'Oh.' She seemed uncertain how to deal with that, then she pulled herself together to adopt a more professional tone. 'Sorry, sir, the Major's in a meeting with all the directors. I've been told not to disturb them.'

Ben was delighted. 'Not to worry. I'll have a wander around until he's free.'

He ran lightly up the broad staircase and started along a corridor where he hoped to find the design department and Roger Hall.

He strongly suspected the directors would be thrashing things out with the accountant and the legal team, leaving the chief designer to find the fatal fault and work out how to put it right.

The design department was at the far end of a long corridor overlooking the runway and two vast hangars. In one Ben could see men working on the *Snowbird*, a white, high-wing, four-seat cabin monoplane which, together with the abandoned *Broadwing*, had made Marshfield a fast-growing company before the war. Maybe Phil Bunyan was right in saying the directors should have concentrated on the commercial market instead of embarking on the more complicated manufacture of the *Lance*.

So far as Ben was aware their designers had had no earlier experience of making military aircraft, and three years devoted to making spares for the blundering biplanes he and his RFC colleagues had flown would have been of little use with the creation of a fast, sleek fighter mounted with four guns and able to outfly any other warplane. However, Roger Hall had produced one which had fulfilled all these demands. Would its failure end Marshfield's venture into military aircraft manufacture? He must do his utmost to ensure it would not.

Ben turned from studying the second hangar where just three workers in overalls were sitting on upturned boxes and gazing at the space where the prototype had stood just a week ago. Across the corridor ten men in the design office were clustered around a large square bench on which was spread a drawing of what was surely the tail section of the *Lance*. Their voices were raised in heated disagreement so they failed to notice Ben enter and head to where Roger Hall sat alone, staring at the wall of his small office at the rear of the spacious room.

Out of courtesy, Ben knocked lightly on the glass panel, although he had no expectation of a response from the man sunk in the depths of depression. Even when he entered, closing the door behind him, it seemed Roger Hall was still unaware of his presence. Ben stood for several moments before deciding he would have to break the hiatus or stand there for the entire morning.

'I'm sorry to arrive unannounced, Mr Hall, but Major Lance is in a meeting and asked the receptionist not to disturb him.' As Hall looked around in a daze of incomprehension, Ben continued. 'While waiting for the meeting to end so that he can give me the guided tour he promised, I've taken the opportunity to offer my apology for not realizing who you were when we spoke yesterday.'

In the face of Hall's continued bafflement Ben approached the desk. 'Only when Julia interrupted our conversation and took me to meet her father did I learn that I'd been speaking to the man who had designed the *Lance*.'

Still no response from someone taking a long time to come from his mental isolation. Better jog his memory.

'Ben Norton. Wartime colleague of Chris's. Flew over from Alex for his funeral.'

Hall's gaze became less distant. 'Ah! Yes. A pilot of considerable experience of aerial combat.'

'Of all aspects of flying, sir.'

Seizing the moment, he gave a rundown of the various aircraft and the type of services he had provided in them over the past twelve years, ending with the same extravagant description of his present commercial activity that he had given the Lances. Best to keep the hyperbole on track!

Like a start button being pressed Hall responded with alacrity, showing his busy brain had stored recognition of someone he had been prepared to confide in yesterday.

'You knew Chris well enough to be sure he would never have made a fatal error; that he would have recognized any kind of problem and ended the flight immediately. Yes? So you said there must therefore be a flaw in the design.'

'Which you emphatically denied,' Ben prompted, praying nobody would interrupt them at this vital time. 'You started to tell me Chris said something but it was too faint for you to hear it.'

Hall got to his feet in his urgency to make his point. 'No! He sounded vague, the words were disjointed, but I heard him mumble that the stick was locked.'

'*Locked*? My God, it would have been impossible to pull up from that dive!'

'Exactly.'

'But surely there was . . .'

'Of course, man,' Hall snapped. 'The *Lance* is designed for speed and immense manoeuvrability. To allow this, I fitted a trim tab to the elevator to cope with the increased loading during excessive dives and low runs, which would prevent this very danger from occurring.'

'So why didn't it?'

The designer threw up his hands in a gesture of disbelief. 'Look, Chris was a damn good pilot. I won't argue with that, but he knew it and couldn't resist showing off. Liked taking chances, especially when he had an audience. Well, you'd be aware of that side of his character.'

Oh yes, Jack 'Farmer' Norton was far too well aware of it, but he maintained his fourteen year silence.

'Having said that, Chris had successfully performed a high-speed dive many times with the trim tab doing its job,' Hall continued. 'I stipulated that the proving flight programme was sufficient to demonstrate the aircraft's true worth without giving the VIPs the fright of their lives with a daredevil dive, but Chris couldn't resist it once he was up there with hundreds of eyes watching him, could he?'

Ben frowned in concentration. 'So what exactly are you saying, Mr Hall?'

'That there's no design fault in the *Lance*. It's a superb aircraft.'

'And?'

Hall flopped back on his chair, his earlier sudden verve fading. 'If the stick was locked during that dive it means somebody tampered with the elevator tab cable to ensure it would sever at some point during the flight. Everything was checked shortly before takeoff, but I know that's what must have happened because it's the only explanation for the tragedy.'

Ben stood quietly for some moments, making no mention of his own similar conclusion of sabotage. 'You said "somebody", sir. Have you any idea who that might be?'

'No. No!' It was almost a cry of despair. 'As God's my witness I don't know how, but a person connected with Marshfield Aviation committed a heinous crime that day against the company and the Lance family.'

And against Captain Christopher George Peterson MC, flawed hero, Ben added silently.

Suspecting Hall of being on the verge of again withdrawing

into morose detachment, Ben asked swiftly, 'You've discussed this with the directors?'

'Wildly melodramatic worldwide news reportage, plus the shocking truth of their own eyes made it impossible for them to accept any excuse for professional failure. The Major listened to me for three minutes then walked away still tight-lipped. He's refused to see me since then.'

Ben believed it. Hugo Lance only allied himself with success; had no time for the mediocre or life's failures. The destruction of the aircraft so vital to Marshfield's future was such a catastrophe it was even likely this broken man might be given his marching orders. Was that the reason for the directors' meeting this morning?

Ben drew up a chair and sat facing Roger Hall. 'You must have an idea of likely suspects. Have you questioned them, discovered their whereabouts prior to Chris's takeoff?'

A slow shake of the head greeted that. A resigned negative.

'You can't just give up,' Ben said with force. 'You told me a moment ago Chris was a damn good pilot who would have recognized any performance problem and landed immediately. You claimed everything was checked as usual, but I believe your assumption that the elevator cable could have been tampered with in a way that would not have been obvious during normal flight conditions yet would snap under excessive loading. Did Chris do the pre-flight checks? Did you?'

Faced with continuing silence, Ben lost his temper. 'Good God, sir, a man was killed while demonstrating the excellence of your advanced warplane this country vitally needs. If you don't have enough guts to defend your creation at least honour the sacrifice Chris made and prove criminal intent was behind the destruction of man and machine. Major Lance must be made to hear what you've just told me.'

Hall's eyes narrowed in speculation as he reacted to this sudden aggression. 'You're too great a firebrand for a man who flew all the way from Alexandria just to attend a funeral. You had no hand in the development of the *Lance*, you didn't witness the proving flight and I never heard Chris mention your name in all the time I knew him. Who exactly are you?'

It was one of those make or break moments. Ben gambled

on the fact that Hall had seen fit to confide in him and decided on honesty. 'I'm a man who fought the enemy for four years, three of them in the air. Since the end of hostilities I've become passionate about the development of aircraft. I've studied their capabilities and their nuts and bolts. I've flown them in all weathers and conditions. When I heard on the aviators' grapevine that Marshfield had stopped production of *Broadwing* to develop a radical warplane, I knew I had to be a part of it. Mr Hall, I want you to assemble another *Lance* and I want to test-fly her.'

Roger Hall pursed his lips and gave a slight shake of his head. 'Right now the directors are meeting to decide the way forward for the company. Sir Edwin can see no future for the *Lance* after this. He wants to revert to the commercial market; start production of the larger, four-engined *Broadwing* that was put on hold four years ago. The Major is adamant that warplanes are the better option in view of the fast-growing number rolling off production lines in Germany and America.'

'He's right,' said Ben heatedly. 'They mustn't give up the *Lance*.'

'They will if there's a majority vote to do so in the belief that the company will otherwise fold. They'll see commercial as a safer bet. Mrs Peterson is likely to support Sir Edwin because of her husband's death. I don't know about young Freddie. I guess he'll go along the route that best ensures the financing of his motor racing and wasteful way of life.'

'There must be other shareholders who have a vote.'

Hall nodded. 'But the family's combined shares can override them. I'd say the decision will rest on whoever manages to persuade Freddie to throw in his lot with them.'

Ben got to his feet restively. 'He must be persuaded to support his brother. Speed is his god, so surely he can see it's essential in the aircraft of the future.'

With a sigh, Hall said, 'What he sees as essential is the wherewithal to indulge his landlocked passion. Marshfield's financial future was tied up in the *Lance*, but reverting to production of the *Mark 2 Broadwing* won't bring a swift turnaround. The design is four years old. Other companies have produced bigger and better passenger aircraft in that time which are attracting steady orders.'

'The family must be aware of that, so why do they consider

it an option? The workshops will have been adapted to production of the *Lance*, and the workforce is only familiar with the smaller *Broadwing*. The obvious way forward is to assemble another *Lance* as quickly as possible, test her until they're confident of her safety in the air, then bloody well invite the VIPs back for another proving flight.' He looked hard at Hall. 'How long would it take to produce another?'

'Working at full strength? About a week.'

'A week?'

Giving a faint smile he said, 'We had a backup machine ready to take over should there be a last-minute hitch.'

Ben thumped his fist on the back of the chair. 'Then there's no question of how they should vote. They have a prototype out in the hangar and they have a test pilot eager to fly her. Not only that, I'll sleep beside her to prevent any other attempt at sabotage. It wouldn't be the first time I've been an aeroplane's bedfellow.'

After studying his companion thoughtfully for some moments, Hall got to his feet. 'Perhaps you'd better have a look at your prospective sleeping partner; see how much of the bed she'll take up.'

Feeling a welcome rapport growing between them, Ben went eagerly with the intelligent, gifted man who understood his passionate nature as his parent never had. The hangar was silent, housing only the silver warplane. The three men who had been sitting on upturned boxes must have found something better to do.

Ben's heart began to race with excitement as he walked right up to the most advanced creature of the skies he had ever seen. She stood bare of those elements which would allow her to move, take to the air, but she beckoned and he responded. Looking a question at her creator who gave an understanding nod, Ben climbed on to the step beside the wing on legs weak with elation and settled in the incredibly small cockpit, marvelling at the sleekness of the fuselage.

He feasted his eyes on dials as yet unable to record data and imagined those indicators moving as he took her off the ground and up to freedom in the skies. He gripped the joystick, rested his feet on the pedals while his imagination had him climbing, diving, racing like a whirlwind mere feet from the ground, suddenly knowing Chris Peterson had died at the zenith of living.

How long Roger Hall stood patiently waiting Ben had no idea, but when he reluctantly joined him it was difficult to express his joy. He had never been good at revealing his intimate feelings; had been taught not to do so as a child. Finally, he said through the thickness in his throat, 'They have to continue with the *Lance*. We'll never have a true fighting force unless we at least match the best being produced by our rivals.'

As if on cue, a young man with a mop of black hair appeared and came towards them holding out an envelope. 'I've been searching for you, sir. Message from the Major.'

Hall read the single sheet with a frown while Ben waited with the same urgency as the bringer of the news. When the designer folded the paper and returned it to the envelope there was nothing in his demeanour to betray his feelings as he addressed the messenger.

'Nothing will be decided until tomorrow, Reggie. Tell everyone they can take the rest of the day off.'

As Reggie walked away Ben asked impatiently, 'What's the difficulty? It's a simple enough choice. Two options.'

Hall nodded. 'It seems Claude Beamish, the company's financial manager, needs more time to prepare the minutiae of comparative costs. He has a lot on his shoulders, poor devil. A little over a week ago he was standing by to deal with the prospect of huge sums being invested or pledged. Now he has to equate the massive loss of those expectations with unknown production costs and phantom income from sales or investment in either option. Nobody can predict the future accurately, Ben. It'll be unfair on Beamish to base a decision on figures he produces under duress tomorrow.'

'I agree.' He noted with pleasure the use of his first name. 'I also think you should be present tomorrow and be given more than three minutes to put your beliefs forward that will vindicate your skill.'

'No, no, finance is not my area. I've been told often enough that I take no account of the cost when I design something. It's true. I create the best machine possible and leave them to find the money to make it. If they can't, it stays as drawings on dozens of rolls of blueprints.'

Curious, Ben asked, 'You've designed aircraft Marshfield has never produced?'

Putting a hand on his shoulder, Hall gently encouraged Ben towards the hangar entrance. 'Trial and error. Trial and error. That's the way it goes until something like the *Lance* is the result.'

'Then some maniac destroys it.'

'Yes. Some maniac destroys three years' work to find perfection. Three years of testing, redesigning, testing again. Sleepless nights while one's mind wrestles with a solution just out of reach; elation when it finally arrives. Watching your creation perform faultlessly time and again, then standing amid a distinguished audience ready to witness a miracle. Standing with a quiet mind knowing the struggle is over. Nothing more to do.' He paused for a moment, then added with a break in his voice, 'It's very hard to see one's brainchild smash to pieces at the moment of triumph.'

They walked back to the main building in silence, until Ben said, 'Mr Hall, I want to help you prove the crash was not through a flaw in the design. I want to fly the *Lance* as many times as it takes to convince the directors, the newspapers and potential backers that she's the warplane this country needs to have superiority in the air. I want to help you track down whoever caused that disaster last week. I want to discover why anyone would contemplate such an evil act.'

'Hmm, after tomorrow there might not be a *Lance* for you to fly; no opportunity for you to do any of those things you mentioned.'

Ben brushed that aside, so sure was he Hugo Lance would prevail. That man had an arrogance that swept aside the desires or opinions of other men without a second's hesitation. He knew!

'You didn't answer my question on who did the pre-flight checks.'

Hall plodded on, apparently having returned to his earlier silent negative mood. Ben grew angry again.

'Mr Hall, please don't ignore me. If you truly believe your claim of sabotage, we have to discover who was responsible. Unless you can offer proof of why the *Lance* crashed, no matter how much effort I put into reinstating the aircraft's superb qualities, doubt will remain. You spoke of wildly melodramatic worldwide publicity silencing your efforts to convince Hugo Lance of the truth. Well, similar wildly melodramatic worldwide publicity revealing sabotage would put an aura of glamour over the *Lance* and create a sensation that would dim the appeal of rivals. Proof of wilful tampering to cause an aircraft to crash, almost certainly killing the pilot, would keep global attention on Marshfield Aviation throughout test flights of the second prototype in case it also flew into the ground.'

Giving a cynical smile, Ben added, 'The world's newspaper barons love nothing better than a potential disaster and a daredevil prepared to risk his life in the process.'

This caused Hall to pause in the doorway and fix Ben with a frown.

'Are you prepared to risk your life?'

'There'd be no risk so long as we ensured it was impossible for anyone to tamper with the aircraft. I value my life, sir, so the sooner we discover the identity of the saboteur who also committed premeditated murder the more relaxed I'll be. We'll make a start by confronting Major Lance first thing tomorrow morning and making him see reason.' He placed his hand on Hall's shoulder and gently urged him through the door. 'If that fails I'll have to bribe Freddie to cast his vote the way we want. How much do you think it'll cost me?'

# THREE

A t nine a.m. Ben walked along to Clanford House where he had persuaded Roger Hall to meet him. Too bad if members of the family were in the middle of their scrambled eggs or kedgeree. The issue was too vital to wait for a leisurely breakfast to end.

The March morning was raw and even his brisk pace failed to keep him from shivering. Too many years in African climates had led Ben to forget how cold it could be in the land of his birth. At the first opportunity he must buy some clothes suited to English weather. And some form of transport, of course. His room at The Dancing Bear was comfortable and perfectly adequate for the few hours he would spend there, but Marshfield was ten miles from Clanford and he could not depend on the village taxi to take him when and wherever he wanted to go.

Rounding a heavy pillar to enter the drive of the Victorian mansion, he saw with satisfaction that Hall had already arrived. Good man! Would he stay focused enough to face down Hugo Lance? It had been difficult enough yesterday to spur the designer into action, because that was what he was. A creator. A dreamer, if you like. A man who conceived clever things on paper but left others to use them. So far as he was concerned his job was done once his creation was up and running. Time to move on and use his vision to invent another wonderful piece of engineering.

'Good morning,' Ben said breezily as he approached the elderly saloon where Hall sat behind the wheel. The man's pale face with dark rings beneath the eyes was hardly suggestive of firm resolution against authority backed by wealth and arrogance, but Hall scrambled from the vehicle readily enough and returned the greeting.

'Sir Edwin's out walking the dogs, as usual, and Freddie never appears until the morning's well advanced, so we should find the Major alone.'

'How about Julia?' Ben asked swiftly.

'I passed her on my way here. She was just turning on to the path that leads up past the quarry, riding her brown mare. I imagine she needs to spend time alone right now to come to terms with Chris's death. Pity there were no children. They would have supported her through these first days as a widow.'

Ben forbore to comment that, from all he had read about her in society magazines and gossip columns in newspapers, he guessed she would manage perfectly well on her own. However, it was good to know they were unlikely to be interrupted during their session with Hugo.

'Did you prepare your case, as planned?' he asked as they waited for their tug on the doorbell to bring a servant.

Hall shrugged. 'It's not much of a case. I doubt he'll pay any more heed to it than he did before. Nobody else heard Chris say the stick was locked, and the wreckage is so total there's no way of checking.'

As footsteps approached to open the door Ben said, 'Put a little more authority in your tone when you face him with it. He can't see your expression so he'll go entirely on what he can hear. Speak with certainty. Don't let him dismiss you before you've convinced him the *Lance* has no design fault.'

A very young maid let them in and asked their business. When they told her she said, while goggling at the well-built stranger with Hall, 'The Major's at breakfast in his study. Can't be disturbed.'

'Tell him Mr Hall and Captain Norton need to speak to him urgently,' Ben said firmly, waving a hand at her as if to help her on her way to take his message.

'I'll ask if he's able to receive you, sir,' she replied primly, still eyeing him with interest.

'We'd be most grateful,' said Hall with a smile, which made Ben wonder if the man had heeded the advice to put more authority in his tone.

The girl was soon back. 'The Major is busy preparing notes for an important meeting. He says he can spare just a few minutes if it's really urgent.'

Ben started towards the door she had come through, saying, 'It is,' just as Roger Hall mumbled, 'That's very good of him,' which added to Ben's desire to inject some fire in him.

Hugo Lance was sitting behind a vast leather-topped desk bearing several telephones and a Dictaphone. Beside these stood a tray holding a coffee pot, cup and saucer, plate, basket of rolls, butter dish and a marmalade pot. So much for scrambled eggs and kedgeree!

'Good morning, sir. Sorry to interrupt your breakfast,' Ben began with the very briskness he had urged Roger to use. 'When we reveal the reason for this early morning call I believe you'll understand our urgency.'

'And shall I understand your involvement, Captain Norton?' came the chilly response. 'Perhaps you're unaware that vital and far-reaching decisions must be made by the company directors following last week's disaster. I really have no time to discuss trifling concerns about your own future business plans.'

'They're linked to the future of the *Lance*, Major,' ventured Hall. 'You should listen to what Ben has to say.'

'Oh? In what way could they possibly be linked?'

Ben swallowed his anger at arrogance reminiscent of their earlier encounter. 'While you tried to reach a decision on the direction your company should now take, I spent yesterday talking to Mr Hall about his impressive one-man fighter and studying the *Lance* in the hangar. Like you, I flew combat aircraft during the war years and, also like you, I'm very aware of how fast other nations are developing military aircraft.'

The hauteur began to fade from the senior man's expression as his attention was drawn to what Ben was saying, so he pressed on with a growing air of command.

'I sat in the cockpit, handled the controls, while Mr Hall gave me the finest details of how the aircraft would respond to the hand of the pilot, and I knew for certain that that machine could prove to be our country's saviour in any future aerial battles.'

Allowing enough time for Hugo to grasp the implication of this eulogy, Ben continued. 'For six months an Australian million-aire has been trying to buy Norton Freight with a view to expanding eastward. Last night I telegraphed agreement to the deal he's been offering. Major, your company was counting on production of the *Lance* to turn its fortunes around. In my opinion it will. To that end I'm prepared to invest heavily in Marshfield Aviation, which should strengthen the case to continue when the directors meet this afternoon. I've booked a long distance call to Australia for ten a.m. to settle a few minor points still under discussion. By noon I'll be in a position to tell you the full amount of my investment if the voting goes the right way. If it doesn't, the offer is no longer available.'

The Lance heir seemed lost for words. Ben felt the warm satisfaction of knowing he held this man in the palm of his hand for a short while.

Hugo finally got to his feet and came carefully around the desk to where Hall stood beside Ben. 'This is an extraordinarily swift decision, Captain Norton. Only a few days ago you were anticipating moving your headquarters to England and setting up freight contracts here. How can I be sure you'll not make another swift decision that will negate all you've just proposed?'

Anger flared again. 'You can't be, but if you want to realize your strong desire to continue production of the *Lance* you'll just have to trust my word as an officer and a gentleman,' he said with heavy emphasis, knowing how this man would respond to such words. 'And you'll also have to trust what Mr Hall is about to tell you as being the truth, because it will also significantly affect this afternoon's discussions.'

After Ben had nudged him into action Roger Hall revealed what Chris Peterson had said before the crash and his own suspicions of the cause. Once started, he put into his account the force of conviction that Ben had wanted and spoke without interruption until he had finished.

Again Hugo was silent for some moments before reacting. 'Chris actually said the stick was *locked*?'

Hall nodded. 'Yes. There was no way he could have pulled out of that dive.'

'My God!' Deeply affected by the implications of what he had heard, Hugo made his way carefully to where a fire burned in a huge stone fireplace and stood grasping the mantel as he gazed sightlessly at the portrait of his ancestor, Sir Godfrey, to whom the house had been gifted in 1862. When he spoke his voice was unsteady with rage.

'That's infamous! We have a traitor in the workshops. A bastard accepting payment from a rival to ruin the company; destroy the *Lance* in a manner that would ensure the greatest commercial loss. All that horrendous publicity in the world press. Guaranteed to show Marshfield as . . . as . . .' He ran out of words in his outrage.

Roger Hall looked taken aback by Hugo's fury, but he must surely have felt the same overriding passion from the moment he had heard those words from Chris over the radio and watched his brainchild plunge into the ground. Ben now understood the designer's sense of shock and disbelief which had taken the fight out of him. He hoped to have put it back by the end of this meeting.

Watching Hugo's hands gripping and releasing their hold on the stone mantel in his rage, Ben wondered when the murder of the man's brother-in-law would enter his venomous thoughts. They were a cold, selfish bunch, these Lances.

Hugo swung round to face them, breathing heavily to control his anger. 'I'll have detectives here by the weekend, grilling everyone in the workshops. I have friends in the Home Office. They have a unit that specializes in industrial crimes. They'll soon identify the bloody culprit and I'll make sure the bastard'll die in prison for this.'

'He'll die on the end of a rope if he's caught,' said Ben quietly. 'Deliberately taking a life is punishable by hanging.'

'What?'

Knowing he had caught Hugo unawares Ben was gratified to see him humbled. 'Whoever sabotaged the aircraft knew the man flying it was certain to be killed. That's premeditated murder.'

'Yes. Of course. That's, that's—'

'Infamous?' Ben let that sink in before adding calmly, 'Do you think it's in your best interests to install an army of harsh-voiced detectives in the workshops? Mr Hall and I yesterday worked out who would have had the opportunity to tamper with that cable and narrowed it down to cover the few men who were in the hangar minutes before the flight. Then we narrowed it further to cover those few who would be familiar enough with the aircraft's specifications to damage it in such a short space of time.'

'Who are they? I'll have them before a panel of police interrogators before they know what's happening.'

Ben increased the pressure. 'This isn't a simple situation,

sir. Your staff are not subject to military law, obliged to obey orders from you. You're simply their employer with the usual obligations to those you engage to work for you. As we've pointed out, an act of sabotage can't be proven, either by witness statements or by physical evidence. Heavy-handedness will achieve nothing but general unrest and resentment at a time when your workforce is already uncertain of a future with the company.'

Hugo Lance was not used to having his decisions questioned, and spoke sharply. 'You've not yet invested in Marshfield Aviation, Captain Norton. You might well have ingratiated yourself with my chief designer but your views will carry no more weight with the other directors than they do with me.'

'That will be a grave mistake, Major,' Ben replied, still unsettled by those grey eyes that appeared to be staring at him in disparagement. 'The directors have, of course, suffered a serious blow, but so have those people who worked with such energy and high hopes on actually constructing the *Lance* only to watch it plunge to its destruction. They would have felt all that adverse publicity reflected on them. Bad workmanship; their fault. Bad design; Roger Hall's fault!' He then took a risk and went in at the deep end. 'Has anyone thought to gather them together and attempt to reassure them that a Board of Inquiry will discover the cause of the accident and put an end to unfounded newspaper reports? Any attempts to boost their confidence!'

'You sound like a damned unionist,' Hugo snapped.

'If I were I'd be organizing a walkout or a body of representatives to disrupt the directors' meetings,' Ben pointed out. 'I'm speaking from the experience of being a member of a squadron. When things were going badly, the last thing a wise commander would do was make a public show of interrogating those men he believed might be behind the general sense of failure. A good leader would first have a quiet word with each flight commander to get their observations, then gather them all together for a morale-boosting talk followed by free beer and a chance to let their collective hair down. It rarely failed.' After a pregnant pause he added, 'I'm sure that's what you did on such occasions, Major Lance. That same course of action surely applies now.'

His words clearly hit home, but Hugo Lance was not a man to be put in his place. 'I'll welcome your proposed investment, Captain Norton, but it won't make you a director or grant you the freedom to dictate company policy. Bear that in mind when you make your call to Australia in half an hour's time,' he said after running his fingers over the prominent hands of a desk clock. 'You must now allow me to finalize my notes for this afternoon's meeting. Good day to you.'

To Ben's surprise Hall spoke up swiftly. 'We need more than Ben's money, Major. All he just said is plain common sense. He knows how to run a company. He's been a director of several in the past twelve years, remember. Successful, profit-making companies. And he's dealt with some slippery customers out there, not your average English businessmen with the law to curb their corporate activity.'

Hugo's mouth twisted in a semi-sneer. 'You've persuaded him you heard Chris speak before he crashed and you're both here preaching sabotage with no way of proving the claim. Of course you speak in his defence. It lets you off the hook, Roger.'

Hall moved forward, red in the face. 'Is that your way of repeating your accusation of a fault in the design which I'm trying to cover up?'

'Read into my words whatever you will,' said Hugo as he felt his way on to the swivel chair behind his desk.

Ben could hardly believe his ears when Hall said, 'You'll have my letter of resignation in time for this afternoon's meeting. As I own the patent for my design there'll be no decision for the directors to make. The company will be obliged to return to manufacturing passenger aircraft from now on.'

This development visibly threw Hugo, but for no longer than a minute or so. Then he reminded Roger of the contract he had signed giving Marshfield Aviation the right to manufacture the aircraft he had designed.

'The company paid you very handsomely, as I recall.'

Ben then saw the other side of his new friend's personality. Dreamer he might be, but he turned into a champion when defending the outcome of that dream. 'You're suggesting I'll break the terms of our contract by resigning and taking my warplane elsewhere? As I recall it refers throughout to an aeroplane to be known as the *Lance*.'

'So?' It was frosty.

'You have declared that aircraft to be faulty to the degree of having destroyed the expectation of vitally needed investment in the company. Because of this there's a strong possibility of the directors voting to cease manufacture of the *Lance*. What happens to the contract in that circumstance? You appear to have no qualms about breaking the terms of the document yourselves.'

'That is highly unlikely, Roger. I have every confidence in the vote being to continue as before.'

He rose again and made his way around the desk towards Hall. That he accidentally knocked over the coffee pot with his outstretched hand was indicative of his pique at how this meeting was developing.

'I . . . we all appreciate how upset and responsible you must feel, but we have to put such things aside and work on seeking the fault and putting it right as soon as possible.'

The hand offered in a gesture of trust and friendship was left in the air as Roger said, 'I've told you the cause of the crash. Chris made numerous test flights after some small adjustments had been made. He performed all the aerobatics that formed the content of the proving flight over and over again without any problems. There is no design fault. If you continue with the belief that there is, I can't work with you. After a short period to allow the findings of the Court of Inquiry to be published, which I'm sure will be an open verdict or one of accidental death, I shall offer my design for the *RH4* single-seat fighter to the highest bidder.'

There was an electric silence until Hugo said, 'I'll see you in court.'

'And set off another explosion of global news detrimental to Marshfield Aviation?' asked Ben, feeling it time to enter the lists in support of the man he turned to with a smile. 'I'll put my money on the *RH4*. Meet me for lunch in The Dancing Bear, Roger, and I'll be able to tell you the full amount.'

Nudging his companion towards the door he had the last word. 'Thank you for giving us some of your precious time, Major. It proved to be very productive. Good day, sir.'

Back on the half-moon driveway Ben gave a soft laugh. 'Well, my friend, you were splendid. All we have to do is wait until this afternoon when the vote to continue with the *Lance* will be unanimous.'

'And if it isn't?' asked Roger, his pugnacity slowly ebbing.

'Then we go ahead with the *RH4*. You took my breath away with that.' He chuckled again. 'Rest assured it won't come to taking that intriguing course of action. I know people like these Lances. I've studied them closely in the past twelve years. They won't allow competition; have to be top dogs. Trust me. Soon after their meeting begins you'll be asked to attend for serious discussion on how soon you can have another *Lance* ready for a proving flight.'

Roger mulled that over. 'I'll insist that you're the test pilot.'

Ben gripped the man's shoulder. 'Thanks . . . but I'm making that a condition of my investment. We'll make a bloody good team, don't you think?'

The bar of The Dancing Bear was quiet that evening but Ben nevertheless asked to have his meal brought to his room. He needed to reflect, plan, make decisions. It had been a momentous day on which those last two had already featured by changing his life very dramatically once more.

John Benjamin Norton, only child of a widowed, struggling farmer, had sold a thriving air freight company in a canny deal with a man on the other side of the world whom he had never met, and in so doing had become a sizeable shareholder in Marshfield Aviation, one of the top five aircraft manufacturers in the country. In addition, he was under contract as the company's official test pilot. The cherry on the cake was the knowledge of having made Hugo Lance dance to his tune. Ben had waited thirteen years for that and the sweetness of retaliation still lingered.

He had left Alexandria fully intending never to return, leaving behind nothing he valued, nobody he loved. He had left with the sole purpose of taking Chris Peterson's job from him, by threat if necessary. He had not intended to sell everything he owned to get what he so dearly wanted, but he could not let it slip through his fingers.

It had not been total victory. The directors had listened to Hall's theory of sabotage but would not accept it. Ben had warned him not to make it a sticking point and lose the battle, so the designer had quietly agreed to take another look at the trim tab and elevator when completing the *Lance* presently in the hangar. Their second stipulation was that all test flights should take place without advance notice and the workforce would be pledged to silence outside Marshfield premises, much as they had been during the war.

Ben's mouth twisted in a faint smile remembering Sir Edwin's penetrating gaze as he asked if Captain Norton was prepared to test the aircraft 'in all conditions and under a cloak of secrecy'. Freddie had forestalled any response by saying loudly, 'By God, the chap fought the Huns for four years in bloody flying deathtraps. He's unlikely to be frightened of anything now!'

Afterwards Ben had gone with Roger to the nearest inn and there celebrated while making plans to discover the identity of the saboteur. They had narrowed suspects down to three: chief engineer Ray Povey, works supervisor Jim Tilbrook and the production manager John Kershaw. These men had been with Roger and Chris in the hour before takeoff and could have seized a chance to sever that cable.

They had agreed to sleep in the hangar before each test flight, mounting two hourly watches throughout the night. While work on the *Lance* was being done to make it fully airworthy, Ben had undertaken to do a little sleuthing into the affairs of the three suspects in his spare time.

He considered that prospect now as he added coal to the fire then placed his dinner tray on the small table outside his door where it would be collected by Mary Bunyan. Returning to his chair he told himself he had no experience at detecting. His only advantage was that he was as yet unknown to the workforce which might make it easy to glean information on the private lives of those three men.

He was brought from his thoughts when the door of his room opened and someone walked in closing it behind them. Getting to his feet in protest he saw a tall, dark-haired woman in a wraparound coat that was surely made from a multitude of minks.

'I didn't hear your knock,' he said coldly.

Julia Peterson smiled. 'I didn't.'

'If what you've come here for is important, we'll discuss it in the bar. If it isn't, come back in the morning. I'll be having my breakfast down there at seven thirty.'

She perched on the end of the bed and pushed open her coat to reveal a close-fitting dark red dress, causing a waft of heady perfume to reach him. 'You intrigue me, Ben Norton.'

'Should I feel flattered?'

Another smile. 'Oh no, you have too high an opinion of yourself already.'

He walked to the door and opened it. 'As I said, if it isn't important come back in the morning.'

She remained where she was, so he went down to the bar and ordered a small whisky and water. When Phil Bunyan glanced across at the stairs Ben said, 'Mrs Peterson will be down in a minute.'

It was longer than a minute. Was she looking through his belongings? Well, she would find nothing 'intriguing' in the cupboards and drawers. All his personal documents were securely double-locked in his briefcase, a habit formed in Cairo after his room in a seedy lodging house had been stripped of everything he had while he had eaten what passed for breakfast.

When Julia eventually descended her mouth was tight with pique. Ignoring Phil behind the bar, she crossed to the alcove where Ben was enjoying his whisky. He stood as she approached and asked what she would like to drink.

'They don't serve champagne cocktails in village pubs, which is why I never drink in them,' she snapped.

'And I never entertain women alone in pub bedrooms, especially those who've recently been widowed.'

For a long moment she fixed Ben with a calculating gaze. 'So let's compromise. My car's outside. We'll talk there. You can leave the door open to satisfy your gentlemanly scruples, if you wish,' she threw over her shoulder as she reached the arched entrance.

He had known from the start that she was likely to be a problem, but he had learned the hard way that it was best to meet problems head on, so he followed her to where a gleaming Lagonda was parked.

The night was chilly and full of stars. So were nights in desert areas, but the smells were very different. In this village was the fresh sweetness of lush pastures, the whiff of warm hides as cows settled to rest in the nearby barn, the dampness of haze above the stream running beside the road. Ben found Julia's perfume alien against these.

'So what's so important we have to go through this charade tonight?' he asked, sinking back against the soft leather that shrieked opulence.

Her expression was in shadow because she had half turned in her seat so her body blocked the light from above the door of The Dancing Bear, but something in her tone suggested she was enjoying the situation.

'Father sees you as a welcome influx of cash and a handy replacement for Chris, Hugo sees the same advantages with the added boon of getting his way over that bloody aeroplane. Freddie regards you as a timely benefactor. I, on the other hand, am uncertain what I see when I look at you. It's all too convenient, isn't it?'

'I'm not sure what you're getting at.'

'I'll make it plainer. You flew from Egypt to attend the funeral of an old comrade. Then you decided to investigate the possibility of moving your headquarters to England. Then you heard there was a dispute over continuing work on the *Lance*. Then you recalled a takeover bid from a man in Australia and completed it virtually overnight. Then you added a condition to your investment: you must be taken on as the company's test pilot. In place of the comrade whose death brought you here.' She paused significantly. 'A comrade whom I never heard mention your name during the entire eight years we were married.'

'You told me yourself Chris never spoke about the war or his friends from that time,' Ben reminded her.

'There's more to you than meets the eye.'

He countered that very swiftly. 'As there is to most people whose activities aren't reported in magazines and gossip columns, and whose picture among guests at this or that social event appears regularly in print. Mostly not in the company of the man you never heard mention my name,' he added.

Unfazed, she murmured, 'Mmm, you're supposed to have been living in some godforsaken Middle Eastern dump chasing debtors through smelly native markets. When would you have seen gossip magazines and bitchy society columns?'

'My dear Julia – I can call you that now I'm a Marshfield shareholder, can't I? – your sophistication is sadly limited to London and the wealthy shires. There's as much opulence in the east as there is poverty. You should go out there. Some parties I attended put your average West End capers in the mediocre category. Too tame by half!'

She let that comment hang between them for a moment or two before saying brightly, 'You can escort me to Bunny Yarland's birthday bash next week and show us all a few eastern delights to spice things up.'

'Aren't you forgetting your widowed state?'

Julia was silent while she took from her bag a jewelled case, opened it and offered it to him. Ben shook his head, so she selected a cigarette, fixed it in a long holder, then gave him some matches and waited for him to strike one and light it for her. Inhaling deeply, she then held the long jade tube away from her face and spoke without looking at him.

'Chris consistently forgot his married status. We'd only been husband and wife for three months when he bedded the daughter of an innkeeper. One in a long line of them. The more innocent and blush-cheeked they were the better.' She drew deeply on the cigarette again. 'Mind you, he had catholic tastes where women were concerned. They were all fair game. He had only to spin the war hero line and they were putty in his hands.'

Angling her head towards him, she said, 'If you really knew him so well you'd have witnessed his greed for conquest. The daring pilot, the dashing hero. He must have played that game with the French demoiselles.'

No, his greed for conquest in those days was centered on killing, thought Ben. His silence brought another challenge.

'Don't tell me he stole your girl and seduced her.'

'No, he didn't.'

'Hmm! Are you married? Divorced? Maybe the reason why he never mentioned your name was because you and he had a loving liaison during the war. Live for today; tomorrow we might die!'

Ben was now angry and tired of her complaints, her posing, her presumptive manners, but he was prepared to let her continue giving him insights to how Chris Peterson had developed over the past twelve years.

'Which came first, his infidelity or yours?'

She smoked in silence for almost a minute then spoke on an entirely different subject. 'Are you up to flying the *Lance*? Hauling freight around the Med hardly compares with handling an ultra-fast fighter.'

'You're a pilot, are you?'

'God no!'

'Then don't babble nonsense on a subject you've had no experience to call on.'

She continued to gaze through the windscreen. 'We'll soon know if you live up to your boasts when you first take her up. Won't worry me one way or the other so long as you don't fly the bloody thing into the ground. In spite of your influx of cash, that really would sink the company. Father would have to sell assets, Hugo would go into a decline, Freddie would be obliged to marry that ghastly Perdita in line to inherit a fortune in a year or so. And I'd have to scout around for a sugar daddy. How utterly boring.'

'Do you actually care about anybody?' Ben asked.

'No. Why should I?'

With that crisp return she threw the butt from the window and started the engine. Before Ben could move, the car shot away into the darkness of the country lanes heading for goodness knew where.

Ben's anger now boiled over. 'Where the hell are you going? For God's sake stop behaving like a mindless idiot.'

Julia merely laughed and sped onwards for about fifteen minutes before turning on two wheels through a grandiose gateway to the large forecourt of a mansion house hotel with lights blazing from every window. She skidded to a halt, grabbed her handbag and climbed from the car.

'Need a bloody drink. Several. And they do serve champagne cocktails here. Come on!'

Ben watched her climb a flight of steps, mink coat flying out behind her, waving to a noisy group arriving wearing conventional evening dress. She was absorbed into their midst with much kissing and cries of delight. Ben slid into the driving seat, turned the car round, and drove himself back to The Dancing Bear.

# FOUR

Once more the solitary guest for breakfast, Ben saw his opportunity to question Phil Bunyan. But he had first to satisfy the innkeeper's own curiosity.

'Mrs Peterson not needing her car today?' he asked as he brought a plate of scrambled eggs and grilled tomatoes to the table, with a brown teapot and a rack of toast.

'She's riding with friends,' Ben replied easily.

Having seen from his bedroom window the Lagonda still where he had left it last night he had been surprised. He had expected one of her socialite friends would drive her over to pick it up. He decided to use it to reach Marshfield this morning and leave it there. It would save him calling out the village taxi.

Getting his own transport was a priority, and maybe it would be sensible to find his own place to live in. A cottage, a small cabin near the workshops. The room he presently occupied here was restrictive and it could be noisy when the bar filled up in the evenings. However, it would do until he had time to search for a home.

'I need to buy something to get me back and forth to Marshfield, Phil. Can you recommend a reliable car salesman in the area?'

'Well, as to that, there's Josh Philips in Lewes. Big showroom, and there's those who say his prices match its size. On the other hand, there's Jimmy Nunn in the next village. He knows all there's to know about any kind of motor vehicle. His main business is agricultural, but them as wants to save a bit of expense tell him just what they want and he gets it in for a more acceptable price. He takes commission, of course, but it's half what Josh Philips puts in his pocket when customers drive away. Leastways, so I've heard.'

'Thanks. I'll have a word with Jimmy on my way back today.'

'You thinking of staying around for a while then, sir?'

The perfect lead in! 'I've offered my services as test pilot to the Lance family. Chris Peterson's tragic death in addition to the loss of their prototype aircraft has left the company in a difficult quandary. As a former friend of Peterson I feel I must do what I can to ease their problem.'

'Now, there's a surprise, sir. You never said you was actually a pilot too. Well I never! There's been fears of heavy job losses. Even closure of the whole works or a company sell-out. But it sounds as if they're not giving up yet.'

'No. No, they're too big an organization to fold, even following such a setback. I've no doubt they'll be back on track before too long. You could help with that.'

Phil looked taken aback. 'Me?'

'Yes. You served an apprenticeship with the company. I understand the upper echelons of management are pretty much unchanged from that time – they weren't called on to fight because they were of more use here – so I'd welcome your impressions of them. I'll be working with them in the coming days and, as a newcomer, I'd welcome some insight into their personalities.'

It was all the man needed. He took a seat at a nearby table, his business protocol not allowing him to join a paying guest at his own table. Folding his arms he leaned back, prepared to stay for a while.

'Well now, I were only a lad when I was at Marshfield. I don't know that what I thought of them back then would fit with the men they are today.'

'On the contrary,' Ben said encouragingly, 'young people are often more perceptive, more honest in their reactions to people they meet. I shall be spending a lot of time with the chief engineer. Tell me what you know of him. Apart from your four years there, you must surely have heard plenty of other people's views when they're gathered around your bar. Praise or disgruntlement over what had occurred at the workshops that day.'

Phil smiled at that. 'You've hit it right on the head, sir. 'Specially on a Friday when they finish early and come in for a couple of beers before going home to their supper. I've certainly heard a thing or two about the bosses.'

'About Ray Povey?'

'Ah! Not lately, I'll say that.' He scratched at his thin moustache with hands that looked unable to remain still. 'There was a time when it seemed he and his missus were buying stuff for their house no man on his wage should be able to afford. My Mary went past there once and saw a big polished chest with gold handles being carried in from a Courtney's van. She happened to visit Lewes next day and saw something similar in their window. They don't put price tickets on their top class furniture, and there wasn't one on that. Word soon went round that there was something havey-cavey about that pair.

'Well, it reached Rita Povey's ears and she let on Ray had been left a tidy sum by an uncle in Australia.' He laughed and gave a wink. 'We've all heard that one, haven't we? Anyway, rumours kept on flying about. Jack Morecombe reckoned Ray was putting in some hours for another company – night shift, like – because he looked under the weather and was extra moody at work.'

'Did the truth ever emerge?' asked Ben.

'No, but things came to a head one day in the works canteen. Ray overheard a young fitter sniggering that Rita was selling her charms for cash. Well, Ray went for the lad and damn near did for him. Both of them ended in hospital, because after the first surprise the lad started hitting back. Turned out he'd been having boxing lessons in the evenings.'

'But it didn't solve the source of Povey's sudden wealth?'

'No-o, but the spending spree ended soon after. Daft thing was, in a year or so, Ray was made chief engineer with a wage that could buy some nice things anyway.'

Interesting, thought Ben. Was Povey doing a repeat perform-ance by taking money from a rival company? 'When was all this bother?'

'About two year ago.'

'So he hasn't been chief engineer very long?'

Phil shook his head. ''Bout a twelvemonth. When I was at the works he'd just been made up to section foreman. He was all right with us apprentice boys, but he could be shirty with some of the men who resented it, 'specially if he had a go at them in front of us lads.'

'What's the general view of him now?'

'It's only what I catch when they've had one or two and get free with their opinions.' Phil played with a coaster as he spoke. 'It's most likely the drink speaking.'

Ben smiled. 'Know what you mean.'

'Whatever else they say they'll never question his skill. Can't fault his technical knowledge.'

'He'd never have earned a top position in a prestige company like Marshfield unless he was able to fulfill its demands. Is the problem still his attitude to those under him? I've known several men whose knowledge was first-rate but who couldn't handle personnel successfully.' One of them lives not far from here, he thought savagely.

'That sounds about right, sir. Forever checking on them. Thinks he's the only one knows what's what. It gets their rag up good and proper.'

Roger Hall's opinion of the man had been favourable, but that relationship was unique. The chief designer was top dog, never to be criticized or questioned on the workshop floor, but Ben felt Povey's habit of finding fault and never praising was worth some investigating. Could the man have driven someone to retaliate in a way he hoped would put blame on Povey, little thinking it would produce such a disaster?

Pouring another cup of tea, Ben asked about the works manager, Jim Tilbrook. 'How do men react to him, Phil?'

'Ah, there's a horse of a very different colour.' Phil folded his arms and leaned back ready for another spell of gossip. 'One of the boys, is Jim. Lord, you should hear him on a Friday night. Has them all in a right merry mood, not anxious to go for their supper until he does. Silver tongue has Jim.' He chuckled. 'Don't know if half the yarns he tells are God's truth, but he holds an audience with 'em. You have to believe there's no woman on earth could resist him. He has the looks sure enough and there's a couple of babbies in the area with the same black hair and blue eyes.' He gave a broad wink. 'The local milkman is blond. His nippers are the same.'

Ben got the message. 'Is Jim married?'

'Never have been, never will be is his boast. Come down to the bar tomorrow and you'll almost certainly meet him.'

'I'll meet him at the works today. I'll be better able to judge him in his office, for that's when I'll have any dealings with him.' And where I'll be able to witness his dealings with the female workers, he thought. That'll give me a clearer idea of his success with women and whether Chris is likely to have been targeted for having stolen some of Jim's conquests. Ben had a theory that the more a man bragged of his adventures with a long list of women, the less likely it was to be true.

'How about John Kershaw?' Ben asked then.

Phil shook his head as he began realigning place settings that were already perfectly arranged on the checked tablecloth. 'Can't help you there, sir. He replaced Fred Kinsley as production manager just four months ago.'

That surprised Ben. Roger Hall had made no mention of it.

'From what I've heard he's something of a toff,' Phil continued, ceasing his fidgeting with cutlery and looking across the table again. 'Bought a posh house over at Fossbeck with stables and a paddock. The wife gives riding lessons. No children, so I'd say they're well breeched, wouldn't you?'

'Inheritance from an uncle in Australia?'

It brought a laugh. 'Daresay they buy everything at Courtney's. And I guess they patronize Fossbeck Manor House Hotel for their food and drink. It's where well-to-do families congregate.'

And where Julia Peterson can get champagne cocktails, Ben thought. The Lance family might well be on good terms with the Kershaws. Was that how John got the job four months ago? Mmm. Worth following up. Where had Kershaw worked before that time?

'Why did Fred Kinsley leave Marshfield, Phil?'

'Industrial accident. Crushed by a runaway pallet.'

'Oh?' This was interesting.

'Faulty brake. Damned thing kept going and knocked poor old Fred over, pinning him against the storeroom wall. Lucky to survive, but he's in a bad way. Three nippers and no wage coming in. Give him his due, Sir Edwin pays all the bills and sends a girl in three times a week to clean and cook while Fred's missus works at a laundry in Lewes.'

*Very* interesting! Generosity to prevent a case being brought against the company for serious injury caused by defective equipment? Was nobody acting for the Kinsley family? Could the apparent accident have been arranged to leave the way open for John Kershaw? The new production manager now topped Ben's list of possible saboteurs. He was anxious to meet the man.

\*     \*     \*

The day passed quickly with no more than a break for a sandwich and cup of tea at noon. Ben was totally absorbed in familiarizing himself with the aircraft he would be test-flying as soon as it was airworthy. Julia was right. The *Lance* was vastly different from anything he had ever flown. He was alternately excited and awed as the full potential of Hall's creation became apparent. He was like a boy with a toy he had longed to possess. The kind of toy young Jack Norton had never been allowed to own; could only feast his eyes on the pictures he cut from catalogues and pasted into a scrapbook hidden under his mattress.

Contrary to his early morning intention, although he was introduced to Ray Povey, Jim Tilbrook and John Kershaw, concentration on the work needed to complete the *Lance* took precedence over any opportunity to study them as possible saboteurs. In truth, Ben was so caught up in the work under way, he gave up thought of anything else.

When a loud wailing sound began he looked up in faint apprehension, then grinned on being told it indicated knocking-off time for the workforce engaged on building the *Snowbird*. None of the men in and around the *Lance* made any move to call it a day and half an hour later Hugo, Julia and Freddie entered the hangar. Ben continued making his personal sketches and diagrams to study in his room at The Dancing Bear, ignoring his new employers.

Hugo immediately demanded if Roger had discovered the design flaw yet. In character, he had made no effort to take his chief designer aside for a private discussion.

'I've been too busy keeping tabs on everything here,' Roger said calmly, much to Ben's relief. 'When I've a free moment I'll take another look at the drawings.'

'Not still holding on to that absurd notion, are you?'

'The good news is that there's less to do than I thought,' he continued, as if Hugo had not spoken. 'She should be ready for an initial trial run in five days. After that, another two or three to fit the guns, add the finishing touches, and serious flying can begin by the end of the month.'

'What does our pilot say to that?' asked Hugo, still staring in the direction of Roger's voice, having no idea where Ben stood or even if he was present.

'I go along with anything Roger says when I'm on the ground,' Ben said, noting that he was no longer Captain Norton but 'our pilot' now he was on their payroll. 'Once I'm in the cockpit with the engine running I'm in charge.'

'Hear, hear!' cried Freddie, who had his head inside the fuselage where an electrical engineer was checking work that had been done some months ago. 'Nobody tells me what to do once I'm strapped in watching for the starter flag to drop.' He twisted his head to look at his brother. 'You should understand that, Hugo. You commanded a squadron, for God's sake. I'll wager every one of your pilots became a law unto themselves once they were up and well away.' He straightened. 'As you most certainly would have been in your time.'

'Shut up, Freddie!' The admonition came from Julia who, like Hugo, apparently thought nothing of demeaning people in front of an audience; a company director in front of employees.

Freddie retaliated. 'It's a different case when people are free to drive away with your car whenever they please. No way can you be in charge then, Julia.'

Ben hid his smile. The appearance of Julia's car outside the works this morning must have prompted questions. What answer had she given?

Hugo was pursuing his theme. 'The entire workforce has been sworn to silence on what we plan to do here. It's essential that no publicity be allowed before we're ready for a proving flight in front of potential backers. We must erase memories of those damning headlines. Never let that fact slip from your minds.'

There was little more than a murmur from men eager to be left alone to do their work, so Roger spoke for them all. 'You can leave everything safely in our hands until the time comes. I'll keep you up to date on progress.'

Hugo frowned. 'There can't be any progress until you've traced that design fault and adjusted the existing components accordingly. Get down to that, Roger. We can't afford unnecessary delays.'

Ben watched as Julia linked her arm through her brother's to guide him across an area with potential hazards for a blind man. She wore wide-legged trousers in claret-coloured wool and a flowing sleeved cape of cream and grey squares. No widow's weeds for the woman Chris Peterson had married and continually betrayed. She had not looked his way just now. Neither had she last night answered his question on who had betrayed the other first in their marriage.

Freddie lingered to chat with the pair of overalled men checking the engine. To a motor racing addict any engine would draw his attention. Ben joined them and smiled at the youngest Lance sibling.

'Thanks for your support today, and at the directors' meeting yesterday.'

'Oh, we hell-for-leather chaps have to stick together,' he replied nonchalantly, turning away and strolling towards the hangar doors through which he could see his brother and sister entering the building housing the head office.

Ben followed, appreciating Freddie's decision to speak more privately to someone who was rather more than just 'our pilot', having invested a large sum in the company.

'Have you never felt the urge to take to the air?'

Freddie shook his head. 'Too risky.'

'What you do on a racing circuit isn't?' he asked with amusement.

'Yes, but it's on firm ground. No danger of falling hundreds of feet before I reach it. I don't like that idea at all, Ben.'

They had reached the hangar entrance well out of earshot, so Ben made use of the moment. 'How do you feel about the theory that sabotage caused the tragedy of the proving flight?'

They halted and faced each other. 'It's been done on the race-track. More than once. No reason why it shouldn't have happened in those circumstances. Look,' he reasoned, 'horses have been doped, saddle girths have been cut. Sprinters have been drugged, their running shoes damaged. Holes have been drilled in boats before a regatta; threatening messages have been sent to force boxers to pull their punches in a vital match.' He gave a rueful smile. 'Someone tried it on me at Monte Carlo last year, but I called his bluff and I'm still alive. Any activity involving large sums of money or professional superiority is liable to encourage dirty tricks. Some of those tricks are so dirty they take no heed of danger to lives.'

Swiftly changing his initial impression of Freddie Lance, Ben said, 'So you believe Roger's claim that someone severed the trim tab cable even knowing Chris was highly likely to be killed in the resultant crash?'

Freddie nodded. 'His purpose would have been to destroy the aeroplane and Marshfield's reputation. The pilot's life would be regarded as an unfortunate complication. I wouldn't care to be in your shoes during the coming weeks. There's every chance he'll do it again.'

With that parting shot Freddie walked off across the tarmac, hands in pockets, scarf flying in the strong breeze.

By eight p.m. everyone decided they were too tired to work productively any longer. Four headed for home, leaving Ben with Roger. They had intended to visit Jimmy Nunn to hire some kind of vehicle until Ben had decided on the car he wished to buy. It was too late for that, so Roger insisted on driving to The Dancing Bear and downing a whisky to keep out the cold during his return journey to join his long-suffering wife.

Once settled in the car, Ben told his companion what he had heard from Phil Bunyan, and quizzed him on his failure to mention that John Kershaw was new to the company.

'A man taking up a senior position just four months ago, who was one of the few people present during the final hour or so before Chris took off is surely a prime suspect.'

'Why?' demanded Roger shooting a swift look at him. 'I'd say the reverse. He'd hardly had time to become intimately familiar with the specifications of the *Lance*. As production manager he's concerned with *Snowbird* output as well. That's a hell of a lot to bone up on in four months. He was invited to be present in the hangar rather than outside with the workforce as a courtesy, that's all.'

'Yet you named him as one of the three who could have severed that cable,' Ben pointed out as they halted at a crossroads.

'So he could have if he had been determined to sabotage that flight. The plans are accessible in the design office during working hours, only locked away at night. Any man familiar with aircraft could recognize and identify what he saw on those drawings. I'm simply saying the premise is unlikely.'

They moved across the busy road to follow the narrow, curving way to Clanford which was unlit apart from lights showing in cottage windows. Ben took up his challenge.

'You said "any man familiar with aircraft", which must mean Kershaw worked in the industry before joining Marshfield. Where was that?'

'South Africa.'

'Did he transfer on recommendation?'

'No, we took him on trust. Same as we did with you.'

Ben could not make out Roger's expression in the shadowy light within the car, but he said, 'Touché.'

'Well, it doesn't do to call the kettle black, my friend. What I heard was that Mirium Kershaw came home last year to help her father recover from his wife's death by drowning when their yacht was hit by a foreign cargo ship riding without lights. Sadly, he then died during the influenza outbreak shortly afterwards, leaving Mirium a large house on the banks of the Thames and a respectable antiques business.

'John then joined her in England. They sold the mansion and bought a large cottage just outside Clanford as their principal home. Mirium also acquired an apartment in Chelsea in the same building as the one Chris and Julia bought three years ago. She still owns the antiques business and spends three days a week there.'

Sifting through all that information as he gazed at the moon through the windscreen, Ben said, 'So Julia met Mirium in the Chelsea mansion block, heard what you've just told me and invited her to visit Clanford House. Shortly after that, Fred Kinsley was injured so John was offered the position of production manager.'

'Something like that, I imagine. Sounds feasible.'

'Do you know which South African company Kershaw worked for and what its latest project was at the time he left?'

Roger turned in his seat. 'What are you getting at, for God's sake?'

'Roger, we're convinced someone sabotaged the *Lance* and killed Chris,' he cried impatiently. 'We cried down Hugo's plan to get policemen swarming all over the workshops. We decided to discover who did it by our own efforts. We agreed to probe the lives of three men who had had the opportunity to commit the outrage. That's what I'm doing.'

After a considerable pause Roger said, 'Yes, sorry. I'm not used to this kind of thing.'

'Neither am I. All I want is to fly the *Lance* and show her off to the world. What I don't want is to find I can't pull out of a dive and end my life in a deep crater filled with a shattered machine and my broken body.'

Roger's estimation of the rate of progress proved to have been over-optimistic. A week passed and Ben had not even taxied the *Lance* across the tarmac, much less lifted it off the ground. Hugo visited the hangar every day with Julia in tow, and each time he demanded to know if the design flaw had been identified. Day after day Roger avoided an answer, until he had had enough and lost his temper.

'There *is* no design flaw. There never has been. I've said it over and over again.'

Ben had backed him up. 'I've studied the plans and the aircraft itself. As soon as Roger gives the go-ahead I shall take the *Lance* on a trial run with total confidence. It's a superb design and we'll demonstrate that to the world before summer's halfway through.'

Hugo had said, almost sneeringly, 'You've been connected with it for no more than two weeks. How can you possibly speak with such bombast on the subject?'

'When we do what I've just said, and orders start coming in, you'll have the answer to that.' Through Ben's anger came a shaft of sudden sympathy. How devastating it must be for Hugo to know he would never fly this advanced fighter; never even see it. 'As one pilot to another, Major, I promise you your company has built a warplane that will alter the way men fight in the air in future.'

That change of approach must have caught Hugo unawares. He walked away without another word. Julia had looked daggers at Ben as she followed her brother. It was the first time she had acknowledged his presence in the hangar, yet he had known she was aware of him during each visit. Did she still mistrust him; believe he had an ulterior motive in joining Marshfield Aviation? If so, why had she not tried to question him again?

Sir Edwin clearly concentrated on the business side of the company, leaving his team of excellent managers to deal with the actual aircraft construction. He spent much of his time in London, staying at his club while he attended meetings and the inevitable lunches, dinners and golfing weekends, where more business was done than in boardrooms.

Freddie was also in London, but he was doing what all his idle friends were doing – rollicking in nightclubs until dawn, staying in bed all morning, frittering the afternoon away until it was time for cocktails and a light-hearted revue or musical comedy, then returning to the nightclubs. What a terrible waste of his youth, Ben thought, having seen too many lives end tragically too soon.

During that week Ben had hired a small van from Jimmy Nunn. He was so busy getting to know the machine he would be flying, he had had little time to think about selecting a car to buy, much less time to look for a place to live. The Bunyans were glad of his continued patronage and made no protest over the clutter in his room, which was inevitable when it was his only home.

Caught up though he was in the pressures of getting the *Lance* airworthy and mentally flying her, Ben did manage to probe the background of the sabotage suspects. What he found merely backed up what Phil had told him. He really needed to get more from the men themselves, but as they were also tied in with the *Snowbird* being worked on in the other hangar, he had little opportunity to corner them for a casual chat.

His chance eventually came two days later when Jim Tilbrook, works manager, came into the hangar to check on progress. Busily making himself some tea, Ben immediately offered the visitor a cup and one of the buns Mary Bunyan had made for him. She was concerned over the long hours he spent at work and had started to mother him. The kind of caring he had not known since he was seven years old.

Jim – he of the black hair, blue eyes and knowing smile – munched the bun with relish. 'Bonny Mary never made buns for me, Ben, yet I've told her many the time that I'd be returning to a cold, empty house with no supper waiting on the stove. Ah, but the girls all go misty-eyed for the daredevils who fly.' He produced the famous smile. 'Small wonder you're still a bachelor. Like me you have a better time keeping them all ready and eager. It's a fool who ties himself to one woman, don't you agree?'

Biting into his bun, Ben said, 'During the war the one thing that kept most men going was having a wife, or a special girl at home. The only thing that made sense to them in a sea of insanity. Of course, that's not needed now.'

The man who had been excused going to war because of the vital work he was doing clearly disliked being reminded of the fact. 'But here you are getting ready to persuade the government to invest in a weapon for another sea of insanity.'

Ben jumped on that. 'You don't agree with the decision to make warplanes rather than the *Broadwing*?'

'Passenger planes are the thing of the future. Bigger and better ones. More powerful. Longer range,' he said with enthusiasm. 'In a decade or two, travelling by air will make ships redundant. Who'll want to spend weeks puking over the deck rails when they can get to the other side of the world in a couple of days?'

He nodded towards the *Lance* in the centre of the hangar where Roger and his team were perfecting what was, in effect, a weapon of war. 'Marshfield might make a few of them for the RAF to fly as justification for their existence, that's all. The Major's living in his past. The money's in commercial craft. The *Snowbird* has kept us afloat and the bloody *Lance* crashed, but if he's determined on sticking with it we'll all be on the dole by Christmas twelvemonth. He's lost his sense as well as his sight, the Major has. And he's talked Sir Edwin into losing his.'

Dipping his hand into the box containing Mary's cakes, he took another and bit into it, giving Ben a calculating look. 'I heard it was you who tipped the scales with a hefty donation. Didn't you have enough excitement fighting the Huns that you want to start all over again?'

'The Huns are building faster and more lethally-armed fighters than we presently have. And they're producing them in their hundreds. I want this country to be able to match them if it becomes necessary.'

The group around the *Lance* had called a break and were making their way across for tea as Jim plonked his tin mug on the metal table top with an exclamation of impatience. 'Ach, you sound like Chris! Went on and on about being prepared. Way he spoke you'd think he couldn't return quick enough to killing other men.'

Ben wanted to offer a defence, point out that in war that was what soldiers were ordered to do, but the words stuck in his throat. The other man took his silence as a sign of culpability, and began to leave.

'Stick to conquering ladies, man. A hell of a lot safer than showing off in that there machine and ending up like your pal Chris.'

The satisfied smile on Roger's face faded as he reached Ben. 'What's up?'

Ben shook off memories of distant ghosts and held out the box of cakes. 'Help yourselves, lads. Mary gave me enough to feed a squadron.' He hardly noticed the use of that last word, but Roger raised his eyebrows.

'Don't get too carried away. You still have to persuade the RAF to buy sufficient aircraft to be able to form a squadron.' Seeing Ben's blank expression, he added, 'You can make a start this afternoon after we've fuelled her up.'

That statement swept all thoughts from his mind except the excitement of achieving what he had abandoned all else in his life for. 'She's ready?'

Roger nodded. 'If you are.'

Despite his eagerness to soar into the April sky and yell his exultation, Ben was fully professional in all aspects concerned with aircraft, so his union with the fiery *Lance* began with 'circuits and bumps' which every flight trainee had to undergo. It consisted of taking off, circling an appointed area, then coming in to touchdown and immediately lifting off again to repeat the process a number of times.

These landings with instant revs causing the aircraft to rise again, known to all pilots as 'bumps', were appropriately named. Beginners often bumped so badly they found it impossible to get off the ground again. Ben was no trainee but he had to learn how to handle the faster, more powerful, unfamiliar fighter that was so very different from those he had flown with the RFC.

His common sense approach paid off. The *Lance* would take some getting used to and he soon realized it would be many days before he would be ready to perform a proving flight as skilled as Chris Peterson's. By the time he switched off the engine and climbed from the cockpit he felt reluctant admiration for the man he was replacing.

He should have felt no surprise to find Hugo and Julia outside the hangar, the former hotly berating Roger for failing to ask his permission for the flight. Angry words left the chief designer unmoved. He was far more intent on hearing the new test pilot's report. Sobered by the thought of the many more hours of practice ahead before he mastered the *Lance*, Ben lost patience with Hugo.

'Major, your instructions were that all flights must be done with as much secrecy as possible, so nobody today was made aware of what was planned. It was a short trial, sir, that's all. A few adjustments need to be made before I take her up again. When I'm ready to make a full test flight you'll be notified.'

'From what I witnessed from the window you'll never make it,' Julia put in icily. 'You should return to flying melons and dates around the Mediterranean. That's probably more your level.'

Ben seized her arm in a tight grip and marched her across the hangar to a far corner. Ignoring his sister's outburst and concentrating on upbraiding Roger, Hugo was unaware of how the brown-haired man in an oil-stained flying suit was behaving. Just as well!

Thrusting Julia against the wall, Ben said, 'Get this into your head, Mrs Peterson. I'm a senior and vital member of Marshfield staff and a shareholder, to boot. Any time you decide to revert to type by insulting me, you'll do so well away from earshot of anyone else. Who the hell do you think you are? You've never learned to fly, nor shown an intelligent interest in the activity that provides the wherewithal for your expensive clothes, your idle life, your flat in Chelsea and your champagne cocktails. You clearly have the impression that, like a car, all one has to do with an aeroplane is get in, start it and whoosh! off you go. You're wrong. I know what I'm doing, and I'll succeed in ensuring the *Lance* is desired by everyone who matters. I'll not do it for Sir Edwin, nor for your brothers. Not to pull Marshfield up by its braces, and certainly not for you. Not even entirely for Roger Hall. I'll do it for me; for the pure joy of flying a machine so spectacular I'll only return to earth reluctantly.'

Julia's cold eyes narrowed. 'Brave words, Captain Norton – if that is who you are. I've been doing some checking. Oh yes, there is a company called Norton Freight which has just been bought by Frank Drysdale of Perth, Australia. The sale was handled by solicitors in Alexandria and a private bank in Cairo. Both sources confirmed they had only seen Mr Norton at the initial meeting. All further transactions were done by letter or aerogram. Their description of Mr Norton could match thousands of men and neither source made mention of his eyes being of slightly different colours.'

Ben grew wary. 'Bankers and solicitors only see the colour of banknotes.'

'You apparently have no wife, fiancée or mistress. You apparently don't even have friends. No letters arrive for you at The Dancing Bear.'

His anger surged again. 'You've been questioning the Bunyans about my private affairs?'

'Strangest of all is the fact that Chris never mentioned you once in my hearing, yet you claim to have been close. How close? I ask you again; did you and my husband share a love that went beyond the bounds of friendship?'

Time to walk away. 'Go to that Chelsea apartment of yours and share the artificial, empty life of those who have nothing but air in their heads and money in their pockets. That's where women like you belong, not here where history is about to be made.'

It was late in the evening when Ben returned to The Dancing Bear after an intense discussion with Roger Hall and the team working on the *Lance*. This had partially mitigated his anger over Julia's probing, but it returned now as he drove from Marshfield in a heavy thunderstorm. It had been an exhausting day and the small tangle with her had taken away some of his elation over what he had achieved in the air. All he wanted now was a hot bath and dinner in his room while he tried to recapture the joy of sitting in that small cockpit communing with the elements.

He parked the van and ran with his head bowed against the

driving rain to the arched entrance of the inn. There were a few people in the bar which tonight had the additional smell of wet overcoats. Phil waved at him as he crossed to the stairs, but Ben decided to tackle the man about Julia's snooping at breakfast tomorrow. However, Phil raised the bar flap and came out from where he had been yarning with a village regular to accost Ben.

'Captain Norton, sir, there's a young lady here been waiting to speak to you.'

Wiping rain from his face Ben saw a very attractive blonde of around twenty-five walking across from one of the booths, a glowing smile curving her scarlet tinted mouth.

'Ben Norton?' she asked eagerly.

'Yes.'

She offered her hand. 'Deborah Keene. I'm a freelance journalist with a contract to write a biography of Chris Peterson, the war hero who was so tragically killed last month. I understand you were a squadron colleague who fought beside him in the air. I'm so thrilled to have tracked you down and look forward to hearing about those daring dawn raids which earned you both the sobriquet The Skylarks. Major Lance has given me permission to interview you whenever you're free.' She gave an understanding smile. 'Mrs Peterson said you're reluctant to talk to her about her husband for fear of upsetting her, so she's also anxious to learn about anything you tell me that will help her through her terrible period of grief.'

# FIVE

Ben had breakfast in his room on the excuse of having vital work he must complete before leaving for Marshfield. Mary Bunyan was by now so fond of him nothing was too much trouble for her.

He had used the same excuse to avoid Deborah Keene last night, but he knew she would not be fobbed off forever. She was doubtless waiting for him to descend right now, with her pencil poised. A young woman who had landed a career-boosting opportunity was certain to want to research her subject down to the finest detail, damn her. And damn Julia who would back her to the hilt.

Overtired by the events of that triumphant day when he had finally flown the *Lance*, Ben had taken a long time to fall asleep. When he had, old ghosts had returned to haunt him. He had known the risks of immersing himself in a situation so closely linked to the past, but he had left his old life in Alexandria fully believing he would have the upper hand over Chris, whatever developed. The crash that nobody was aware he had witnessed had changed the emphasis completely. Chris still held the aces in death.

The generous cooked breakfast grew cold as Ben stared from the window cursing this unforeseen obstacle. The Keene woman wanted an account of derring-do in company with Christopher George Peterson MC. If Ben told it how it had really been it would bring the end of the exciting future he had set his heart on. He was thirty-two and had sacrificed a great deal to get where he was now. No way would he let Chris snatch it from him posthumously. Yet he refused to weave a fabric of lies. Keeping silent all these years was one thing. He had no intention of enhancing the heroic myth that had been perpetrated so shamelessly.

Getting to his feet he thought of the only other option which, in truth, was an impossibility. How could he possibly get rid of

Deborah Keene? He had no influential acquaintances as the Lances had, someone he could persuade to offer the girl a more prestigious and lucrative assignment for which she must drop this present one. He could only dodge her for so long and, with Hugo's backing and prodding from Julia, there was no chance of the project being dropped or even deferred.

Catching sight of the time, Ben hastily slurped some tea and ate a slice of cold toast smeared with fried egg before collecting the thick folder holding all his notes and sketches, his wallet, loose change and keys to the hired van, then shrugged on the thick overcoat he had bought at the weekend. Leaving his room he quietly trod the corridor leading to the rear entrance of the inn. As he slid on to the driving seat he told himself the Keene woman would soon catch on to this means of escape, so the sooner he found a place to live in the better. At Marshfield he could plead pressure of work to keep her at bay and in his own home he would have the option of not answering when she knocked on the door.

Nearing Marshfield Ben saw, with a lift to his spirits, pale shafts of sunshine penetrating the fine drizzle. If the rain cleared by this afternoon he would make another flight to test the modifications they would implement this morning. Then, through this pleasant thought came the reminder of his biggest problem. If someone was still determined to destroy the *Lance*, even with him in the cockpit, he should concentrate on identifying him. That person could end his beckoning future more drastically than a blonde with dreams of a journalistic coup.

These worries must have etched themselves on his expression because Roger greeted him with, 'Out on the tiles to celebrate, were you? If so, you're not taking my baby up today.'

'I was working until all hours,' Ben protested as he dumped his briefcase and overcoat on a chair in the screened area they used as an office in the huge hangar. 'I wasn't entirely happy with the angle we reckoned would adjust the problem with the gun housing. I worked on the figures and I've come up with something more satisfactory. The pilot has to press the button with short jabs and he needs to know the angle of fire will be one hundred per cent correct. Here's my diagram.'

They bent together over the sheet of paper Ben rolled out

across the drawing board as the rest of the team began arriving for work. One by one they clustered around the two senior men ready to study and comment, but Ben's firm statement that he was the person who would fly the machine and he damn well knew what he wanted soon had them all nodding in agreement.

They worked on that and several other small changes until both Ben and Roger were satisfied that another test flight could be undertaken. The clouds had cleared away leaving a pale blue spring sky and a gentle breeze.

Gazing up as he stood at the entrance to the hangar, Ben murmured, 'It's enough to make any man yearn to be up there as free as the birds.'

'Not me,' declared a hearty voice he recognized. 'There's far more attractions down here.'

Jim Tilbrook had one of them with him. Deborah Keene was wearing a red coat fashionably too large that hung straight to mid-calf. A black cloche hat hid most of her hair; overlarge black spectacles hid most of her face. Over her shoulder hung a businesslike camera, and a fat notebook in her black-gloved hands completed the image she clearly wanted to portray.

Ben had met many journalists both during the war and in the Middle East, none of them in the least like this young woman. He suddenly wondered if she was merely a wealthy ingénue who had persuaded a besotted sugar-daddy to give her the opportunity to realize a dream. Had she ever actually worked for a living?

Her smile washed over him as she came forward eagerly. 'I intended to join you for breakfast, Captain Norton, but I'm afraid I overslept. It must be the country air, so relaxing after the fog of London.' She glanced at the men who were setting out mugs and packets of sandwiches on the bench outside the office. 'I see you're going to take a break for lunch, so now would be a good time to get from you a brief résumé of how you and Chris Peterson came to be known as The Skylarks.'

'Not a good time, Miss Keene,' he responded crisply. 'While I snatch a quick bite I'll be getting ready to fly as soon as she's fuelled up and towed out to the airstrip.'

'Gosh, how thrilling!' she enthused. 'To actually see the *Lance* in the air! I'll take masses of pictures. Before, during and after!'

'No! Major Lance won't allow that.' Ben began walking back into the hangar to grab a mug of tea and a couple of someone's sandwiches. His secretive (unnecessary after all) departure from The Dancing Bear meant he had not picked up the usual lunch pack Mary provided.

Deborah trailed after him. 'He was quite happy about it when I gave him a brief résumé of how I've planned the book.'

Ben grunted a reply. Obviously, she had picked up the phrase 'brief résumé' from someone and believed regular use of it would sound authentic enough to enhance her pose. He then recalled that last night she had described herself as a 'freelance journalist', which meant she was not under contract to any particular editor or publisher. It could also mean no one would employ her.

Reaching for the mug Mary had given him with a picture of a dancing bear on it, Ben deftly extracted a cheese and pickle doorstep sandwich from Roger's lunch box and faced Deborah again.

'Try using that camera now and it'll be confiscated. Have it out with the Major. He'll explain why pictures of the *Lance* ready for takeoff, in mid-air and landing are taboo. That also includes shots of me engaged in such activity.'

Her cheeks flushed with anger. 'That's ridiculous! Photographs will be a major aspect of the book. Mrs Peterson has agreed to let me use snaps from the albums her husband kept, showing him from boyhood, through the war years and up to his tragic death.'

'And that's where a biography ends,' snapped Ben waving a half-eaten sandwich in her direction. 'I'm not Chris Peterson. Images of me would be irrelevant.'

'No,' she argued. 'I'll include old wartime shots of you together, so present day ones of you preparing to launch the aircraft that killed him will be compellingly emotive for my readers.'

Savage anger rushed through him. 'If it killed me too, think how even more compellingly emotive those pictures would be for them, Miss Keene. Your biography would be an overnight bestseller.'

Roger grew aware of Ben's fury and swiftly intervened. 'He's not being uncooperative, Miss Keene.' Putting a hand beneath her elbow he led her away from the men intent on their snack.

'I'm about to telephone the Major to tell him Captain Norton will make a short flight at two o'clock. You can speak to him about photographs and he'll explain his ruling on test flights.'

'That's a well-known technique, man. They try harder to capture your interest.'

Ben turned to see Jim Tilbrook replacing a cork in a small bottle from which he had tipped something in his tea to enliven it. Jim winked. 'I'm not playing the heroic flyer, so a little boost sharpens my wits during a long working day.'

Still unsettled by the spat with Deborah Keene, Ben nodded at the mug in Jim's hand. 'Better not let the Major catch you. He's a stickler for obeying the rules. All the more so when they're his rules.'

The other man's eyes narrowed. 'You've learned a lot about him in just a couple of meetings.'

'That's right,' he returned. 'It's one of my talents, so watch out if you're in the habit of breaking any more rules. I'll surely know about it before long.'

He would have moved away to mingle with the men he had been working on the *Lance* with, but Jim's next words stopped him.

'Cocksure bastard, aren't you! Just like him.'

Oh no, very definitely not like Chris. He gave a sour smile. 'Was it his arrogance or something else that made you despise him so much?'

'You should have the answer to that. Close mates, weren't you, when you fought the Hun together?'

Time to walk away from this conversation. Ben joined the others who were now laughingly squabbling over ownership of a banana, and he picked it up.

'Mine, I think!' He started to peel it. 'You're all ready to sit back and relax. I've got to fly the machine you've been tinkering with all morning and trust you knew what you were doing. I need this extra sustenance.'

Amid the joking responses, Ben was aware of Roger returning with a visibly chastened girl by his side. The Major had lived up to his expectations! The camera no longer hung from her shoulder and she stayed beside the works manager as Roger came to join them all.

'Has Major Lance been fully informed of the flight this time?' Ben asked. Roger nodded. 'Wanted to delay it an hour because he had a visitor, but I told him cloud was building up in the east and three o'clock would be too late.' He grinned. 'Load of tosh, but we don't want to kick our heels for half the afternoon when it's not essential. Besides, you're all keyed up for it. Doesn't do to hang about getting edgy.'

Ben took him up on that. 'I'm not edgy, Roger. I've had my eye on her the whole time. Nobody could have jinxed her before the flight.' He swallowed the last of his tea and put the mug back on the table. 'I suppose Julia's planning to come and watch.'

'Already on the way, no doubt. Ben, make it a little more exciting this time, then she might believe you're fully qualified for the job.'

He ignored Roger's teasing smile. 'Damn Julia. I'll fly the way I think best at this stage. With just a meagre forty-five minutes at the controls so far, the only way I could emulate Peterson would be to end up in a hole in the ground and I've no intention of risking that to make a point with my employers. Or to make that irritating woman's biography sell worldwide.'

He strode away to the small partitioned area at the rear of the hangar which housed toilets and washing facilities where pilots could also don their flying suits in private. Despite his denial, Ben was feeling edgy. Test flying was demanding at the best of times. A man could do without the presence of hostile spectators . . . and women who had no experience of flying making stupid demands.

When he was ready he stood for a while breathing slowly and steadily as he had always done before going off on those unforgettable milk runs, when he and Chris had emerged from the half-light, very low and fast, to take the enemy by surprise and shoot up their aircraft on the ground. It had been very effective. While it had lasted.

The sound of the *Lance* being towed out to the airfield caused him to blink away those images and remember what he was about to do. Very tame by comparison. Ah, give him just a few weeks and he would show anyone Flight Sergeant Norton could match the very best of them.

Outside the hangar was a small group of spectators. Ben identified Ray Povey, chief engineer, who had overseen the work being done after that first experimental flight, and John Kershaw, production manager, who was present purely because of his status. The latter was talking animatedly to Julia Peterson, who appeared to be wrapped in Joseph's coat of many colours today. Hugo was alongside Roger, probably still badgering him about the supposed design fault, and on the Major's other side Deborah Keene was scribbling furiously on her notepad while Jim Tilbrook spoke with much waving of hands. As Phil Bunyan had said, the works manager had a silver tongue, and that girl was fool enough to believe all he told her.

A small spurt of excitement returned as Ben walked out to the silver aeroplane; a fresh sense of arriving where he had so much wanted to be. He climbed into the narrow cockpit and fastened the straps. The engine fired and the propeller began to spin faster and faster, banishing all thoughts except concentration on taking this beauty into the air. A few circuits and bumps to get the feel of those changes wrought since the first flight, then he would put her through her paces. Gently.

The sky remained clear save for a few fluffy white clouds tinted here and there with gold as sunrays caught them. God, it was the true essence of freedom to race across the sky leaving all the complexities of life on the ground. There had been times, even during the war, when it had been possible to forget all else while he was up where birds never ventured. Just a man in an aeroplane, like all the others. Until the shooting started.

The preliminary circuits and bumps were pleasingly smooth, although the *Lance* seemed heavier to take off the ground each time today. Nothing to worry about. The slight readjustments they had made would have altered the balance. He would take that into account.

After several low passes at moderate speed, Ben climbed to test the aircraft's performance at higher altitude. He was delighted at the ease of this manoeuvre. He headed towards the sun with no loss of speed. What a beauty this machine was! She responded to his lightest touch as if this was her rightful element. A pilot could make her do anything he wanted with split second timing. Once armed he could outwit and outfly an enemy in aerial combat without being vulnerable himself. Roger Hall was a genius.

The urge to continue climbing before rolling over to execute an exhilarating dive had to be suppressed. He was too responsible to embark on aerobatics before he was well and truly familiar with this advanced warplane. So he continued to effect passes and gentle climbs until he felt truly as one with the *Lance*.

It was while circling on the far side of Pitman Hill that he saw the altimeter was responding erratically and the false horizon had become a wavy line. They had certainly worked on the instrument panel this morning, but he knew everything had been securely fitted back in place. He had checked it himself. What could have caused something to work loose? None of his manoeuvres had been extreme enough to shake the aircraft to that extent.

Pushing the nose down as he passed over the hill the altimeter jiggled between four and six thousand feet, and the lower he dropped the more it jumped from numeral to numeral. The artificial horizon was now so indistinct as to be almost unreadable. With growing concern Ben noticed that the fuel gauge was also moving erratically. He knew the *Lance* had been filled with more than enough to cope with a short test flight, so what was causing this drastic reaction?

Creeping into his mind came an unwelcome thought. Flying as extremely as Chris Peterson had on that day, faulty instruments could have led him to misread height and speed during that last fatal dive. Did the *Lance* indeed have a design fault? Today, even this careful experimental flight had exposed some flaws. Anxiety hovered as he headed towards Marshfield. Would the stick also lock before he could land safely?

Deciding to go straight in as soon as he approached the landing strip he assessed his chances. Visibility was perfect, weather conditions the same, and he was experienced enough to make a calculated landing without instruments. He had successfully carried off more than a few risky returns to earth during the war and more recently along the Mediterranean coast.

Gazing down to assess his height, the devastating truth hit him. The hangars looked shimmery; wobbled as if made of jelly. The instruments were not faulty; it was his eyesight. Dear God, was he in the initial stage of some frightful destructive disease that attacked a person's vision? Was it imagined or were sharp spasmodic pains starting to attack his temples?

The prime impulse of a pilot, whatever his condition or circumstance, is to get down as swiftly and safely as possible. Men had been seen to do the almost impossible by Ben, who had been inspired by their courage and skill. In this instance it would need determination, steady nerves and enough resolution to put aside fear to do the job successfully.

Concentrating hard, Ben was unaware of murmuring the mantra he had chanted when making hairy landings in France, and since. He kept the nose down regardless of the fact that the altimeter appeared to be recording a climb, one made in a series of short upward surges. But the ground was definitely coming up to meet his defective view of the mown strip running through the longer grass. His heartbeat thudded against his ribs, his throat grew dry, and his hand gripped the stick so tightly his wrist ached. If he levelled out too high he had a second chance. If he left it too late . . .

Suddenly, everything made sense. Engine noise, the change in the rush of air around the cockpit, the nearness of the stand of trees at the end of the runway all told him he could breathe easily again. A few moments later a jolt told him the wheels had made contact and the *Lance* was running smoothly to a halt on the exact spot he would have chosen.

Sweating heavily, Ben stayed in the cockpit until the maintenance crew in the tow truck began to cross from the hangar; a shimmering shape emerging from a mirage. His heartbeat still thudded, his throat was still parched, but he now had just the one fear lying like a dead weight on his chest.

The affliction had started so suddenly and severely. There had been no hint of anything wrong with his sight. At his last medical check in Alexandria, Dr Kaseem had declared it to be perfect. A fresh surge of fear ran through him. Please God he was simply suffering from the onset of a particularly virulent fever, nothing more. Something that would pass leaving him fully fit. The alternative was beyond acceptance.

The blur of a human face appeared beside him. The voice was that of young Felix Stroud and it held a note of anxiety.

'Everything all right, sir?'

'Absolutely,' he replied with an effort.

'You came in earlier than we expected . . . and in a bit of a hurry.'

'Yes.'

After a moment or two Felix asked, 'Are you going to drive her to the hangar or shall we tow her in?'

Ben cast him a bleary look. 'What's the hurry?'

'Well . . . the Major's waiting to have a word with you.'

'What about, for God's sake?' he demanded. The pains in his temples were fast developing into the kind of headache that needed peace, quiet and a darkened room. 'As he couldn't have seen any aspect of the flight what can he possibly have to say about it?'

Another moment or two of silence from the mechanic. 'I believe it concerns the young lady journalist.'

'In that case I'll stay where I am while you tow her to the hangar. I need to report to Mr Hall before listening to more nonsense about her book.'

'Righto, sir,' came the amused comment. 'We'll take her a good way in so's you can go direct to the office where Mr Hall's taken cover. She tried to take snaps of him while he was watching your flight. He wasn't best pleased.'

Felix's indistinct features disappeared and Ben soon heard the towline being attached. He automatically released the brake, his chaotic thoughts unable to come up with what he could say to Roger that would not bring about the end of his status as Marshfield's test pilot.

Sudden dimness after bright sunlight told Ben they had reached the hangar. Only after several voices asked if he was all right did he register the fact that they were waiting for him to climb from the cockpit. All his limbs acted normally, but he had difficulty seeing where exactly to put his feet. The floor was further down than it had looked. He stumbled and would have fallen if the table holding their mugs had not been there for him to grab for support. The weighty jolt set the mugs rattling against each other and several fell over.

'Watch out, sir, there's hot tea in them,' warned someone nearby. 'We thought you'd like a drop when you got in.'

Still gripping the edge of the table, Ben stared at the earthenware mugs, two of which were now rolling on the surface spilling brown liquid over the oilcloth. One of them was decorated with a dancing bear and an image rose up in his mind to make appalling sense of what had happened. He then knew exactly what he was going to say to Roger waiting in the office for his report.

Roger looked at him from beneath furrowed brows. 'That's a hell of a conclusion to draw.'

'Not at all,' Ben countered wearily, the effects of whatever Jim Tilbrook had laced his tea with making rational thought an ongoing effort. 'We've been on guard against someone having a second go at sabotaging the *Lance*, so he sabotaged the pilot instead. He confessed he's against Marshfield producing warplanes. He also made it clear he was not an admirer of Chris Peterson. Very much the reverse. And he's not afraid to air these views down at The Dancing Bear.'

'Yes, but . . .'

'Roger, I saw him putting a cork in the neck of a small bottle from which he made no secret he'd poured something to keep him going during a long working day. My mug had been standing next to his.'

'Even so . . .'

Sharper pain began lancing through Ben's head making him lose control. 'For God's sake, man! You swear there's no design fault. I've flown the aircraft twice to prove your point. There's nothing wrong with the instruments – Felix just checked them – and I had twenty-twenty vision at my eye test just before Christmas. I tell you that bastard put something in my tea before I took her up.'

'Why would he be careless enough to let you see him with the bottle in his hand? As you say you did, there's no chance he'll hang on to it as evidence. Your successful eye check's no use in building a case against him. Even if the local doctor examines you right away and says your condition is due to ingesting some noxious substance, how would you prove it came from that bottle?' He frowned. 'You should let Dr Gaines give you the once over, Ben. You could have developed . . .'

'I haven't developed anything. I just need to sleep this off before rumours that I'm unfit to fly start circulating. Hugo would fire me on the spot. If he should hesitate, Julia would push him in that direction.' Eyes half closed to counteract the pain in his temples, he challenged his friend. 'Is that what you want after I helped you fight the battle to get the *Lance* relaunched and into full production? After I proved my readiness to defy the Lance family's lack of faith in your design? Is it?'

Plonking on to an old wicker chair, Roger wagged his lowered head. 'No, Ben, by no means. I just don't understand what's going on here. I've known Jim Tilbrook for years. Yes, he's smooth-tongued, but surely not a black villain.'

Silence hung between them for a moment or two. 'Well, I don't believe he wanted to kill me, or to wreck the aircraft. He was simply giving a warning of what might come if we don't heed his message.'

'Which is?'

Ben was reaching a stage past remaining on his feet. He needed bed and darkness. 'Damned if I know . . . or care,' he mumbled. 'I'm going to fly the *Lance* before an audience of potential investors before the summer's over and create triumphant headlines worldwide which'll be my message to anyone who tries to stop me. Now, for pity's sake set up that camp bed, cover me with a blanket, send word to the Major that we'll be working all night, then bugger off home, Roger. We'll talk more in the morning.'

Ben awoke in a strange room. The small clock on the dresser told him it was six a.m. He lay for a while listening to cockerels crowing and the dawn chorus of smaller birds, then he moved his head warily. Good! He slowly sat up. Marvellous! He felt clear-headed and very refreshed from a deep sleep. Even optimistic. Which was surprising after yesterday's events. He certainly remembered those hairy minutes when his sight of the instruments and everything on the ground blurred. He vaguely recalled his efforts to convince Roger of Tilbrook's implication while fighting the growing effects of whatever the works manager had poured in his tea. After that there was a blank, but he guessed he was now in the Halls' spare bedroom.

His clothes, along with his flying suit, were draped over a chair but a dressing gown hung on the back of the door so he put that on over his underpants and went in search of a cup of tea. In the kitchen he found Roger, also in a dressing gown, careworn and heavy-eyed.

'You look better than when I put you to bed,' he said by way of greeting.

Ben sat on a ladder-back chair. 'It's good of you to bring me here. How on earth did you manage it without causing a ruction with Hugo?'

Roger gave one of his rare grins. 'After finding the courage to threaten him with taking my design elsewhere I find I can now lie to him with great firmness. Fortunately, he had that journalist woman hanging round his neck so he limited his language and unwillingly accepted what I told him. I think he's wary of causing too much aggravation in case she puts something in her book he won't like.'

Not half as wary as I am, thought Ben. 'What about Julia?'

Roger crossed to the range where a kettle was emitting steam and poured water into a brown teapot. 'You'll discover Julia does as her brother dictates when he's there, but she's a vixen if he's not.'

'And she's encouraging the Keene woman to disrupt our work in order to get tittle-tattle, which has no place in a biography of Chris Peterson, the renowned airman. Can't Hugo put a stop to it?'

Roger gave the tea a stir. 'The sooner she's got what she wants, she'll leave us alone. Keep dodging her and we'll never get rid of her.' He poured the dark brew into large cups and pushed one towards Ben. 'We have to accept that Julia will want the book to be a worthy tribute to the husband who died in such a horrific manner. She's hiding her grief in the way women of her standing do. Recapturing his life in league with the journalist will maybe ease the pain of loss a little.'

With the cup halfway to his mouth Ben stared at Roger in amazement. 'What tommyrot! Theirs was a showcase marriage, nothing more. She kept up a pretence in public as women of her standing do, to use your own words, but from what she told me herself it's obvious the union was arranged purely for the benefit of Marshfield Aviation. No, Roger, she's colluding with Deborah Keene to suit her own agenda. I know very well what it is and I won't have our progress with the *Lance* delayed by her. It's too important.'

It was Roger's turn to stare. 'You will have to see Dr Gaines. You're hallucinating.'

'Ha! No, no, my friend, I did that once when I flew too high and suffered from lack of oxygen. My feet are firmly on the ground now. The trouble with you is, you're a dreamer. Your head's full of facts, figures and statistics, and your eyes see only mythical, magical flying machines. That's why you're a champion designer. We salute you for being what you are. But you lose out on recognizing human complexities, adverse personality undercurrents. Our employers are devious and totally self-centered. I've seen little of Sir Edwin, but the man who fathered them all must be of that ilk. I don't trust any of them to look beyond their own desires.'

# SIX

Gently refusing the Halls' offer of a bath and breakfast, Ben called a taxi to drive him to The Dancing Bear, where he entered by the rear door after spotting Deborah Keene at a table in the eating area. Treading the upstairs corridor he decided to trade on Mary Bunyan's good nature to bring to his room eggs, bacon and everything else she could fit on a plate as soon as he had had a bath and dressed in fresh clothes. Only then would he turn his thoughts to how best to deal with Jim Tilbrook's malicious move yesterday.

That problem was swiftly driven from his mind on entering his room. It was clear someone apart from the young girl who made the bed and dusted the dresser each day had been in there. Even the dusting had become perfunctory now he had brought in additional boxes of personal items and piles of professional manuals, which stood on the floor, on the two chairs and along the dresser top.

Cynthia, the chambermaid, was Mary Bunyan's niece; an ingenuous sixteen-year-old who seemed in awe of Ben whenever they happened to come face to face. She would not be bold enough to go through his personal possessions, but they were definitely no longer as he had left them yesterday morning. Anger surged through him as he checked the contents of each box, then of each drawer. Nothing had been taken, but the intruder had made no attempt to disguise this invasion of his room. Only the double-locked briefcase would have defeated her, but for how long?

His rage now focused on Phil Bunyan as he strode the corridor and leaped down the stairs two at a time. His headlong progress drew the interest of the Keene girl, who began to rise from her breakfast table.

'Sit down!' he ordered, heading for the small office behind the bar where Phil was making a telephone call. Pressing his finger on the cradle Ben effectively cut him off, saying, 'I want a word with you and it won't wait. How much did she pay you to give her the key and turn a blind eye?'

Phil remained seated holding the receiver, looking bemused. 'Key?' he mouthed.

'The thing that opens locked doors,' Ben snapped. 'My locked door. I carry mine with me, but the master key hangs on that board above your head.' He pointed to it. 'How much was her bribe to hand that over? Come on, man! It was a breach of trust; serious professional misconduct.'

'What?' Bunyan rose clumsily, pale-faced. 'Bribe? What're you talking about? That key hangs there so Cynthia can go up and clean the rooms every morning. She puts it back when she finishes. Why would she pay me to give it to her?'

Ben flung out his arm to point in the direction of the dining area. 'I'm talking about that woman eating breakfast. She's searched my luggage and been through the drawers in the chest. Someone gave her the key. If not you, was it Cynthia?'

'Certainly not.'

'Then who? Your wife?'

The other man now grew angry. 'I'll thank you not to drag Mary into this. I say again, I've no idea what's going on here. Far as I'm aware that key's been on the hook since young Cynthia cleaned the rooms yesterday. We didn't see you for supper and your van wasn't parked outside all night, so we guessed you was elsewhere. I see you arrive in a taxi just now and walk round the back to come in, which I thought was odd. Now you're laying down the law about this danged key, saying your luggage has been gone through. It don't make any sense, I tell you.' Recalling his status as innkeeper he adopted a more conciliatory tone. 'You've been under a strain, working all hours on that warplane, Captain. Could be you've been a bit hasty when looking out what you wanted and left your things in something of a muddle.'

Ben also calmed down. He knew men well. Phil Bunyan was genuinely confused by his accusation. 'I spent the night with Mr and Mrs Hall. He and I had things to discuss. I went upstairs intending to take a bath and change my clothes, then found evidence that my boxes had been opened and searched. Tell me, Phil, when did Miss Keene come back here yesterday?'

Responding to Ben's friendlier attitude, he said, 'Latish. She and Mrs Peterson had taken their evening meal at Clanford House, but they had a nightcap here before they went upstairs for Miss Keene to show Mrs Peterson something in her room. I never saw them come down again. I was on the go at the bar last night. Charlie Drew's booze-up with his pals before he goes off to be a soldier. Daft young bugger!'

Ben hardly registered those last words. His anger rose again at the news that Julia had been here last night. Having a nightcap; something she told him she never did in a village pub because they didn't provide champagne cocktails. Turning abruptly, Ben rounded the bar and headed for the solitary guest just finishing her breakfast.

Standing beside her, Ben demanded icily, 'Are you prepared to sink that low in order to boost your career? Whose idea was it; hers or yours?'

She gazed up at him calmly enough, but evidently puzzled. 'Hers . . . but I don't accept that there's anything discreditable about using pictures of him in my book. It's a biography. He was a war hero. Without photos of his early days the book wouldn't have as much impact.' She stood to confront him, her cheeks faintly pink. 'I'm not doing this to boost my career. It's a kind of labour of love. I was twelve when the war ended. From the age of ten Chris Peterson had been my hero. I collected pictures and newspaper cuttings about his exploits to put in a scrapbook. I sent letters to France hoping he would somehow get them. I knitted a scarf and socks for him at Christmas. There was an address people could use to send presents to the Front.' Her eyes began to sparkle. 'I bought chocolate with my pocket money and persuaded my father to give me five Woodbines in a packet to include in the parcel. Mother made a cake for him. We all wanted to show our pride and gratitude for what he had done.'

My God, thought Ben, this girl is in love with a man who never was. Her revelation drove from his mind her invasion of his room as he recalled that battle-torn Christmas two days before Chris had joined Hugo Lance's elite squadron. The officers' mess was stacked with hampers filled with gourmet food and wine, boxes of cigarettes and cigars, gifts of warm underwear, expensive leather gloves and shoes, bespoke shirts and even silk dressing gowns. They had been arriving all that week.

There had been a separate delivery brought on a battered carrier drawn by a mud-splattered horse sagging between the shafts: brown paper wrapped parcels sent from strangers to the brave pilot who had shot down the enemy ace Gustav Blomfeld. Ben remembered passing the officers' mess that evening and seeing Chris standing atop a table conducting an auction of the contents of those parcels, some drawing roars of laughter at their awfulness. Deborah Keene's knitted scarf might have been one of them. That was the night Ben had come dangerously close to killing him.

'You would have been there, too,' said a tender voice bringing him from the past. 'Julia hasn't any snaps taken at Christmastime. Do you have any I could use?'

Mud, despair, the incessant sound of gunfire, the sight of that bastard denigrating the kindness of strangers all faded to leave the eager face of a young woman who had no idea of what she was asking him.

'Is that what you were searching in my room for?' There was no anger in the words now. That flashback had shaken him too much.

Her brow furrowed. 'Searching in your room? No. How could I?'

'So what were you and Julia doing here last night?'

'Having a drink. She kindly invited me for dinner at Clanford House, then drove me back. I took the opportunity to show her the shots I've chosen from the collection she lent me. We went to my room to get her approval and she took the rest back with her.' She gave a tentative smile. 'We wanted to ask your opinion and get from you some background description to match the pictures, but Mr Bunyan said you were still out. Would you care to do that now?'

'No. Julia was with you the whole time?'

'Yes. She left at around eleven.'

'Did you go out and wave her off?'

She frowned. 'What is this? A police interrogation?'

'Did you?'

'No. She said it wasn't necessary. You're being very aggressive for no reason I can see. Why're you always so rude, Captain Norton?'

Ben studied her silently for several moments, trying to get his thoughts straight. 'During my overnight absence someone broke into my room and made a thorough search of my belongings. Bunyan denies giving the master key to anyone, so it must have been taken from the hook in his absence from the office. There's only one person I know who would have done that, and she must have had it planned when she dissuaded you from seeing her drive away.'

Deborah sank back on the chair, still frowning. 'Why would Julia want to go through your things? It doesn't make sense.'

'Oh yes, it does. She's playing along with you because a biography of her vaunted husband will be good for Marshfield, that's all. That woman has an agenda of her own, believe me. Don't be taken in by her bereaved widow act. That marriage was a sham; just another boost for the family business. You'll find out before long.'

'But . . . but what has that to do with the alleged invasion of your room?'

He turned away, having gained the information he wanted. The priorities of a bath, fresh clothes and breakfast returned.

She called after him, 'Will you be free for an interview this evening?' He ignored her and headed back to Bunyan's office. The innkeeper glanced up warily. 'I'm going to use the bathroom for half an hour to freshen up, Phil. Could Mary then provide some breakfast in my room? I need to work on some details before going over to Marshfield.'

Relieved by the return to normal relations, Phil agreed with a smile. 'The wife knows you're back. Said to me, "He'll want a nice big plate of eggs, bacon, sausage, tomato and mushrooms, I know." I told her I'd give her the nod to start on it.'

'Thanks. Sorry about the misunderstanding earlier. Tell me, did you see Mrs Peterson leave last night? About twenty-three hundred.'

Bunyan shook his head. 'I told you, sir, last night was Charlie Drew's farewell party. At that hour I was having to put the lads on their feet and steady enough to walk home. If they remembered where their home was.' He chuckled.

'So you weren't behind the bar here?'

'Not for some fifteen minutes, I guess.'

'I see. Someone could have taken that master key during that time without being noticed?'

'Oh,' he said catching on to what Ben was suggesting. 'Well, I . . . such a thing never entered my head, you know. Why would anyone—?'

'Thank you, Phil,' Ben said, putting an end to the subject and heading for the stairs and his hot bath. Even after it, and after having eaten Mary's promised large breakfast, anger was still bubbling beneath his surface calm. The single redeeming fact was that Julia had gone home none the wiser. What she had been seeking was stored in his memory and she could never invade that.

It was past noon when Ben parked the van at Marshfield, entered the main building and headed for the design office where he hoped to find Roger. His friend was engaged in a mathematical exercise which looked to Ben no more than a jumbled mass of figures that would surely make sense only to another aircraft designer. The man deep in discussion with Roger was John Kershaw, the production manager.

They both looked up as Ben entered. Kershaw smiled a greeting and straightened up.

'I'm poaching know-how from Roger, Ben. Some *Snowbird*s appear to have developed occasional loss of thrust, for no apparent reason any of our workforce can pinpoint. Two aircraft have been returned to us for examination, so I asked Roger if he has any ideas on the problem.' He smiled again. He did it too often for Ben's liking. Kershaw was very good-looking, with red-gold hair, tawny eyes and muscular grace, but that smile held a hint of calculation Ben found disturbing. He thought himself a balanced judge of men, yet John Kershaw had him puzzled.

Julia had encountered Mirium Kershaw at her Chelsea mansion flat and invited her to weekend at Clanford House. That had led to Mirium buying a luxury cottage at Fossbeck, which in turn had led to John, who had just joined her from South Africa, stepping into Fred Kinsley's shoes when he was crushed by a runaway pallet. All too convenient?

Ben had resolved to investigate the man in the next day or so and had the means to do it, but the advent of Deborah Keene had added unwelcome complications which had to be dealt with first. Hence, he had in his pocket the key to the door of a large apartment over a coach house in Fossbeck Camden, the offshoot village five miles beyond Fossbeck itself. Ben planned to move into his new home at the weekend.

Returning Kershaw's smile, he said, 'And has Roger given any input on your problem?'

Kershaw waved a hand at the sheet of paper he and Roger had been studying. 'That's worth a try. It makes sense, so I'll take these calculations down to Ray Povey; get him to have his engineers make the adjustment and test it out.' He began rolling up the large sheet covered with figures. 'The two machines with the problem have each been in operation for eight years. If it's something that develops after long service we need to get to the bottom of it before we have a stream of aircraft being returned.'

He nodded at Roger. 'Thanks. I'll let you know how we get on.' He turned back to Ben. 'No flying today, eh? That mist rolling in looks as if it's set to stay for a day or two.' The smile appeared again. 'I can't get used to the weather in this country, can you? Been in the East for some years, I heard.'

'That's right,' said Ben. 'Too bloody hot in a cockpit there. In France it was too bloody dangerous. This climate suits me fine.'

Kershaw gave a brief grunt and departed. Roger looked hard at Ben and said, 'What don't you like about him?'

He made a face. 'When I find out I'll let you know. Maybe it's because he seems too good to be genuine. Far too handsome, far too genial, and far too wealthy. He and his wife own two expensive homes and a lucrative antiques business in London. They're personal friends of Julia so, presumably also of Hugo. In most situations that would make the employer–employee relationship somewhat awkward on the social level, yet there's no evidence of that. And I have to wonder why, with all that wealth, the Kershaws are not Marshfield shareholders.'

Roger wagged his head. 'You think it's because he knows the company won't survive? You have *him* as the saboteur?'

Ben sat heavily in the chair beside Roger's desk. 'I've been thinking deeply about Tilbrook's inane trick yesterday and I've reached the conclusion that it was merely the act of a resentful character with a serious inferiority complex. Add the inborn distrust of the English ever present in the Irish and we have someone who needs to make a statement whenever he feels his opinions are being dismissed or ignored.'

Roger wagged his head again. 'That's too fanciful for me.'

'I'll put it another way then,' Ben replied, leaning back in the chair and indicating the photographs of the *Lance* hanging on the wall. 'An aeroplane is a complex machine, but you understand all the fine details that make it work and also the miscalculations that make it malfunction. Men are all much the same when it comes to self-worth, Roger. Jim wants to be fully involved with aircraft manufacture, but he's against production of the *Lance* because he believes the future for Marshfield lies with commercial aircraft. He also believes that he's right and his wisdom is being ignored.

'He's apparently said so to the Lances, to his colleagues over a few pints in The Dancing Bear, to me and to anyone who'd listen. He links the decision to continue with the *Lance* to warmongering. Imparted that opinion to me yesterday as we drank tea. Claims we're all eager to kill and become heroes. He had no respect for Chris Peterson; accused me of being as arrogant as he was.'

Ben gave a slight smile. 'He also has the firm conviction that women swarm around airmen like bees on a honeypot. For a man who likes to boast of a reputation for charming every female in the locality and beyond, this fancy deepens his resentment. He even made an issue of Mary Bunyan's generosity in making cakes for me, but never for him.' At Roger's raised eyebrows, he added, 'Oh, said jokingly, but it clearly rankles.'

After a short silence Roger asked, 'What are you trying to tell me in this roundabout manner?'

Ben sighed. 'First you say I'm too fanciful, now I'm too complex. Roger, yesterday Jim Tilbrook doctored my tea. There's no way of proving it, but I know he did. He even confessed to "putting a little something" in his own mug when I spotted the bottle in his hand.'

Roger's eyes hardened. 'I've known Jim for years. Never

thought him capable of doing something like that just as a man's about to make a flight.'

Ben realized Roger was still loath to accept what he, himself, knew for certain, but he pushed on with his thoughts. 'There are two explanations. Because what he dropped into my tea was only designed to make me dizzy enough to blur my eyesight a little, his aim could have been to degrade my reputation as a pilot before the Lances. Perhaps to rob me of my position as test pilot for the company, although that seems rather extreme if his motive was simply masculine jealousy.'

'Mmm, so what's the second explanation?' demanded Roger tetchily.

'It was a warning. Stop now or else!'

'Oh, really, Ben, that's the stuff of fiction.'

'No, my head-in-the-clouds friend,' he returned with some heat. 'I know what that dope did to my system very quickly; what it could do if taken in a greater quantity.' He left a long enough pause for that to register with the other man, then said quietly, 'What if Chris had imbibed a massive dose just before the proving flight?'

Roger countered that angrily. 'He spoke to me. Said the stick wouldn't move.'

'Said *he couldn't move it*. Different emphasis, Roger.' As his friend continued to stare with angry disbelief, Ben pushed his case further. 'You've been adamant there's no design fault, so someone must have severed the elevator tab cable minutes before takeoff; a very precisely timed risky piece of sabotage. There's no way of proving that, either, as we've admitted to Hugo, but you firmly believe that because you see it as the only explanation for what happened. My theory is more plausible. Much easier for someone to slip a drug in Chris's tea during those last vital moments, yet you refuse to go with it.'

Watching the older man struggle with a premise so deadly simple, Ben said firmly, 'You *must* consider it. Christ, you gave me the names of three men who could have cut the cable. Why do you find it so hard to believe one of them used a drug to bring the destruction of the prototype and Chris's death?'

Sadness and anger put lines of stress across Roger's face and his shoulders hunched as he drooped in his chair. 'You could have ended the same way yesterday afternoon if your theory is correct.'

The truth of that hit Ben anew. He had lived for four years with the threat of dying clouding every day, but that had been war and every man waging it had faced the same possible fate. This was different. This would have been murder.

Mist merged with low cloud to make even driving the narrow lanes hazardous. Flying was impossible and likely to be so for at least forty-eight hours, so Ben took the opportunity to buy two easy chairs, a desk and a wireless set from stores in Lewes and arranged for them to be delivered to his new home on Saturday.

Before he took the train to London he visited a doctor's surgery, was accepted as a new patient, and underwent a basic health check which included reading from an eye chart on the wall and completing a simple colour identification test. Eyesight twenty-twenty. General physical condition A1. Well, he had known all along it was Tilbrook who had caused the problem with his eyes.

On reaching London, he went first to a Lyons Corner House for a meal and was swamped with memories. He and his NCO pals had descended on the popular café when they had finally been given Blighty leave and had ordered everything on the menu. Most of them had then gone home; others had had a riotous time flirting with admiring and willing girls, going to peep shows and the music halls, sleeping for hours and eating.

He had spent the week on solo pub crawls during daylight hours, dossing down in Salvation Army hostels each night. He had narrowly missed being picked up by redcaps on two occasions, but by the time he reported to Victoria Station for the boat train the desire to seek a cave, any kind of basic shelter where he could never be traced, had faded leaving the determination to make Chris pay for what he had done. Well, the bastard had, but not through Ben's hand. Someone had beaten him to it.

He got heavily to his feet and went out to the busy street. Dismiss the past. Concentrate on preventing that same person from putting an end to him as well.

In a nearby post office Ben wrote a lengthy cable to a former RFC colleague in South Africa, who had offered partnership in a venture to fly mail across Natal. Desperate to cut all links with the legacy of battle, Ben had declined and headed for Egypt. Their paths had nevertheless crossed during the intervening years as those of men in aviation frequently did, and each had been of use to the other in the way of business. Ben hoped George would turn up trumps on this subject. Adding the word URGENT, he gave the return address as that of his new flat. No chance of anyone at The Dancing Bear being aware of its arrival and spreading the news.

Leaving the post office, he hailed a cab and asked to be driven to Knightsbridge. En route he asked the driver if he knew the exact location of an antiques establishment of some quality.

'Blimey, sir, there's a dozen or more of 'em. Which one are you after?' came the amused reply.

'Oh . . . drop me at the first one you come to. I'll take it from there.'

'Righty-ho. Lookin' for something in pertickler, sir? Some of them specialize in silver or china or the old sparklies, if you gets my meaning. I could put you right on that, if it'd help.'

'My plan is just to browse, thanks all the same.' Ben smiled inwardly. Reminiscent of Cairo where every other man offered to take strangers to the best vendor of what they were looking for. Human nature. Couldn't resist it.

Within twenty minutes, Ben alighted outside double-fronted premises painted black and gold, with a legend above the imposing door that stated the proprietors were under appointment to His Majesty. Rejecting that one as too unlikely, he walked along one of London's famous streets rejoicing in the fact that the city's just as famous fog had lifted enough to see clearly ahead.

After rejecting another establishment as too highbrow, Ben came to an unpretentious frontage with window displays of beguiling clutter. This looked much more likely.

Greeted by the familiar smell of antiquity he began to wander, stopping every now and again to study price tickets as the other five people present were doing. A thin, sallow-faced man in a black suit and bow tie was keeping an eye on them all without making it too obvious. A woman in a dark dress with a wide white collar was sitting in a small cubicle. Presumably a cashier. Nothing so public as a cash desk at which to pay for purchases. Ben left empty-handed deciding that an owner was unlikely to be the one waiting for payment. She would be advising prospective purchasers out front.

He found her in a shop around the corner, in a narrow but exclusive arcade where shoppers who needed to ask the prices would never go. Ben's instinctive belief that his search had ended was upheld on entering and hearing the woman of an elegant couple say, 'It's perfect! Exactly what we asked you to find for us. You're a genius, Mirium darling.'

While the women cooed compliments at each other, the impeccably dressed man walked to a small table at the rear to write a cheque for a china epergne covered with growling tigers, elephants and half-naked men with spears. Ben thought it hideous, even more so when the woman cried, 'It's a perfect match to the one Bertie brought back from India.' Good God, they now had two of the monstrosities!

He was pretending to admire a polished wood table when the effusive pair departed, leaving him alone with John Kershaw's wife. Only when she came up to him did he get the full impact of her attraction and catch his breath. Dark auburn hair in a chignon, amber eyes, classic features, she was truly beautiful. What a handsome couple the Kershaws were.

'Good afternoon, sir,' she greeted smoothly. 'Can I be of any assistance or would you prefer to browse in peace?'

Ben smiled as warmly as he could. 'A bit of both, actually. I think it'll be a case of only knowing what I want when I see it. Perhaps you'd browse with me; offer your superior knowledge of anything that catches my eye.'

Her smile was a knockout. Surely it lured many a male into buying a piece he didn't really want. 'If you'd care to give me some idea of the reason for the purchase I could make sure your eye catches the appropriate articles.'

He gave a light laugh. 'Yes, how very sensible.'

'Are you looking for a gift? For a lady, perhaps?'

'No, nothing like that. Truth is, I've just bought a little place in the country. Filled it with the basics for a bachelor, but I can see it's too impersonal. Needs a human touch. An ornament, a lamp, a clock, a painting? I just don't know which would do the trick, I'm afraid,' he ended with the right amount of male helplessness when it came to homemaking.

It worked. 'Any one of them providing it melded happily with the character of your home. And if you buy it because you simply have to have it.' She smiled again, laughter lighting her eyes. 'An elderly gentleman comes in nearly every month; a charming man with a burning desire to fill his house with beautiful antiques. Therein lies the problem. On each visit he proudly carries off a jug, a miniature, a vase, a jewelled box, and I suspect he never looks at them again once he has placed them on a shelf, sill or tallboy. He has filled an empty space and fulfilled his accumulative drive.'

Ben used that confidence to further his plan. 'Then you really must browse with me to prevent me from buying something totally unsuitable, deemed to be unloved,' he said with amusement.

She responded as he had hoped. 'Tell me a little about the style of your house as we wander.'

'It's a large apartment above a coach house in a pretty village not far from Lewes. Stream running alongside it, sheep on the slopes, meadows filled with wild flowers, and rosy-cheeked residents who will doubtless refuse to acknowledge me until I've been there at least seven years. It's that kind of place,' he finished with a grin.

'That's extraordinary!' she exclaimed with a curious suggestion of excitement. 'I recently bought a house in Fossbeck, a large village near Lewes. Do you know it? My husband was recently offered a post as production manager at Marshfield Aviation, so we moved there for his greater convenience.'

Ben looked suitably astonished. 'Your husband is John Kershaw? I was speaking to him just this morning.'

'You know John?'

'I've also just accepted a post at Marshfield.'

'What an astonishing coincidence!'

'It's a small world, Mrs Kershaw.'

'Oh . . . Mirium, please.' This was said with more persuasion than another man's wife should use, Ben thought. Then it dawned on him that he was making quite an impression on her which he could use to advantage. He'd had a great deal of practice at that over the past twelve years.

'We pilots are a superstitious breed. Too many strange coincidences during the war. I believe in unknown forces guiding our lives.' He gave another warm smile. 'I walked past three antique shops before deciding to enter yours. It must mean what I'm looking for is sitting here waiting to enchant me enough to make me on fire to own it, don't you think?'

'You're a pilot?'

He nodded. 'The replacement for Chris Peterson. John would have already been with the company when that disaster happened. He must have wondered how long his job would last given the rumours flying around about Marshfield's uncertain future.'

'Not really. We're friends of Julia and Hugo Lance, who assured us there'd be no problem. Merely a temporary hitch.' She moved closer to him. 'You're Ben Norton, then. John has spoken about you. Says he doesn't envy you the task of testing that fighter after what happened to Chris. It needs courage to take on what you have, Ben. You were great friends, I believe.'

He was saved from a response to that by catching sight of something that attracted his attention. Moving through the curving aisle he halted before a small painting on an easel to gaze at it without speaking. Against a background of swirling beige, yellow and amber surrounding a great ball of shimmering gold was the figure of a muscular, young, half-naked Greek whose great feathery wings were fast melting in the heat from the sun to send him plunging to the earth. The picture was titled *The High Flyer*. The artist's signature was illegible.

'He's attempting to make a name for himself.' Mirium came alongside Ben. 'Has a penchant for mythology which I think more suited to illustrations for children's books. Only because I like the colours he's used as a background to Icarus falling to his death did I agree to display this one to gauge public reaction to it. The more I study it, however, I can see the symbolism somehow shines through the picture book simplicity. Would you agree?'

Ben was lost for words to describe how the painting affected him. Memories crowded in of returning over the devastation he and Chris had just created, when flames from enemy aircraft on the ground had reached almost high enough to burn their own wings. The sky had been all of these colours and the cockpit like an oven on those early days in Cairo, when he had battled to drive Chris's betrayal from his mind and soul with almost non-stop flying. Oh yes, the bloody symbolism here had him by the throat.

'Are you all right, Ben?'

Without looking at her, he murmured, 'This is what I want for my flat; the element it presently lacks.'

He caught the last train back to Lewes, carrying the securely wrapped painting. He had anticipated travelling with Mirium, but she was to spend the next two nights at her Chelsea flat as she did every week. So Ben invited her to have dinner with him. Not a Lyons Corner House this time. Afterwards they took a taxi to her flat where Ben collected the picture she had taken there on closing the shop premises. As they parted, Mirium said she would be sending him an invitation to dine with herself and John at Fossbeck soon.

It was too dark to watch the passing scene, so Ben closed his eyes and reviewed what he had learned from a woman who had shown all the signs of being far more attracted to him than she should be. Was the Kershaw union on the rocks? Had it been yet another marriage of commercial convenience? According to Roger, Mirium had inherited the antique business and a very large Thames-side house when her father had died shortly after her mother's death in a nautical accident.

Of John's background he had learned very little. On asking if her husband had enlisted during the war Mirium had simply said his work in the aviation industry had been too vital to the war effort. He was South African by birth; she had grown up there in the home of her mother's sister, now deceased.

'Father was an inveterate seafarer. He and Mother had no sooner completed a long voyage than they were planning another. I was something of a hindrance so I was taken to live with Aunt Helen.' She smiled a trifle wanly. 'I never saw my parents again.'

'Until your mother was killed and you came to England to console your father.'

'Well . . . yes, but he was already very ill and he died within a few days. There wasn't time for me to get to know someone I hadn't seen for more than twenty years. He was a stranger to me.'

'All the more praiseworthy of you to leave your husband to comfort someone who had virtually abandoned you as a child,' he had been unable to resist saying.

As the train rattled through the late hours Ben told himself the promise of a large inheritance can arouse a surprising filial sense of duty. And a proposal of marriage from a man whose lofty ambitions needed financing on a large scale.

Before driving to The Dancing Bear, Ben took his painting to the empty rooms above the coach house. In three more days he would be living here, and the picture would be on the wall as a constant reminder of his own ongoing need to defy Hugo Lance. Fog still made visibility hazardous so he drove the van with great caution. By the time he reached his room in the darkened inn and climbed into bed, he was firm in his belief that Mirium Kershaw was a person whose social facade hid a secret or two. Rather like Captain Ben Norton, of course.

In the morning, the fog had thinned to a hazy mist, but the cloud base was too low to allow flying so he drove to Lewes and bought a bed, a wardrobe, a chest of drawers, four rugs, bed linen and towels.

In time he would get a table with a set of chairs, but a lone bachelor could live without them quite comfortably. Although all these things wouldn't arrive until the weekend, Ben drove to the flat, unwrapped the painting and hung it above the mantel-piece. Then he sat on the floor to study it anew while he ate a meat pasty and an apple washed down with ginger beer that he drank from the stone bottle.

His rambling thoughts were interrupted by a loud knocking sound and it took him a while to register that someone was hammering on the front door. Thinking it must be a representative from the large estate which the coach house had been part of until Ben bought it from an elderly, eccentric widow who was hard pressed for money, he was surprised and delighted to find on the doorstep a young lad dressed in a uniform reminiscent of bellboys in luxury hotels.

'Cablegram for Mr Jack Norton, sir,' he said, glancing inquisitively beyond Ben at the empty room with paper bag and ginger beer bottle on the floor. 'Is you living here?'

'You should instead be asking if I is Mr Norton,' Ben teased with a smile, taking the cable and feeling in his pocket for a small coin.

'What's your name?'

'Henry Jenks, sir.'

'Right, Henry, I'll be moving in on Saturday. If you're free and would like to earn more of these, come along and give me a hand for an hour or two. Free buns and ginger pop.'

An eager smile lit his face. 'I'd like that, sir. I'm saving to buy a pogo stick, but I ain't got far with it yet.'

'Come any time after ten.'

Giving a parody of a military salute Henry departed, jumping the last three steps and mounting his bicycle like a Cossack leaping astride a horse.

Thinking George must have something worthwhile to tell to come back so soon, Ben opened the envelope and read the brief message.

*J.K. co-designer of Sturt and Cleeves' Duiker monoplane. Production ceased after 2 crashes. J.K. hit the bottle. Last seen heading across the veldt 1926. Why your return to roots? Partnership still on offer.*
   *Cheerio. G*

Ben reread this message several more times, his thoughts racing. Well, well! John Kershaw had once been a designer, not a production manager in South Africa. Sturt and Cleeves was a relative newcomer to aircraft manufacture; started up at the end of the war. So Kershaw had not been too valuable to the industry to enlist, unless he was at that time working for another company. Of great interest to Ben was where the man had been since 1926. Four years of self-imposed absence from the social and industrial scene. Because he'd become a raging alcoholic?

More questions followed. How long had Kershaw and Mirium been married? Had she been instrumental in getting him back on the wagon? How had they managed to persuade the Lances to offer him the prestigious post of production manager when Fred Kinsley was hit by a runaway pallet just four months ago? Ben then recalled Roger saying they had taken Kershaw on trust, as they had taken him. That comment was incontestable.

Leaving the empty apartment, Ben drove to Fossbeck and asked the postmistress how he would reach the home of Mr and Mrs Kershaw who had recently bought a large house in the village. To counter her suspicious look he claimed to be an old friend from South Africa passing through and hoping to spend a day or two with John and Mirium.

The excitement of speaking to a good-looking stranger from a country that held an aura of romance and mystery for her did the trick. After several attempts to divert her from accounts of ferocious animals, flat-topped mountains, wild areas where people got lost and were never seen again, and the relief of Mafeking, Ben finally gained directions to the Kershaws' residence.

Set back among trees, and appropriately called The Chestnuts, the house was in cottage style; long and low with a thatched roof and enough windows on the upper floor to suggest four or five bedrooms. A very large home for two people. Were they planning to produce several children? His knowledge of property prices in England was limited to how much he had paid for his apartment, but Mirium's inheritance must have been gratifyingly large enough to buy this and the mansion flat he had glimpsed yesterday. The antiques business would provide mere pocket money, he guessed.

To the left of the house was a row of six stables fronting a medium-sized paddock. Not a horse was in sight so Ben supposed Phil's comment that Mirium gave riding lessons was slightly premature. No doubt it would happen in time. Mmm, an intriguing couple, the Kershaws.

It was not until he had taken a walk along the softly rounded hills known as the South Downs before seeking a good hot meal at a village inn that Ben realized the most significant fact he had learned from George. Two of the light aircraft Kershaw had co-designed had crashed leading to the cessation of manufacture, the end of his job as a designer, the road to alcoholism and hopelessness. Put a man who had suffered all that back in the same environment, where laurels were being heaped on the designer of a new supreme aircraft, and maybe he would be driven to destroy it like the one he had created.

And maybe destroy any more that came off the production line.

# SEVEN

He could no longer avoid it. Deborah Keene was waiting for him in the bar. Julia Lance sat beside her with a large photograph album. His activities of the past two days had relaxed Ben enough to resign himself to doing this difficult interview. The Keene woman was, in all innocence, intending to write in homage to her hero. Ben could cope with that more easily than with Julia's lascivious suspicions. What a detestable creature she was. Small wonder Chris had strayed from the marital bed. As a fellow male he could accept that without condemnation. The rest he could not. Crossing to where they sat he saw in the younger woman's eyes uncertainty; in Julia's the light of challenge.

'I hope you're not going to be aggressive again,' said Deborah. 'I need your input and if you continue to avoid talking to me about your friendship with Chris Peterson, I'll start thinking you have something to hide.'

So Julia had already put that idea in her mind. He gave a twisted smile. 'Miss Keene, I'm employed by Marshfield to examine and test-fly their new fighter until I'm ready to prove to investors, the Press and the world's aircraft manufacturers that the tragedy of the last proving flight was not due to faulty design or careless workmanship.'

She stood angrily. 'You're putting the blame for it on Chris?'

'No, I'm not,' he countered. 'What I'm trying to get over to you is that I do have more responsible things to do than to sit and chat to you about an experience you can't possibly imagine. I put it behind me, as most of us did.' He turned to Julia. 'You told me on the day of his funeral that Chris never talked about the war or his colleagues from those years. Trying to drag up things better left buried in the past is a mistake.'

Leaning back in an attitude of relaxed enjoyment, she smiled. 'You speak and behave as if what you think should remain buried in the past could be highly entertaining, if revealed.'

Holding down his anger with difficulty, Ben said, 'You find Hugo's blindness amusing, do you? Have Miss Keene include in her book the full details of how he lost his sight so the readers can have a good laugh. All those deaths, all those damaged minds, all those limbless and sightless poor devils,' he added losing his temper completely. 'You have absolutely no comprehension of what went on out there in Flanders, you ignorant, pampered creature. And to think we did it all to keep women like you safe and free. You make me sick.'

Although he had spoken with quiet venom, total silence fell over the drinkers around them as he walked away and took the stairs two at a time to reach his room. Once there he stood gazing at rural serenity as moonlight began to silver the countryside beyond his window. He was breathing fast; his heart was hammering against his ribs, his brain felt as if it was on fire. Would she find the truth about her husband 'highly entertaining' if he ever told it? He knew with sudden certainty he now never could.

He didn't hear the quiet knocking on his door fifteen minutes later as he lay fully clothed on the bed, still lost in the past. The first he knew of her presence was when the mattress dipped and he realized she was sitting there with a glass held towards him. The contents smelled like whisky.

'She's gone,' said Deborah as he sat up to take the drink. After a moment or two she added, 'I had no idea she could be so insensitive. She must have hurt you deeply. And I'm sorry for what I said to you.'

Oh God, he thought despairingly, is she going to start turning me into a hero now? How do I get out of that? Swinging his legs to the floor he left the bed swiftly and went to open the door. 'Thanks for the drink. Give me ten minutes and I'll come down and chat to you while we have a nightcap.'

The drinkers again fell silent when he appeared, but Phil came from behind the bar with a tray and followed to where Deborah sat waiting. Putting a gin and tonic before her and another whisky on the table he told Ben they were on the house. Adding a dish, he said, 'Some of Mary's cheese sticks warm from the oven. She says you're fond of them, sir.' He returned to the bar and normal service resumed.

Deborah gave a hesitant smile. 'His wife's taken a fancy to you.'

'She'd have been a wonderful mother if she'd had the chance.'

They fell silent and sipped their drinks. Ben then guessed it was up to him to start the ball rolling. 'Look, as I said once before, your book is to be a biography of Chris Peterson. I only touched four years of his life along with many, many others during that unnatural period. I know little of his childhood and early youth; even less of the years since the war ended. You should concentrate on quizzing those people who can give you the kind of input that would truly describe the subject of your book.'

'But you were his close friend,' she protested.

'We were all friends. Had to be,' he countered swiftly. 'Nearly every morning there were empty chairs at the breakfast table. Didn't do to rely on having one special pal.'

'But you both survived.'

'Yes.'

'So please tell me about him. How you met; how you paired up to become known as The Skylarks.'

Tossing back the rest of the whisky he sat gazing into the girl's dark blue eyes and told her what she wanted to hear. When he later lay in bed listening to owls hooting and the cry of a distant vixen it was impossible to pull his thoughts away from those distant years she had forced him to relive.

Those two fresh-faced sixteen-year-olds from good families who had lied about their age to enlist Ben had described to Deborah, in reality had been the desperate son of a harsh-tempered widower struggling to make a living from a rundown smallholding, and an orphaned lad being raised by a social-climbing aunt with ambitions for him above his station. Far from finding immediate rapport at the recruiting office, as Ben had claimed, the pair had only become aware of each other three months later when the orphan was picked on for being too namby-pamby to be a brave soldier.

Chris had been skinny and hesitant then, which made him the ideal target for bullying. Having been driven from home by Jeremiah Norton's violent temper and his contempt for his son's aptitude for learning, Ben's anger had risen at any behaviour that dominated and ridiculed. He had defended the victim and eventually floored the bully who had forcibly removed Chris's trousers and combinations to find out if he was really a girl, causing ribald laughter from others.

Thus, the unlikely friendship between the pseudo-posh Christopher George Peterson and John Benjamin Norton, the brainy yokel with the powerful physique of a farmhand, had begun. When 'Farmer' Norton was around, Chris was left alone. In return he offered his pal the pleasure of talking about books and foreign lands and the history of their country they were about to fight for.

And fight they did. In the mud, in debilitating heat, in disease-ridden trenches, across meadows littered with dead men and horses, and they were no braver than the next man. But they lost their enthusiasm for war, so when they went home on leave and saw at Victoria railway station a sergeant in the handsome uniform of the Royal Flying Corps recruiting volunteers to transfer, they exchanged swift, eager nods and signed up without hesitation. By that time they were both the legal age to fight the enemy and they knew they would rather do it in the air than in the trenches.

On gaining their wings, the elegant, well-spoken Peterson was given commissioned rank. Jack Norton, who looked and spoke like the farm labourer he was, would surely be out of place in an officers' mess; feel happier with others of his class. This division could have put a strain on the bond between them, especially as they had earned similar marks and commendations during their flying training, but it had grown so strong it seemed nothing would ever break it.

At that point Ben came from the past with a deep sigh. He had led Deborah to believe the jingoistic fiction of two true blue sons of England who had done their duty side by side with courage and honour to the bitter end, but he told himself the biography of a dead war hero should be mainly laudatory so the pack of lies he had told would be swallowed up in the entire panegyric.

When sleep came it was filled with curious dreams of tigers, elephants and half-naked men trying to kill them. Those bloody hideous epergnes! Waking thoughts soon told him the men with spears had surely represented soldiers with bayonets, the tigers were cunning female predators, the elephant's huge obstacles to be overcome.

During his breakfast Deborah appeared and sensibly interpreted his nod and gruff greeting as a message that he did not want company. She settled at a corner table and made much of studying the pages of her flip-over notebook. Phil also apparently read the mood between his two residential guests and served them with just the basic verbal exchange.

Outside, the air was clear, the sky a milky blue. A perfect spring day in the making. Ben's spirits rose. He would take the *Lance* up and push her further than he had so far, but not before he'd checked her thoroughly. There was little chance of Jim Tilbrook dosing his food or drink after that obvious warning, but what he had learned of John Kershaw now made him more suspicious of that man. Enough to cause him to ensure all was well with the machine he planned to fly this afternoon. Maybe the time would soon come for him to sleep in the hangar.

So much for his plans. A setback greeted him on arriving at Marshfield. With Roger Hall were John Kershaw and Ray Povey, the chief engineer. Ben had had little to do with Povey, the unpopular boss once suspected of putting in night hours with another company to earn enough to allow his avaricious wife to buy expensive things for their home. An inheritance from an uncle in Australia, as sudden new wealth was often explained away. Nobody had believed that; had had more earthy ideas on the subject. And had expressed them to rile a man who had shown little respect for them.

A large, brusque man with a quick temper, Povey was nevertheless well qualified for the position he held and he presumably met with Sir Edwin's and Hugo's approbation whatever the workers thought of him. After the round of greetings, Povey put a meaty hand on Ben's shoulder.

'Got a treat for you this morning. The lads are fuelling her up now so she'll be ready for takeoff in the half-hour. Get your clobber on smartish, then come through so's we can give you a quick rundown of what we want from you.'

Ben was puzzled. The ground crew were certainly not fuelling the *Lance*. There was no way he intended to fly until the morning was well advanced, in any case, and Povey's attitude irked him. Get your clobber on! The bastard wasn't addressing a young apprentice, for God's sake. But he was known for lack of respect for those he worked with, along with his cocky attitude.

Moving away so that Povey's hand fell from his shoulder, Ben said, 'You're talking in riddles. I won't be taking the *Lance* up until Roger and I have had a discussion on my flight plan.'

'No, no, man, you're flying *Snowbird* in thirty minutes from now.'

'Your mistake, I'm afraid,' Ben countered sharply. 'My commission is to bring the *Lance* up to peak performance in the shortest possible time.'

'Your *commission*,' he heavily accented the word, 'is as Marshfield's test pilot. That means whenever there's a need to check out alterations, repairs, replacement components, you test the aircraft before I sign it off as airworthy. That applies to all machines on these premises.'

Kershaw attempted to mediate. 'I mentioned the problem when we were in Roger's office the other day, if you remember, Ben. A simple adjustment was needed, that's all. No call for a full aerobatic test. Basic manoeuvres, that's all. *Snowbird* isn't the *Lance*.'

'Which is why somebody else could do it. How about you, John? Unless you've let it expire you must have a pilot's licence, albeit a South African one. You could take *Snowbird* up.'

Kershaw's mouth tightened, his expression grew speculative. 'Ray's in the right here. You are the company's test pilot. That title covers all company aircraft. The accent has been on the *Lance* because of the disastrous proving flight, of course, but other work goes on in these hangars. It doesn't do to forget that.'

'And it doesn't do for anyone to forget the *Lance* takes priority over all else. Check with the Major.'

'We already have. He's given us the go-ahead.'

Ben took that badly. Did a house with stables in Fossbeck, a mansion flat like his sister's and antiques in Knightsbridge count for more with Hugo than the ability and desire of someone determined to prove the worth of the aircraft on which Marshfield's future depended? The answer was obviously yes. The war, his legacy from it, had not changed Hugo's arrogance that sorted what he regarded as the wheat from the chaff of society.

'So, as I said just now, get your clobber on and come through so's we can give you a quick run through before you do the test flight,' said Povey with more than a touch of smugness. 'You RFC blighters are all the same. Think you're God's gift, don't you?'

'You're including Major Lance in that biased opinion, of course. Have you expressed it to him?'

Povey turned away. After a short hesitation Kershaw did the same, but Ben caused him to halt by calling after him, 'Don't you have a current licence, John? You surely must have tested the *Duiker* before it went into production. Although not thoroughly enough, apparently.'

For a moment it seemed Kershaw would turn aggressively on Ben, but he clearly thought better of it and followed Povey into the next hangar wearing a grim expression.

'You've made a pair of colleagues very annoyed. Was that wise?'

Ben had forgotten Roger's presence. Still gazing at the doorway through which they had gone, he said, 'They both had the opportunity to sabotage Chris's proving flight, according to you. I should have annoyed them long before this.' He turned to his friend. 'Povey's attitude echoes Tilbrook's and lends credence to the possibility of guilt. You must have been aware of his resentment of men who fought in the war, even though he was doing a vital job here. As for the newcomer, Kershaw, apparently being the less likely culprit, I'll tell you about him when I've done this bloody simple test flight.'

Roger looked worried. 'You've not yet flown *Snowbird*. She's not the *Lance*, remember.'

'Roger, in my time as an RFC blighter and an aviation pioneer all along the Med, I've flown enough different ramshackle machines to enable me to take even a bathtub off the ground without lessons on how to do it,' he said, heading for the toilets and washroom where he kept his flying kit.

Only as he taxied the light aircraft out into the sunshine did it strike him that the pair he had just classed as possible saboteurs had had ample time to tamper with this monoplane he was about to take into the air, thus ensuring there would not be another proving flight to sell the *Lance* worldwide. Not with him at the controls.

Ben's fears of sabotage proved groundless, yet those forty minutes in the air produced an unexpected and very unwelcome one. Flying an aircraft as basic as the little monoplane highlighted the superb complexity of the *Lance* which continued to thrill him each time he settled in the cockpit. His every action had been concentrated on working towards a proving flight so successful the fighter would enter the annals of aerial history at the end of that day. He had given no thought to what would follow.

He had left his life in Alexandria with no loose ends to tie; he had sold the results of his years of risky investment and dogged, hazardous slog to get where he wanted to be; he had signed a contract agreeing to work for a company owned by the Lance family as their test pilot. All that he had done for the chance of a lifetime and the very thought now put a chill around his heart. Once production of the warplane began, the glittering bubble of achievement would have burst and he would be left with the daily tasks any qualified pilot could handle. Sitting at the controls of this compact small craft he had a sudden sense of returning to where he had started.

The downbeat mood remained as Ben signed his report on the test flight before leaving Povey's small office in the second hangar without another word to the man who had treated him with disdain. There was no sign of John Kershaw, but the desire to quiz him further had faded, and since Roger began telling him that Sir Edwin had received a large order for *Snowbird* from a Norwegian who wanted the wheels replaced by skis, their conversation over a lunchtime sandwich centered on that welcome development for Marshfield.

'Will it take you long to adapt the design?' Ben asked.

Roger smiled. 'I did that a few years ago. *Snowbird*'s very name suggested to me it would be an ideal form of transport in bleak, isolated areas. Sir Edwin turned it down because at that time the order books for the standard model were full. The universal desire was for speed. The Schneider Trophy events had all manufacturers excited and they concentrated on that factor. The Major was caught up in the general enthusiasm, hence why my design for the *Lance* twelve months later got the thumbs up the first time I offered it.'

'And a good thing too,' said Ben, driven into once again imagining Hugo's sense of loss on not being able to see the fabulous flying machines he could only hear. It banished his own period of hollow reflection.

'I spoke to him an hour ago and fixed the time of your test this afternoon for fourteen-thirty. If Sir Edwin arrives back from London in time he'll also come. If not, John Kershaw will accompany Hugo. Julia's taken off for a few days at the Chelsea flat and Freddie's in Scotland with friends.'

Roger accepted a couple of Mary Bunyan's cherry buns from Ben. 'Still in favour with your landlady, lucky devil!'

'Not for much longer.' Then Ben changed his mind about telling Roger he was leaving The Dancing Bear on Saturday. As usual, his companion's thoughts were purely on aerial matters so he passed no comment. For Ben, the news of Julia's absence was welcome and he asked if Deborah Keene had gone with the widow.

Munching his bun with appreciation, Roger shook his head. 'Saw her with Jim Tilbrook earlier. He can't resist a pretty face, although she didn't look all that enchanted with his company.'

'Huh, I'm not surprised. We know his opinion of Chris – of anyone who flew in combat – so she won't like what he says about the man she aims to eulogize in her biography.' Ben screwed up the paper bag now empty of buns with some force. 'By the way, I've put myself on the list of a doctor in Lewes. He pronounced my physical condition as A1 and my eyesight as twenty-twenty. Happy now?'

Roger gave him a straight look. 'You can't let Tilbrook get away with it, then. What he did amounted to a criminal act.'

'If I'd damaged the aircraft or myself on landing it would have been. It was a bloody vicious thing to have been done by a man who has never flown. It's not like driving a car, when it's possible to park by the roadside in tricky situations, if that's what he imagined.' He sighed. 'All I can do is make him aware that I know what he did. We can't prove it any more than we can prove the *Lance* was sabotaged when Chris was killed.

'Ray Povey feels a similar disparagement for wartime fliers. You heard what he said about the RFC this morning, Roger. In my book he's well in the running for what happened on the proving flight. Tilbrook could have drugged Chris prior to take off, but Povey's an engineer and could easily have tampered with the aircraft.' He gave a grim smile. 'His attitude made me distinctly apprehensive in the *Snowbird*.'

Still looking very serious, Roger pursed his lips. 'That monoplane is his baby. When he hears about Sir Edwin's contract in Norway, he'll be pushing for the workforce to concentrate solely on production of a model with skis, maybe even with floats. Povey wouldn't destroy a *Snowbird*, Ben.'

'I was thinking more of myself being destroyed,' he returned harshly.

'You're not the target, lad. It's the *Lance*. If we get as far as a proving flight that's when you will be vulnerable.'

'There's no "if" about it. I'm planning on being ready to stun spectators with a full display by the middle of June. By Christmas the workshops will be at full production level.'

His spirits plunged again. And the bubble would have burst!

When Ben taxied the *Lance* out to the main runway dead on the proposed flight time, there was a sizeable group of spectators. Sir Edwin had accompanied his blind son and along with ground crew that serviced the fighter were Kershaw, Povey, Tilbrook and Deborah Keene, whose slender body was swathed in an oversized green plaid cloak which made her look ridiculously out of place in a group of men in serviceable garb. In black gloves decorated on the cuffs with mock emeralds, her hands were fiddling with the flip-over notebook, as usual. No sign of the camera. The message had got through to her.

Following last night's interview, her flamboyant presence acted as a spur to Ben. Flying conditions were ideal. No cloud cover, visibility perfect. As the wheels left the ground he caught himself smiling. So he was Marshfield's test pilot who must fly any and every machine he was told to, was he? Well, he'd been told to fly this one so he'd give them a demonstration on how bloody good an 'RFC blighter' was in the cockpit of an aircraft to beat any other.

After being grounded for three days, he revelled in the freedom he always felt with endless space around him and the rest of the world in miniature below. Knowing in his heart he was already master of the *Lance*, he literally waltzed around the blue infinity, diving and climbing, circling and swooping, in the culmination of their unity. The *Lance* responded to his slightest touch on the stick as if she was as exhilarated as he, and Ben forgot all else but that perfect moment.

He was eventually brought back to reality by Roger's voice advising him that Sir Edwin had seen enough and wanted him to make his descent.

Still in a bravado mood, Ben touched down and fast-taxied towards the watching group until the *Lance*'s nose was less than fifteen feet from them. It amused him to watch their hurried retreat into the hangar before he cut the engine. Climbing from the cockpit he took time to make a few observations on the flight to the ground crew, then he pulled off his helmet and gloves to approach Sir Edwin and Hugo, the latter looking happier than his father. Maybe his heightened sense of hearing allowed this former pilot to identify what an aeroplane was doing by the engine sound.

'Well, Captain Norton (Sir Edwin was always formal towards staff members), that was quite a display! You've made astonishing progress while I've been in London, which must mean the design fault has been identified and corrected.'

It would be far easier to agree, but Ben was staunchly behind Roger on the subject. 'There's never been a design fault, Sir Edwin, as we've said many times. In my opinion, the sooner we prove that to prospective investors the better.' He hurried on. 'I had mid-June in mind but the *Lance* is ready now, and by the end of this month I can have planned and rehearsed an impressive proving flight to my satisfaction.'

The earlier bonhomie faded swiftly. 'That has to be a decision taken by the shareholders. We cannot have a repetition of the disaster that heralded worldwide disparagement of our prototype fighter.'

'And the death of your son-in-law.'

'And that . . . of course,' the older man murmured through lips drawn tight against Ben's reminder of his insensitivity. 'Caused, without a doubt, by the design fault which you claim to have been corrected,' he added pointedly.

Ben decided against going down that road again. 'I'm claiming your outstanding new warplane to be ready to perform before even the most sceptical aviation expert within two weeks.'

Hugo took him up on that. 'But are *you* ready? A proving flight is only as good as the pilot at the controls. The *Lance* can't do it unless she's in the right hands.'

That comment made in the man's usual autocratic manner revived all the resentment Ben had felt at their encounter all those years ago, but Roger, for once highly perceptive of undercurrents, stepped in before Ben could react.

'She is in the right hands, Major. If anyone had doubts about that, they would have been dispelled by the brilliant display Ben has just given. I thought I knew that machine better than anyone until he took her up and demonstrated how wrong I was. Yes, I created her, but he brings her to full-blooded life as never before.'

'It was so thrilling I was brought to tears,' said a female voice that caused all heads to turn and stare. 'I so clearly imagined the aeroplane diving and being unable to stop. I'll be able to write up that tragedy so believably in his biography.'

Into the stunned silence Jim Tilbrook said quietly, 'I'll drive you back to Clanford, Deb.'

She looked over her shoulder as he led her away, perhaps belatedly recognizing her terrible gaffe. Or perhaps not. That patriotic fiction she was told last night had apparently intensified her passion for the man she had sent presents to during the war.

Ben was more concerned about a discussion that appeared to be ending without a definite decision being made. He overheard Sir Edwin say sotto voce to Hugo, 'Who allowed that young woman to join us? She's far too garrulous. We are striving to keep these test flights a secret, but she's likely to tell everyone she meets, and in melodramatic manner. It's bad, Hugo. Put a stop to it, at once.'

'Julia's made a friend of her, sir.'

'Then send her to join your sister in Chelsea. What we're doing is far too important to be interrupted by silly females.' He put his hand on his son's shoulder and began guiding him away from the hangar. 'We must talk about Captain Norton's claim. He's impetuous. When we invite VIPs here again it's imperative that nothing goes wrong. That would really bring the end of Marshfield.'

Ben turned to Roger with a resigned shrug and they both walked to the table where tea had been brewed by the young apprentice offering mugs around.

'Thanks for your support just now. We might have got somewhere if that stupid girl had kept quiet,' he said. 'Tilbrook was responsible for bringing her to watch. Is it possible he's stopped drugging my tea and intends instead to let her loose among her journalist friends who'll revive their campaign against the *Lance* before we can prove them wrong?'

For once Roger recognized the mockery in his words and continued in the same vein. 'Easier for him to persuade her to seduce you and render you so exhausted you're unable to get yourself off the ground, much less the *Lance*.'

Smiling his thanks to the apprentice as he accepted his Dancing Bear mug filled with tea, Ben grunted his disagreement. 'Tilbrook's set his sights on her. If she showed signs of favouring me I'd really start worrying about my future.'

'Then you'd do well to start thinking about it.'

'Eh?'

'A little bird has put around the rumour that she took whisky to your room, then you both came down and spent an hour together in the bar.'

'Who the hell told you that?' he demanded fiercely.

'It's going the rounds, along with the news that you first told Julia what you thought of her and both of you stormed off in full view of the customers.' Seeing Ben's expression, Roger wagged his head. 'Marshfield employs over a thousand people. The Dancing Bear is the local watering hole for some of them.'

After taking that well and truly in, Ben lowered his voice to tell Roger he would not be living there after Friday. 'I'm moving into a flat nearer to Marshfield. Despite my failure to bring things forward just now, the proving flight date is getting close and I intend to keep my whereabouts a secret from everyone save you. That should put an end to pub gossip and keep the Keene woman out of my hair.'

Roger sighed. 'I wish we could pin down whoever caused that disaster and deal with him before we embark on another public display. Sir Edwin is right. Marshfield would be finished if . . .' He broke off and hid his embarrassment behind his mug of tea as he drank lengthily.

'Once a date has been set I shall sleep in the hangar,' Ben told him. 'And I'll have a word with young Felix Stroud. He's enthusiastic and completely trustworthy. It'll be easy to persuade him to ensure the *Lance* is never standing here unobserved during working hours. It might be a good idea to get him to share the after dark vigils. He's single and living with his sister, so no problem about being out all night now and again.' He grinned. 'Good looking lad like that is probably in the habit of doing so already.'

Roger then shook him by saying, 'You should be doing a bit more of that, Ben. All work and no play will start taking its toll soon.'

He responded sharply. 'Who d'you have in mind? Julia? Deborah Keene? Maybe Cynthia Bunyan, chambermaid at The Dancing Bear?'

Roger disconcerted him further. 'Chris tried his luck there. Her father came after him with a shotgun.'

'What!'

'It all blew over. The girl knew of his reputation and read more into his words than there was. Sincere apologies, bouquets of red roses to Cynthia and her mother, a case of whisky for the father. Chris never went near The Dancing Bear after that.'

'Bloody fool! If the father worked for Marshfield I'd say there was a perfect suspect for sabotage, but he wouldn't have had the opportunity to tamper with the cable before takeoff that day.' He edged Roger away from the other tea drinkers. 'I've learned something about somebody who did have; which increases my suspicions of him.'

He related the information George's cable from South Africa had supplied. 'I'm sure the account given by the Kershaws of his years with Sturt and Cleeves artfully suggested he was their production manager and, as you once told me, he was taken on trust, as I was. The problem over the *Duiker* wouldn't have made worldwide news. The company was in its infancy and was a small set up. Still is, compared with Marshfield.'

Roger was frowning. 'Is your pal in a position to verify this?'

'Absolutely. Clearly he has no way of tracking where Kershaw went in 1926, but he wouldn't have lied about the man hitting the bottle after the veld-hopper he co-designed was scrapped. To my mind a festering sense of failure could have prompted in him a dangerous resentment of the *Lance*'s success which found an outlet two months ago, especially if he's still a heavy drinker. Any hints of that?'

'None have reached my ears, Ben, but it's possible to keep such habits secret by tanking up at home. Even their wives are unaware of the problem until they find bottles hidden behind books in the study or in the hen house.' His frown deepened. 'This is extremely unsettling.'

'On the contrary. I think we're making progress with our investigation into the three men you named as being able to cut that elevator tab cable. We now know Tilbrook has no qualms about using some kind of drug on a man about to take an aircraft off the ground. It wasn't potent enough to cause me to crash, but enough of that same stuff could have destroyed the *Lance* and the pilot two months ago.'

Roger nodded, his lips tightly closed, and Ben continued. 'We have to decide if my dose was deliberately small enough to be no more than a peculiar type of warning, or if on both occasions it was used Tilbrook misjudged the quantity. Had he intended only to warn Chris? Had he intended to kill me last week? And did he bodge both attempts? Whatever the truth we can't pin down his reason for doing it, but it was certainly the easiest method of sabotaging the proving flight.'

'But there's no way of laying the crime at his door.'

'Not yet. So let's consider Povey. As chief engineer he'd be familiar with the *Lance* right down to the last nut and bolt. Which means he'd know the ideal way to make it impossible for the fighter to pull up from a steep, fast dive, and he'd be able to cut that cable so swiftly nobody would be aware of it.'

'I suppose so,' Roger said heavily. 'In that half hour before takeoff we were clustered around Chris and the *Lance*, very tense and issuing ridiculous last minute reminders to him. Any one of them could have done it unnoticed by the rest of us. But I still can't . . .'

'I know,' said Ben. 'It's an appalling thing to suspect of anyone, much less a trusted colleague. But you believe it did happen, so one of those three must be guilty. Let's consider Povey. He disliked Chris, but that on its own was surely not enough to drive him to want him dead. Povey's "baby" is *Snowbird* – you've just affirmed that – but, again, that wouldn't lead him to risk his job and position here by destroying the *Lance*. So, unless there was some hidden agenda between Povey and Marshfield or Chris, which had to be settled so criminally, I'm inclined to put his name at the bottom of the list.'

'Which leaves John Kershaw.'

'Yes, Roger. As a relative newcomer to the company he seemed the least likely culprit, but this new information about him changes that. As a partner in design of the *Duiker* he's more knowledgeable about aircraft construction than the average production manager would be. He'd almost certainly have a pilot's licence, too. When I quizzed him this morning on the subject his reaction confirmed the fact. Stands to reason, in a country as vast and thinly populated as South Africa flying is the quickest means of travel for men in business. Add the facts that he has concealed his past from the Lance family, stepped into his job here through his wife's convenient friendship with Julia at the Chelsea mansion flats, and has a history of being a hard drinker, he goes to the top of my list.'

'I'm afraid I have to agree. He only joined Marshfield several weeks before the proving flight. Not long enough for Chris's death to be his aim.'

'Unless the bastard had seduced Kershaw's wife.'

'No, not enough time for that.'

Ben said stonily, 'It takes less than half an hour if the woman is willing.'

Roger studied him in silence for several moments, then quietly agreed. 'Even so, most husbands would go no further than giving the cad a beating in a dark place one night. If Kershaw caused that crash it's more likely to have been on the grounds you gave just now. An act devised by an unstable mind rather than a criminal one.'

'All the more reason to start sleeping in the hangar. He might not wait until my own proving flight to vent his sense of injustice a second time.'

After the elation of the flight the rest of the afternoon seemed flat, and disappointment over the question mark on the proving flight led Ben to call it a day and leave early. Roger was not as upset as he. The shock and sense of responsibility after Chris's crash put a brake on the urge to rush into another test of his design. Although he had total confidence in the *Lance* and Ben's talent as a pilot, the fear of another inexplicable failure hovered. Don't tempt fate just yet, he thought.

When Ben reached his van in the car park he encountered Jim Tilbrook returning from delivering Deborah to The Dancing Bear. It had taken the man long enough to allow him to linger there with her in an attempt to further his cause, unless he had pursued some other business on the way back. Whichever it was, he looked very pleased with himself.

'Would you believe it, now,' he commented in his Irish brogue, smiling knowingly. 'All that piloting bravado zooming up and down, here and there, did nothing more than give the lady enthusiasm for writing about diving into the ground and dying.'

Ben halted on the point of entering his vehicle, hand resting on the roof, door open. 'There was no valid excuse for her to be watching. She's besotted with the dead hero of her proposed biography. His life was in the past. What I do right now has nothing to do with Chris Peterson's life. Or his death. Don't bring her again when I'm test-flying. Her stupid comment put an end to a discussion of great importance concerning the next proving flight.'

Again the knowing smile. 'To be sure it did, but I can't control what the darlin' says, can I?'

'Yes, give her a dose of the stuff you put in my tea. It'll keep her quiet . . . but it won't make her see you in a better light. It just makes everything blurry and induces a thumping headache. She'll want you even less after that.'

Sliding behind the wheel he started the engine and pulled away, leaving Tilbrook watching him go. The smile had gone from the man's face and been replaced by a scowl of pure venom.

# EIGHT

K nowing Sir Edwin was going to delay the proving flight – for how long was anyone's guess now – Ben spent the morning in his room preparing to move his possessions to the coach house after breakfast the next day. Most of them were already boxed and simply had to be packed more tidily. He had so few clothes they could be laid in the van on a rug covering the floor. Socks and underwear could fill the spaces between manuals, logbooks, a number of aviation charts and flight instructions pertaining to every airfield he had used since 1918. Much would have changed over the years, but a freelance pilot's inclination was to keep such information because it might help in an emergency.

Once he had marked the boxes according to their contents Ben opened his briefcase, his mouth twisting in a wry smile. If it had not been double-locked and alarmed with a device to deter attempts to get at the contents, he would not have left it on the wardrobe shelf. In Alexandria some of the contents had been placed in a safe-deposit box at his bank, but he had not seen the need for that in a quiet Sussex village. All the same, Julia's search had been unsuccessful due to the security attached to the leather case. How delighted she would have been with the contents.

Along with the usual social and financial documents were a passport in the name of John Benjamin Norton, a birth certificate showing the father as Jeremiah Frederick Norton, farmer, and mother as Mabel Norton, formerly Jakes, housemaid.

The sepia photograph of Mabel Norton was dog-eared and faded. Ben had handled it so much, especially during those first months in the trenches when every man had needed an image of mother, wife or sweetheart to keep him sane. Although Ben barely remembered her, he treasured that early picture of the woman who had brought him into the world. She had surely been the one parent who had loved him.

Other photographs were in the large manila envelope. Jack Norton, sixteen years and five months old and looking at least eighteen due to his physique, dressed in ill-fitting, mud-stained uniform like the others standing glumly with him in a Flanders village. Another of Jack 'Farmer' Norton in a different uniform, standing beside a *Nieuport biplane* and grinning from ear to ear. Another showing him seated in one, still grinning, but wearing Flight Sergeant's rank and the coveted wings on his tunic. In one of the several squadron pictures George Marshall, his informant in South Africa, was standing next to him. Lieutenant Peterson was seated with the officers in the front row, of course.

Ben's hand stilled over the next image and left it lying where it was. It had been taken on return from their last early morning raid together, two days before it had happened. He had once considered cutting Chris from the emotive scene, but they stood with arms across each other's shoulder, laughing and full of elation, making it impossible to separate the two figures with scissors. Ben kept it to remind him never to grow close to a man again. Beside it, a mounted sepia studio portrait showed a bride and groom. He kept that to remind him never to grow close to a woman again.

The revolver was for his personal safety. He had used it twice. Once in Cairo, once in Alexandria. Never thought he might need it in Sussex, but when he started sleeping beside the *Lance* he would have it with him. Although he was fairly certain no attempt would be made to destroy the fighter or himself until it would have the greatest effect, Ben was going to take no chances.

Tilbrook's hostility was surely born of inflated masculinity. His performance yesterday had been further evidence of a jealous, thwarted lover. A middle-aged one who ought to be better able to handle it. However, men of that type continued to believe in their personal magnetism until the truth of a mirror image one day destroys it. They then become pathetic old moaners everyone tries to avoid. Apart from the mild doping aimed at reducing his professional appeal, Ben didn't suspect Tilbrook of planning the destruction of another *Lance* despite the man's opposition to the production of warplanes. His aim was just an immature urge to ridicule and hamper someone who might invite more female interest than he.

On arriving at Marshfield after a quiet lunch at a pub along the route, Ben walked smack into another confrontation of even greater hostility. As he crossed to the hangar housing the *Lance* John Kershaw came from the other one, manhandled Ben into the space between the two buildings, then stood blocking any escape. Having deliberately provoked the South African about the *Duiker* yesterday he had half expected a comeback of some kind, so Ben stood passively on the overgrown area between the dark, rearing concrete walls.

'What's your game, Norton?' Kershaw demanded belligerently.

'It's called aviation. You should know.'

'Don't get clever with me, you cocky bastard.' He thrusted Ben against the wall and kept him there with hands on his shoulders. 'You discovered where Mirium works and went there pretending you didn't know who she was. Told her a yarn about looking for something to put in your apartment, which we all know is non-existent, and bought a gross picture she's been trying to sell for months. You then let slip you work here, and the rest was easy, wasn't it?'

'The rest?' Ben was taken aback by this line of attack.

The pressure on his shoulders increased as his assailant grew even more aggressive. 'An invitation to dinner in an expensive restaurant, then a taxi back to the Chelsea flat where you'd left the picture to be collected later hoping you'd laid on enough charm to get what you wanted and stay the night.'

'Is that what your wife told you?' Ben didn't believe she had and Kershaw ignored the question.

'I ask you again, Norton, what game are you playing? You've been to Fossbeck asking where we live. The woman in the post office asked me last evening if my South African friend had found our house with her directions, and hoped we'd had an enjoyable reunion. She described the man with eyes of slightly differing colours, so don't deny it was you who's been snooping around.'

'I wouldn't describe it as snooping, Kershaw.' Ben used the same aggressive formality of surname. 'When I collected my picture from Chelsea before catching the last train back here, Mirium said she would organize an invitation to dinner very soon . . .'

'You can forget that!' Kershaw snapped.

'. . . so when I found myself in the Fossbeck area I took the time to locate the house. The postwoman obviously mixed me up with someone else on the subject of a reunion.' Ben looked him straight in the eye and added coldly, 'If you don't take your hands off me right now you'll get my knee in your balls. Hard! And when you double up in agony you'll get a neck chop that'll lay you out long enough for me to get on with the work I came to do.'

Eye contact was held for no longer than three seconds before Kershaw stepped away, lowering his arms to his sides. 'Just stay away from Mirium or you'll get worse than that from me, d'you hear?'

Ben studied him with optical disparagement. 'What I hear is someone so unsure of himself he thinks every man who has some kind of contact with his wife will lure her away. Grow up, Kershaw!'

Leaving him in the claustrophobic gap between hangars, Ben approached the *Lance* trying to fathom the meaning of what had just occurred. Admittedly, Mirium Kershaw had shown a warmer interest in him than he expected from a married woman, especially when she learned of his close connection with her husband, but she had not sent a sexual invitation with her behaviour.

What was Kershaw afraid of? And how did his violent jealousy tie in with his professional failure, leading to drunkenness and an absence from the aviation world and the social scene for several years before reappearing in Sussex? Most curious of all, why had he shown no reaction to the evidence that Ben knew about the *Duiker* disaster? Most men would surely need to discover just how much he knew and how he had come by the knowledge.

Pulling up beside the sleek fighter, Ben's eyes studied her with possessive admiration. Was Kershaw, in fact, unstable enough to support a theory that he could be driven to destroy any man's successful aerial creation in retaliation? Ben decided Kershaw would need careful watching in the days leading up to the *Lance*'s second proving flight.

The move to the coach house was achieved without a hitch, although not without some hurt feelings. Phil Bunyan was sorry to lose his prestige guest; Mary shed tears enough to drive Ben to promise he would call in to enjoy her meals on a regular basis. Husband and wife were overtly put out by not being given the new address, certain it was that of their rival The Green Man up on the South Downs, but Ben was not going to go so far as to give in on that. He just said he was moving nearer to Marshfield and gave Phil a generous gratuity as he said goodbye.

Deborah Keene was an interested spectator but stayed in the background throughout. Ben was not fooled into believing it was because of her insensitive gaffe after his test flight. Besides, she knew where to find him during the working day. Unfortunately, Hugo did not appear to have done as his father advised and sent her to stay with Julia.

Henry Jenks, keen to increase his savings to buy a pogo stick, turned up as arranged and proved to be very ready to sweep, wash and polish before the furniture was delivered. For his efforts he was rewarded with ginger pop, doorstep sandwiches and slices from several cakes of the varieties beloved by small boys and their adult version. As they ate, sitting together on the floor, the thought entered Ben's head that this was probably like having a son to share things with, but he hastily pushed that away.

On that Saturday evening, sitting in the new armchair before a small fire lit to drive away the chill of inoccupation for a considerable time, Ben gazed at his picture of Icarus and told himself this was the true beginning of his new life. For as long as it might last.

Living so much nearer to Marshfield gave Ben more free time at the end of his working day. Evenings were staying light for longer, and the second half of May brought soft, balmy weather to coax him to explore the beautiful green ridge behind the villages straggling along at its foot. After so many years in the Middle East he found great contentment in walking through what was truly England's green and pleasant land.

He also revelled in flying in ideal conditions. During that next week he tested another two *Snowbird*s and had an instructional flight in a *Broadwing* with a visiting pilot from a company using them. Ben found the larger passenger aircraft ponderous and uninspiring, but valued the experience in a machine he was unfamiliar with.

The fact that Ben had left The Dancing Bear was no secret. Mary Bunyan's mouth-watering buns were no longer passed round when tea was made, and his sandwiches had the same filling three days in a row. However, his address remained known only to Roger. All contact with Tilbrook, Povey and John Kershaw was kept brief and official. Any prospect of a warmer relationship growing between them had been halted with no apparent regrets on either side.

Julia was still in Chelsea, so far as Ben was aware, so his sole problem was Deborah Keene. At the end of that first week of what Ben thought of as his new life, she was waiting on the passenger seat of his van in the parking area at the end of the day. He studied her through the open door and said he thought Sir Edwin had banned her from the premises after her last visit.

Her bright eyes sparkled with challenge. 'I'm not in the buildings. There's a difference between them and an open space outside. Lorry drivers come in all the time, delivering things. Complete strangers. But they're not "in the premises" are they?'

'How did you get past the guard on the gate?' he demanded.

The sparkle remained. 'I asked to interview him for the book, so he invited me into his little shed for a cup of tea while he told me his life story. At the end of it I said you were going to drive me back to The Dancing Bear and walked across to your van. He doesn't know you're no longer living there.'

He got in beside her, started the engine and drove across to where the burly, middle-aged Thomas Gladstone stood ready to open the gate for departing workers, most of them on bicycles.

Ben nodded his thanks as he drove through. 'Goodnight, Tom.'

'And to you, Captain Norton,' came the cheery reply, with a knowing grin at Deborah. 'Look after that charming young lady, sir.'

Three miles along the road Ben pulled up by the hedge lining it and switched off the engine before turning to the girl who was wearing another eye-dazzling coat of clashing colours, with a matching band around her head that resembled a hat without a crown. He thought she looked silly, yet curiously attractive, which annoyed him further.

'I saved old Tom from embarrassment by driving you out, but this is as far as we go. The bus stop is over there on the corner. The little green bus goes past every half hour. It'll take you all the way to Clanford, Miss Keene.'

She stayed there beside him and her attitude completely changed. 'I know I was incredibly stupid to say what I did. It's haunted me ever since. I'm terribly sorry, Ben. Please forgive me.' She put a hand on his sleeve. 'I thought we'd become friends during that evening when you told me about those thrilling days with Chris. How you met, and those daring dawn raids on—'

'There's no more to tell,' he interrupted sharply. 'When will you get into your head that the book's about him, not me? I suggest you join Julia in Chelsea, as Sir Edwin told the Major you should be persuaded to do. She married the bas . . . man,' he amended swiftly. 'She knows more about him than anyone else.'

'No. I asked her why Chris was transferred to Hugo's squadron and you weren't; why the RFC saw fit to split up a hugely successful duo. She didn't have the answer. Said her husband never spoke about his life before they met, and the first she knew about those dawn raids was when you mentioned them at the funeral.' Tipping her head to one side, she said, 'Julia's suspicious of you.'

'I know.'

'Does she have reason to be?'

Catching sight of a flash of green between tree trunks up ahead, Ben nodded in that direction. 'Here's your bus approaching.'

Deborah stayed where she was. 'She's gone to Chelsea with the intention of asking her influential friends to check you out.'

'Why doesn't the bloody woman do something useful, like telling her "influential friends" I've invested heavily in the company and will soon be displaying another prototype that's faster, more manoeuvrable and able to outfly any warplane yet built?

'General opinion has Freddie as a selfish wastrel, but he at least gets the Lance name lauded in motor racing circles, and he mixes with wealthy men dedicated to the development of speedier machines than our foreign rivals, whether on land, sea or in the air. Julia simply takes from the Marshfield coffers to spend on champagne cocktails with a gaggle of people as useless as herself.

'Sir Edwin and Hugo are striving to keep the company solvent and several thousand people in jobs. Why isn't Julia in the boardroom with them, or using her privileged status to promote *Broadwing* and *Snowbird* from her Chelsea flat? She's nothing more than a social parasite.' Seeing the bus drawing to a halt at the stopping place, Ben added sharply, 'Get over there before it drives off.'

'No. I want to know why you and Chris were separated. Tell me, Ben.' He put the van in motion and drove it forward to park right across the narrow country road to prevent the bus from moving off. A car approaching from behind them was also blocked by Ben's van. He sat back in his seat with folded arms. 'Goodbye, Miss Keene.'

For a moment or two he believed she would call his bluff, but the sight of the bus driver climbing out, red-faced with anger, and the loud, continuous blare of the car's horn behind them set her moving.

'I don't give up easily,' she hissed at him.

'Neither do I, believe me.'

Watched by two angry drivers and a young woman looking daggers at him, Ben made a three-point turn and drove off more disturbed by the encounter than he had shown. Why was the wretched woman pestering him on that vital fact? Her biography needed only to record that Chris Peterson had begun operating with a newly formed elite squadron after ridding the skies of the German ace Gustav Blomfeld, for which he had been awarded the Military Cross and promotion to captain.

Deborah had approached Julia, presumably by telephone,

because her appalling want of tact last week had put an insur-
mountable barrier between herself and the male Lances, which
Ben had welcomed in the belief that she would return to London
for further research.

Reaching the coach house he put a match to the kindling in
the grate, poured whisky into one of the two cheap tumblers that
served until he got around to another shopping trip, then sat
before the infant flames cursing the fact that he'd ever mentioned
those dawn raids. Chris's death in the *Lance* had forced an
immediate drastic change in tactics. No longer able to use the
threat of exposure and character assassination to gain what he
so badly wanted, Ben had had to trade on that early wartime
friendship, never foreseeing where it would lead. But how could
he have known some gullible young woman swayed by hero
worship would decide to put it all in a book?

He raised his eyes to the painting of the young God falling
to earth with wings melting and faced what he had too long
ignored. If that biography ever went into print, the truth about
the lad who had been dubbed 'Farmer' Norton because of
his country burr and ignorance of town ways would become
known.

Julia had no interest in wartime exploits, but she was equally
dangerous. Piqued by his aggression she was pursuing a different
line altogether. Ben's apparent lack of a wife, fiancée or mistress
suggested to her that he was either homosexual or playing out
some kind of complex charade at the Lance family's expense.
Depending on how influential her friends were, heartless, self-
absorbed, air-headed Julia could set in motion an avalanche that
could overwhelm them all.

For some minutes he contemplated all the problems he faced
and evaluated ways of overcoming them. The possible threat
to his life by displaying the *Lance* he and Roger were dealing
with together, more vigilantly as the proving flight neared.
Publication of that biography would have to be stopped, and
that would be up to him alone when the opportunity arose. If
it came to the very worst with Julia she would have to be
silenced with a counter threat. Keep quiet or I'll reveal something that will be irreparably damaging to all that you and your
family value.

Pouring more whisky, Ben felt the force of those weights that were tipping the scales against him and knew he must bring forward the date of the proving flight, before another thing he wanted with all his heart and soul was denied him at the eleventh hour. Gazing at the glowing pictures in the fire, his raw spirits recalled that first devastating loss.

He had lost his virginity at a village in Flanders, and had enjoyed several liaisons with girls who admired English soldiers, particularly les aviateurs. Ben had treated them with rough affection and respect, but his overriding passion was flying so he didn't lose his heart until some years later.

During that period in Cairo, Jack had become Ben and acquired a cultured accent to go with the manners and sophistication that allowed him to be accepted by those who could further his plan for the future. His prime passion was still flying, but he continued to treat his sexual partners with respect while using them to get him those things he wanted. He eventually departed from them and the Egyptian capital without regrets.

Society in Alexandria had accepted the good-looking, polished pilot without reservations, crediting him with the kind of background he must surely have. By carefully offering vague replies to awkward questions, Ben had allowed people to read into them what they chose, and it worked. Without actually lying, he became a young man sought after by prominent hostesses as a possible suitor for their daughter, niece or young sister once Norton Freight was well established and profitable.

Marriageable girls came and went but not until four years ago, when Ben was twenty-eight, did one take him by storm, suddenly and overwhelming. Stella was the niece of a rich widow, in Alexandria for a six-month holiday, but she could have been a relation of a bazaar stallholder for all Ben cared. He wanted her, longed to possess her, could concentrate on nothing else. Norton Freight was doing well. He had just extended his routes to include Tunis, so he was well able to offer a decent home and financial security to a wife.

By the end of the first month Stella was to be seen everywhere on Ben's arm; by the second she was wearing his ring and making wedding plans. In the third month they found a secret hideaway and made passionate love whenever Ben had a break from his demanding flight schedule. He was deeply, deeply committed to spending the rest of his life with this girl he adored.

Two weeks before the wedding he returned from a three-day long haul along the Med to find a letter and a jeweller's box among his correspondence. Stella wrote that she had come to Alexandria to recover from a broken engagement, but her lover had telephoned to beg forgiveness and ask her to return to England to marry him before sailing with him to Bermuda where he was to take up a diplomatic post. So sorry, but Ben was sure to find someone else before long.

The bridegroom in the photographs sent to her aunt was not Ben, but the smile on the duplicitous bride's face had led him to steal one of them to remind him never again to be bewitched by a woman. And it had worked. Instead, he had been so bewitched by the lure of the *Lance* he had abandoned everything to pursue his old passion to its fulfilment.

Sitting in that sparsely furnished room, shaken by those memories from the past, Ben gradually realized what he must do without delay. He had come this far; he was damned if he would let Deborah, Julia or Sir Edwin stand in his way.

For the next three days Ben took advantage of clear weather to fly the *Lance* every morning and afternoon. Sir Edwin had been invited to a shooting party in Scotland, Julia was in London and Freddie was burning tyres around Europe's race tracks, so Hugo had to rely on his managers to escort him to the hangar. As Ben hoped, the frequency of this quickly led to the man abandoning his practice of being present for every flight. He couldn't see the manoeuvres anyway.

On the fourth morning Ben divulged his intention to Roger. 'I'm ready. The *Lance* is ready. We need to show her off to men who matter. No point in kicking our heels. It'll possibly support the theory that there was a vital design fault which is taking an age to put right. I'm going to start rehearsing my programme for the proving flight.'

'Good time to do it. The Major's seen sense and given up his demand to be informed each time you take off. Get up there and do what you want.' Roger smiled. 'You're every bit as confident as Chris, but more controlled. Don't change that, Ben. Put her through her paces without using her to show off your personal brilliance. A proving flight is exactly that: a display designed to support the truth of what we claim about the aircraft, not about the bloke flying it!'

Ben chuckled. 'Yes, sir!' Then he sobered. 'I've been flying for fourteen years in all manner of machines, but this will be my very first proving flight. Something of a milestone. I get butterflies whenever I remember the significance of it.'

'Me too, lad.' Roger's voice grew unsteady. 'You're going to vindicate my worth as a designer.'

Those words stayed with Ben as he took off and headed for Pitman Hill. Like Chris he would make his approach from there and fly fast and low over the airfield. From then on his display would be entirely different in performance yet include every manoeuvre that would excite spectators. As he experimented with the possibilities, Ben repeated some movements with variations to decide which one to adopt. Although he had planned it on paper, it was a different matter in actuality, so he eventually landed eager to discuss it with Roger and produce fresh diagrams.

It was soon apparent something had developed while he had been ranging over the sky. The three managers were in the hangar and the ground staff had clustered around Roger talking energetically.

Pulling off his leather helmet Ben crossed to join them. 'What's going on?'

The group turned to him. All were smiling, so it could not be something bad. 'Come on, then. Tell me what's made you all so happy?'

Roger went to him. 'The Major's received the report from the Board of Inquiry on the crash.'

'And?' he asked urgently.

'After careful examination of the wreckage and checking the medical history of the pilot, they've brought in a verdict of accidental death possibly caused by the pilot losing consciousness due to the speed and extremely precipitous angle of the final dive.'

Ben's gaze locked on to Roger's. This decision would be published in the same newspapers that had damned the designer and the manufacturer. This verdict would go a long way towards boosting Marshfield's hopes for the future of the *Lance*, but one of the three managers celebrating here knew, as did Roger and Ben, that Chris Peterson's death had been no accident.

# NINE

There was a headline in most national newspapers on the following day. Ignoring that they had blazoned their opinion that the *Lance* was badly designed and a complete white elephant, they now stated that Peterson had clearly misjudged the speed of his final dive and suffered the consequences, which had also destroyed Roger Hall's splendid new fighter that could match any being produced in other countries. Rumours of a second prototype already being tested in preparation for another proving flight before VIPs suggested Marshfield Aviation would lose no time in issuing invitations.

Ben read this while he ate breakfast. His anonymous call to the *Daily Express* two days ago had not been taken up until news of the Board of Inquiry verdict had been made public, but Sir Edwin and Hugo would surely now be dragooned by this press coverage into setting an early date.

An hour after Ben arrived at Marshfield he and Roger were called by Hugo's secretary to report to his office. They were discussing a revised flight plan Ben had supported with diagrams, and they exchanged satisfied smiles.

'Looks as if we're in business again,' said Roger. 'I wonder who spread the rumour about a second prototype being tested.'

'Mm, I wonder,' Ben mused as he rolled the charts and secured them with an elastic band. When they set out along the inner corridors, he said, 'Of course, the Board's decision kills their claim of a design fault, but it also kills ours of sabotage. They'll never heed a request for constant surveillance on the *Lance* once the proving flight is fixed and VIPs invited. The blame for the crash is credited to a man who can't defend himself, which suits them perfectly. We'll have to mount vigils ourselves, with the assistance of Felix Stroud.'

'I'm happy to do that,' Roger returned, pushing open a swing door giving access to the top managerial offices. 'What we have to decide is if and when another attempt is likely to be made.'

Ben shook his head. 'There's no if about it, in my opinion. He got away with it once, he'll try again now the official verdict has put fresh verve into the Lances. If the saboteur is in the pay of a rival company the aim is to prevent manufacture of the aircraft for all time. Another public disaster would certainly do that.'

They approached Hugo's office suite through more swing doors. 'And if he has other reasons?'

'That would possibly dictate when he would strike. A pacifist is likely to use any opportunity offered from now on. He sees the *Lance* as a weapon of war being offered to men who would use it against an enemy. To destroy this prototype after all the money and work spent on creating it would have a good chance of causing the Lances to give up on the project and concentrate on *Snowbird* and *Broadwing*. Killing a pilot would not be necessary. Just destroy the weapon.'

Ben slowed to a halt and faced Roger frankly. 'If our man is Kershaw he's the most tricky. A person of sudden violent temper, as I experienced. Someone with a history of failure followed by a period of instability. He could well be driven to make any new design fail, as the *Duiker* did, the more publicly the greater his sense of revenge. Add to that the belief that I have designs on his wife and we have an answer to all our theories. I'd guess Chris Peterson might have made a play for Mirium Kershaw, which sealed his fate. He had to die with the aircraft.'

'You're saying he'd try again on the day of the proving flight?'

'Yes. He was there when Chris flew into the ground, and his name is on the list of three who could have severed the cable during the last tense minutes before Chris taxied from the hangar.' Ben raised his hands in appeal. 'Roger, that list is yours – I wasn't there – and one of those three men must have been guilty. Tilbrook is anti-war, a womanizer and vocal in his vehemence that Marshfield should concentrate on commercial aircraft. We're now aware that he could have drugged Chris to achieve his ends, which would have been easier for him than to disable the *Lance*. Ray Povey has the professional knowledge to tamper surreptitiously, he wasn't an admirer of Chris's cockiness, and he has an expensive, demanding wife. But would he commit such appalling crimes for payment?'

Roger frowned. 'There's strong evidence he still lives beyond his means, but he's not corrupt enough to do that. I've known him for years. Maybe he occasionally works night shifts somewhere, or he gets lucky at racetracks now and again. There's nothing vicious about his character, Ben.'

'Which brings us back to the man the cap fits perfectly. Someone you've known just a month or two longer than I have. Kershaw's the one we need to watch closely in the coming days.' He began slowly walking towards the door of Hugo's office. 'One precaution we can take is to have nobody around during the final minutes before I take off.'

Roger nodded agreement. 'After this meeting we'll work out how to keep the *Lance* constantly under observation by us or Felix.' He pushed open the door and smiled at Hugo's secretary. 'The Major wants to discuss something with us, I believe.'

'Yes. Go through. He's expecting you, Mr Hall. And Captain Norton.'

It came as an unpleasant surprise for Ben to find Julia sitting beside her brother. Just why had this meeting been arranged? Had he and Roger misread the situation?

Hugo was a bundle of brisk energy and authority as he greeted them and invited them to sit. The Board of Inquiry report had clearly put new life in him; Ben now saw the man he must have been before Chris crashed. Julia's stony expression remained as she made no attempt at a greeting to either of them. Was she going to produce some damning evidence that would shake even Hugo's optimism and bring the carefully built house of cards crashing down?

Hugo began speaking expansively about the *Lance* as if he had never doubted the fighter's spectacular properties. Then he concentrated on Ben. 'I've heard you putting her through her paces morning and afternoon these last three days, Captain Norton, and you'll continue that routine until I'm satisfied you're fully confident in the cockpit.'

'I am now,' he returned swiftly. 'By the end of next week I'll have a display ready for anyone you choose to witness it. Roger's creation is a pilot's dream to fly. She's the perfect machine for RAF fighter squadrons.' He went on to compare the *Lance* with aircraft they had both flown during the war, enumerating the vital points that made this new combat aircraft so superior.

Hugo's expression showed his complete understanding of all Ben said, and once again thought of the injury that had overtaken this distinguished pilot overrode Ben's dislike of him.

'Set an early date for the proving flight and take advantage of this new press interest, sir. Strike while the iron's hot,' he urged. 'There'll never be a better time to counter the earlier universal disparagement. We can erase all memory of it with a display that'll put Marshfield back with the giants of the aviation world.'

Controlling his exuberance, Ben added quietly, 'I want the *Lance* to triumph as much as you do. I'll fly my heart out to make it happen.'

Into the resultant silence Roger murmured, 'He will, Major. I think we should do as he suggests.'

Hugo sat for some moments, twisting a gold fountain pen in restless fingers. Then, without turning to or consulting Julia, he nodded. 'I'll speak to my father this afternoon when the guns return to the house. Work towards a date in early June, gentlemen. That's all, thank you.'

By evening the Marshfield workforce was informed that Captain Norton would make a proving flight in the *Lance* before an invited group of spectators on the second Wednesday in June. Everyone except those who were closely involved were granted a holiday on that date.

Twelve days in which to perfect a dazzling display. Twelve days only if the weather allowed flying on each of them. Ben and Roger knew how much depended on success so they stayed well into the evening in Roger's office working on a plan to guard the fighter from any attempts at sabotage before the flight took place.

Roger insisted Ben must have adequate rest, so they recruited young Felix Stroud and divided the night hours into three watches, two of which would last four hours and the third for only two, which Ben would take. Another camp bed could be placed with the one already in the hangar, and the man on watch would occupy the cockpit from where he would see anyone approaching;

during normal working hours one or other of them would be within sight of the *Lance* the whole time.

They agreed that if an attempt was made, it was most likely to be near or on the vital day, but they cornered Felix and found him agreeable to start on the morrow. Ben deplored the lad's attitude of treating the whole business as a bit of a lark, but Felix was steady and reliable, regarding the *Lance* with a young man's avid passion for machines that flew, so he would play his part with dedication.

Ben vowed to eat and drink only items he had prepared himself and kept in a locked drawer until needed. No chance of dope being added. After telling Roger this he gave a wry grin.

'Taking it too seriously, d'you think?'

Roger shook his head. 'This is far too important. Ben, I'll do my utmost to keep you safe. I want you to leave the ground that day in prime condition to fly an aeroplane that'll bring you back triumphant after getting both our names in the record books. No one will be allowed to prevent that, I swear.'

Ben was so moved he found himself offering his hand in a gesture of true friendship. Roger clasped it tightly. No need for words.

It was almost fully dark when Ben went out to his van deep in thoughts of the next twelve days, so much so he belatedly registered the sight of a Lagonda parked in direct line with his vehicle among those few still to be collected by workers. The glow of a lighted cigarette told him Julia was there waiting for him. He should have known her silence in Hugo's office didn't mean he was off the hook. His pulse quickened. He would not let her ruin everything when he was so near to achieving it. He held the ace. If she forced him to play it he would, but he wanted to have that supreme experience first.

'I want a word with you,' she said stridently as he neared.

He halted but didn't bend to look at her. 'More than one, I imagine.'

'I have influential friends.'

'So Miss Keene told me.'

She ignored that. 'Hugo thinks of nothing but getting the company back on track. He's put the war out of his mind – it robbed him of sight – and concentrates on the future he can create for himself and Marshfield. No use involving him in this, so I've pursued it myself.' Her hand came through the open window and her fingers elegantly tapped ash from the end of a cigarette in an amber holder. 'No Ben, Benjamin or Benedict Norton appears on the list of commissioned officers in the Royal Flying Corps, or the Royal Air Force as it became, who served in the same squadron as my late husband. Your tale of dual derring-do which earned you the name The Skylarks was complete fabrication. You never knew Chris Peterson, did you?'

Ben said nothing, waiting for what else she might come out with.

'I don't know what game you're playing, but it'll soon be over. You're a liar and a fraud, and I mean to expose you as such. Unfortunately, my brother is hell bent on instigating another proving flight, acting on the assurances of his managers that you can handle the aircraft expertly. While you're important to him and the company I must keep quiet, but once that's over and done with I'll reveal all I know and make it very public. Then I'll sit back and watch the consequences with immense pleasure.'

'Have you finished?' he asked, knowing she had discovered very little and was exaggerating its importance.

'I've only just started, believe me. My friends are continuing to be busy on my behalf. You have twelve days, Mr Whoeveryouare. Twelve days, that's all.'

With a roar she drove away with a speed and panache her brother Freddie would surely have admired.

Sleep was a long time coming. Ben's brain was teeming with facts and figures, plans and fears. Riding above all else was the possibility of his life ending very shortly. A determined saboteur could overcome their careful daily security. There would be brief times when he was alone – he couldn't glue himself to Roger or Felix – and he'd need to come home for a bath and change of clothes. He'd also need to collect his mail from the village store he'd used as a poste restante from the day he had booked into The Dancing Bear.

Almost certain Kershaw was the villain, Ben suspected he would wait through the coming twelve days before making his move, but it would be foolish to depend on that. A fatal crash during any one of his flights would create enough press coverage to destroy all hope of launching the *Lance*, and he would be dead or so badly injured death would have been kinder. He lay in bed until the early hours cudgeling his brain for a means of getting Kershaw out of the way during this vital time. The further the better. South Africa would do nicely.

Mirium had revealed that John had no close relatives in his homeland, so no likelihood of one falling ill and demanding the man's presence at their deathbed. Mirium herself had not looked pregnant, so little chance of a miscarriage that would demand all Kershaw's attention. At that point in his rambling thoughts Ben told himself to stop thinking like a thriller writer concocting a plot for a book, and get some sleep.

He left the bed and padded to the tiny bathroom for a couple of knockout pills. They had been his saviour in the first weeks after Stella's desertion and marriage. On returning to his bed he heard the sound of a car starting up just outside the front window. Curious, he walked to look from it. The nearest neighbour was two miles away so who would be about at two thirty?

The car had been backed into the entrance of the drive leading to the manor house, and was half hidden by the wall of flowering rhododendrons. The vague figure in the driving seat lit a cigarette then put out the match, suggesting there was nobody else in the car. Had someone lost his way in the maze of lanes hereabouts? When the vehicle slowly moved forward in the direction of Marshfield which connected with the main thoroughfare to Lewes, Ben guessed the driver had pulled up to consult his road map.

He returned to bed but another hour passed before his weary brain decided that enough was enough and he slept. During the war years and those erratic ones spent building up Norton Freight, Ben's sleep pattern had fluctuated so much his body was used to the demands he made on it.

Woken by the dawn chorus, as he had been since arriving in Sussex, he first made tea then began assembling blankets and a pillow for the coming nights in the hangar. He also packed a bag with spare clothes to keep at Marshfield in the event of not being able to come back often during the next twelve days.

Once everything was ready he decided to stow it all in the van before cooking a decent breakfast and cutting a pile of sandwiches to take with him. He passed a bakery on the journey, so he'd buy a bagful of sausage rolls and some fruit to supplement his rations.

Gathering up the bedding and his thick overcoat to wear while doing his two hour watch in the cockpit, Ben opened his door and stepped out to the small platform at the top of the exterior wooden staircase that gave access to his new home. His next step sent him plunging towards the large concrete yard where coaches had once stood to be washed and cleaned. He hit it with a force that drove the breath from his body, and pain rioted through his limbs until he lost all awareness.

'Captain! Captain! Oh jeepers, what should I do?'

The scratchy voice of a boy in the throes of losing his soprano and gaining a baritone penetrated Ben's unconsciousness. He opened his eyes. Henry Jenks, who delivered newspapers as well as letters and telegrams in Fossbeck Camden and its environs, was kneeling beside him ashen with fright.

'Oh, you're not dead, are you!' the lad declared.

'Not yet,' Ben murmured.

He gazed at a greenish blur that danced up and down until it turned into a clear image of a coach house. At its side rose a flight of wooden steps. Oh yes, he had crashed from top to bottom. Something had prevented him from . . . At that point the image began to blur again and he closed his eyes to ease his dizziness.

'Oh jeepers, I'll fetch Dr King.'

Ben vaguely heard the clatter of a bicycle being righted but he was too winded to call the lad to stay. Slowly he became aware that he was lying on something soft, but how could he be? His hands moved experimentally along his sides and felt woollen cloth bearing big buttons. His overcoat! He had been carrying it with several blankets. Further experimental fingering discovered them, layered beneath the coat. It then dawned on him that his head was resting against a pillow. Dear God, it had saved his skull from being cracked open on the concrete. Was that friendly spirit which had been with him during four years of battle and twelve of further risks and uncertainty still watching over him?

The nausea of shock assailed him when he rolled on to his side and pushed himself into a sitting position, but, he seemed not to have broken any bones. Sensibly deciding to give himself time to recover his equilibrium before getting to his feet, he was still resting on his overcoat when a car drew up and a thin, moustached man carrying a medical bag got out and approached with a smile.

'I always advise patients if they plan to fall down a flight of stairs to be sure to carry blankets and a pillow to land on.'

He squatted, took a small torch from his bag and shone it in Ben's eyes. 'You've been damned lucky, Captain Norton. Young Henry saw you come down as if you were diving into a pool of water. You could have broken your neck, and that would've been that. Now, follow my finger with your eyes. I'm Reginald King, by the way.'

Dr King went through the routine of discovering if any limbs were broken, if the spine had been damaged and if Ben's heart rate gave cause for concern. At the end of it all he gave a nod of satisfaction.

'You'll be black and blue by tomorrow, but you're still in one piece. Let's get you on your feet and back up those stairs for a cup of strong tea and a rest to recover from the shock of soft body hitting hard ground.'

He took Ben's arm and helped him to stand rather unsteadily for a moment or two. Henry arrived back just then. His cheeks were pinker than before and he managed a smile for Ben.

'As you have this young lad to thank for fetching help so soon, don't you agree he deserves a cup of tea and perhaps a biscuit or two? Take the Captain's other arm, Henry, just to ensure he doesn't give a repeat performance when we reach the top.'

More to please the boy than because he needed the additional prop, Ben allowed them to help him. He was annoyingly shaky on climbing the steps, but that was nothing to how he felt on nearing the top one to see it hanging loose in two splintered sections almost torn away from their holdings.

'Ah, now we see the cause of the problem,' declared the doctor, halting to stare at the damage. 'So rotten you only had to put your weight on it for it to go. Let me help you over it.'

He used the banister to pull himself up to the square landing, then turned to offer Ben his hand. 'Better get Syd Moss to test the rest when he comes to replace this one. I'll drop a word in to him on my way back, if you like. Anyone coming here at night could be badly injured. And you'd be liable, Captain Norton.'

Sending a reluctant Henry to make tea – 'A spoonful for each person and one for the pot, lad' – King took from his bag a small vial of amber liquid.

'No doubt you've had this before,' he said to Ben. 'It'll make you dozy so don't take that flying machine off the ground for a day or two.'

Once he was alone ostensibly to rest and recover, Ben took a closer look at the cause of his fall and saw what he had suspected. The top step had been sawn almost right through and the nails on each side had been loosened. They stood proud on the splintered wood, several having been torn completely free. The minute he had put his foot on it the breach would have widened and sent him headlong. If he had not been clutching all those soft articles which had cushioned his fall John Kershaw would have probably achieved his aim.

Returning to make toast which was all he now felt like for breakfast, Ben told himself this was the method used on the *Lance*, cutting almost through something so it would break under extreme pressure later – at a time when Kershaw himself was nowhere near! The bastard had been here during the night and used a fine saw to make an almost invisible cut across the step. How the hell had he known where to come? Only Roger knew about the coach house, and he would never have given the information away.

He left the toast half eaten as nausea returned. He had not taken King's bromide because he fully intended to take the *Lance* up later this morning, but he was still shaken by what had happened. He had not expected Kershaw to act so immediately. So much for all those security plans they had dreamed up!

The morning was halfway over by the time Ben drove through Marshfield gates, dosed up on an analgesic which did not cause drowsiness. He knew; he had used them a number of times in the past and still been in control of his aircraft. Aware that tonight and tomorrow would be the times when bruised, protesting joints and muscles became acutely painful, Ben had no intention of losing this one day of the precious twelve. Or of giving signs of unfitness to the Lances. Too much was riding on the proposed date for the proving flight.

Weather conditions were favourable and he needed to iron out any slight refinements to his planned display during the two flights scheduled for that day. After he had done that he would decide on whether or not to tell Roger what had happened, and then discuss what they should do about Kershaw.

That second uncertainty was resolved when he parked and started to walk towards the hangars. Kershaw must have spotted the arrival of the van from the window of his office for he suddenly appeared at the entrance to hangar one and watched Ben for every step of his way to where the *Lance* had been towed out and fuelled up in readiness. The mere fact of his presence, apparently unharmed and ready to fly, visibly rattled Kershaw so there was no need for a confrontation for which Ben had no proof. An opportunity would surely come to make the man aware that the malicious attempt to cause injury, if not worse, had been attributed to him and retribution would eventually follow.

Amid chaffing from the ground crew, and worried questioning from Roger about his tardy arrival, Ben swiftly donned his flying suit silencing everyone by saying he needed to get aloft before the sun reached its zenith.

With inborn determination he took off and flew the entire programme at three-quarter power. He would have done this anyway for a couple of days until he was totally satisfied that he would fully demonstrate to the men on the ground the *Lance*'s superb qualities. For those twenty-five minutes Ben forgot all else but the urgency to complete what he had set out to do, at all costs.

When he landed and climbed from the cockpit, pain and stiffness reminded him it was time to take more pills to help him through his second flight early in the afternoon. Roger beamed as he embarked on an enthusiastic rundown of each manoeuvre, which persuaded Ben to keep quiet about his headlong fall just four hours ago.

'Your decision to end with a tight, descending spiral out over the sea before disappearing behind Pitman Hill then skimming the crest to swoop low over the runway with guns blazing shows what my aircraft truly is. A warplane.' Roger cocked his head. 'You've done that manoeuvre in conflict, haven't you?'

Ben managed no more than a nod, knowing why he had chosen to conclude a flight he had so much wanted to make he had been prepared to ruin the life of the man who had flown alongside him during those risky days. If Chris could look on from wherever he was now, would he recognize the significance of that mock strafe and finally weep?

'Hey, why the frown?' Ben came from his thoughts as Roger led him to the table where tea and sandwiches were laid out. 'Young Felix's sister supplied the food and Felix brewed the tea. All perfectly edible, Ben,' he finished with a slightly anxious glance at him.

Ben shook away memories. 'Sorry I didn't contribute any victuals.'

'No need, sir,' put in Felix as he poured tea. 'Connie's a good cook and offered to keep us supplied. She'll even deliver as we're going to stay here overnight.'

At that point Ben realized he had forgotten to bring his pillow and blankets. Henry had carried them back to the flat and probably put them in the bedroom. 'Does she know why you're going to sleep here?'

The red-haired young man grinned. 'Told her a yarn about overtime because of the proving flight, but I think she's suspicious I've really got a girl on the go.'

Ben nodded. 'Natural enough, but it's not necessary to put her to the trouble of bringing food here every day. We can go in relay to the works canteen. I'll have a decent dinner at home tonight. It happens I have to meet a chap who's going to do some work for me and he's only available this evening. I'll be back in time to do my two hour early morning watch.'

The always eager Felix said, 'If I did the first watch I could get in four hours of sleep then do yours, sir.'

'No,' Ben returned sharply. 'We need to be fully alert during these next days. Each of us will do whatever's necessary.'

His tone registered with the lad, who asked, 'D'you really believe someone'll try to destroy the *Lance*?'

Or me, thought Ben, but said, 'Yes, I do. And so does Mr Hall.'

Felix flushed with excitement. 'Cor!'

Fully dosed with painkillers, Ben prepared for his afternoon flight and emerged from the changing room to discover a small audience lined up outside the hangar. Julia, Deborah, Hugo and John Kershaw, the latter probably included as a professional pilot who could give Hugo knowledgeable descriptions of what the former squadron commander was unable to see.

Obliged to acknowledge Hugo's presence, Ben crossed to where they all waited, and said what was necessary. He ignored the two women but fixed Kershaw with a challenging look which matched the other man's as he turned away. That optical encounter drove Ben to revise his plan to repeat the trial run of the morning and boost the engine power for this one.

Once in the air all negative thought evaporated to be replaced by the familiar surging elation of travelling high above the earth. In consequence, the final appearance over Pitman Hill to swoop mere feet above the ground was almost as spectacular as it would be when he actually fired the guns, starting two days before the vital day.

Taxiing back along the grass runway, Ben was aware that the group of spectators had enlarged considerably, and also that he was beginning to experience the full physical toll of that fall of more than twenty feet on to concrete that morning. Wanting to hurry home for a hot bath and an hour or two on a soft bed, Ben sighed when Hugo looked set on further conversation when he climbed from the cockpit. A short retinue followed to cut off Ben's access to the hangar, the faces of all but two wore smiles. The expressions of Julia and Kershaw were unreadable.

Hugo Lance was more affable than Ben had ever known him to be. 'I'm impressed by your decision to revamp the previous display flight plan, Captain Norton' (Ben was no longer 'our pilot'). 'Very circumspect under the circumstances. You've taken into account the aircraft's specific properties and used them to best advantage, John says. Good! Good! I also understand you intend to close your programme with a low-level strafe firing live ammo at two dummy trucks. I'll have to clear that proposal with my father before I give you the go ahead. He'll be back at the weekend, but please continue as things stand for the time being.'

He prepared to leave, yet lingered to say, 'Invitations have been issued and the response so far has been excellent. Just pray to the God of meteorology for clear skies on that day.'

Julia, arrayed in wide-legged turquoise trousers and a silvery silk tabard, murmured as she turned to follow her brother and Kershaw, 'I'll concede you're a pretty damn impressive pilot, but thirteen days from now all hell will break over your swollen head, I promise you.'

Deborah was being led away by Jim Tilbrook who had joined the group, but she shrugged off his hand on her arm and stopped to look back at Ben in appeal.

'Please talk to me. I'll meet you anywhere at any time you choose.'

'He's too busy playing hero of the day, me darlin',' Tilbrook told her sourly, clasping her arm again. 'Stick with me. I can tell you about things he can only dream of.'

Ben turned into the hangar fully understanding the maxim *coming down to earth*. Up there he was the man he wanted to be; a high flyer. Down here he had to deal with the human race.

Despite throbbing pain and aching limbs Ben stopped at an inn for a good hot meal on his way home two hours later. It was essential to keep up his strength over the coming days. Arriving at the coach house, he looked up at the door of his flat, realized how far he had fallen, and shivered. How close, how close he had been to . . .!

The top step was new, fitted by an expert. On the floor inside the front door was an invoice with a handwritten note attached.

*No need to examine the other steps. This one weren't rotten, sir. Someone had cut through it with a fine saw. Something not right there. I'd have a word with Constable Frith, if I was you.*

Suddenly depressed, Ben gazed at his painting of Icarus and wondered why the hell he had bought it. Was it trying to tell him something?

A long, hot bath and a few more painkillers dulled the feeling of impending danger enough to allow Ben to fall asleep almost as soon as he settled in the softness of his bed. He slept too well. It was two a.m. when he roused and remembered his promise to be back at Marshfield for his early morning watch. His attempt to roll out of bed set him yelling. Every joint, every muscle protested. However would he climb into the *Lance* in this state and hide his unfitness from Roger, who would ban him from flying his precious prototype? Only eleven more days! He needed every one of them.

Hobbling into the small kitchen to make tea, Ben became conscious of heavy drumming on the roof. Rain! He had not prayed to the God of meteorology, but he had better start now. So much could happen between now and that vital day.

Carrying his mug to the window where he could better gauge the severity of the deluge, he was acutely shaken to see that same car backed into the main driveway as before. Good God, was Kershaw set on finishing what he had started last night? Going to the wardrobe he took out the revolver, swiftly pulling on trousers and a pullover, then he returned to take up a position beside the window which would give him a clear view of Kershaw mounting the steps.

The driver was still in the car, however. Would a potential killer be deterred by heavy rain? Ben relaxed slightly, then received a shock as the man he was watching struck a match to light a cigarette. Last night he had remained no more than a dark shape. Now, as he bent forward, the brief flare of light clearly identified Ray Povey.

# TEN

At the main gate of Marshfield the night security guard greeted Ben with surprise. 'You're never going flying in the dark, Captain Norton.'

'Just need to get in early,' he replied. 'We're all working odd hours at the moment. Did Mr Povey go through earlier?'

'No, sir. Went 'ome 'is usual time and I've not seen 'im since then. Is you expecting 'im?'

Ben shook his head. 'Thought he might be putting in some overtime on the new *Snowbird* contract.' He drove between the opened gates. 'Thanks, Maurice.'

As soon as he entered the hangar, Ben was temporarily blinded by a beam of light from the cockpit, which caused him to shield his eyes with linked hands until it vanished.

'Sorry, Ben,' Roger called out. 'Saw a figure materialize in the shadows and went into action with my torch.' He prepared to climb from the *Lance*. 'Expected you back before this.'

Ben moved forward and helped the older man jump down. 'We need to talk seriously, Roger. I know who wants to prevent production of this lovely aeroplane for all time.'

'You do? How?'

Ben led his friend to a chair beside the table bearing tea mugs, then sat close beside him. Felix was fast asleep in the office, but Ben was taking no chances of being overheard. This was strictly between the creator of the fighter and the man determined to launch it in fitting style.

After relating the details of the sawn-through step causing his fall, Ben told of his certainty that the person in the car that night had been Kershaw, this premise being borne out by the man's reaction to seeing his victim appearing apparently unharmed to fly as planned.

'The car was there again tonight, at roughly the same time. The driver struck a match to light his cigarette and I saw his face clearly in the glare. Not Kershaw. It was Povey.'

'Ray?' Roger was plainly upset. 'I might have believed almost anything of him but that.'

'Before I could go down and confront him he drove off. I checked every one of those steps before I put my weight on them. I also searched the van, but all seemed fine. Unlikely though it seems, the downpour apparently prevented his second attempt to put me out of the picture, maybe permanently.'

'No! Ray would never contemplate doing that.'

'Roger, he knew what would happen when I started to descend that flight of steps; fall more than twenty feet to a concrete yard,' Ben said insistently. 'He's trying the easy solution first. Kill or damage me and the proving flight would have to be postponed until Hugo found another test pilot willing to brave the jinx on the *Lance*. More overblown, speculative press reportage which would be almost as damning as another crash.'

He sighed heavily. 'We've no need to mount a twenty-four hour watch until his attempts on my life have all failed, leaving him with no alternative but to do what he did before.' Sensing Roger's reluctance to accept this, Ben resorted to plain language. 'He destroyed three years of concentrated work on your part, and he murdered Chris Peterson. He's capable of repeating that double crime, without doubt.'

Into the long silence Ben added, 'He's not unstable, like Kershaw, so he must be doing it for money. Why else? His job would be safe due to that gratifying contract for *Snowbird*, which you say is his baby. Someone's paying him to sabotage production of an aircraft that would outshine all others in that category.'

After considering all this Roger said, 'We must inform Hugo and Sir Edwin.'

Ben shook his head. 'They didn't believe us last time and, like last time, we can't prove it. No, Roger, they're both presently buoyed up and enthusiastic. I don't want to chuck cold water over their faith in us to pull off a complete reversal of corporate opinion in eleven days' time, because that's what I bloody well intend to do. I want that day of recognition and glory. I want my name in the record books along with yours. I want Hugo Lance to shake my hand and present me to VIPs and the media with obvious respect.'

After a moment or two, the man he could barely see in the darkness said quietly, 'I see.'

Realizing he had exposed too much of himself, Ben tried to sound more rational. 'We have the advantage of knowing who we're dealing with; something Povey doesn't suspect. I intend to turn the tables on him. Lie in wait in the van and catch him at whatever the rain tonight prevented him from trying.'

'I can't condone that, Ben.'

'All right.' He got to his feet. 'Time you got back on that camp bed while I do my two-hour watch. We've no firm guarantee he won't attack the *Lance* next time. I'll wake you and Felix if he comes, but it's still pouring out there so I doubt he will. More likely he'll plan something for tomorrow night.'

Roger stayed where he was. 'I can't get back to sleep after hearing that news. You require a twenty-four hour bodyguard, Ben. The devil's trying to kill or maim you! We have to tell Hugo right away. He might not believe you, but he could send Ray off on some pretext until the proving flight is over; get him out of the area during these vital days. Marshfield's future relies on the *Lance*. The Major knows that.'

'The *Snowbird* contract has staved off the worst threat of job losses, and he's on a roller right now. I know his type. He'd translate this information as an attack of nerves by the pilot, an excuse to postpone the flight on which so much depends.' Seeing his friend's negative expression he said insistently, 'He has no real faith in me, no sense of fellowship. And Julia has fed that inborn aloofness in retaliation for my failure to dance to her tune. I'm under no illusions. After the acclaim for your splendid design has died down, I'll be replaced by a professional test pilot. Someone who fits their narrow requirements and isn't a shareholder in the company, with a tendency to do as he pleases. No, Roger, I mean to deal with Povey myself.'

Roger got to his feet and confronted Ben. 'Has it occurred to you that unless everything goes to plan next Wednesday I shall also no longer be required by the Lance family, and with little likelihood of persuading anyone else to take interest in my designs?'

'Yes, that's occurred to me on and off during the past weeks, which is why we have to keep any hint of trouble away from any member of the Lance family.' He put a hand on Roger's shoulder. 'You befriended me when I most needed it. Trust me to get us through this successfully. I won't let you down.'

Still edgy, Roger chose to brew tea rather than return to the camp bed beside the one on which Felix was sleeping with the soundness of the young and healthy, and as dawn had broken to provide enough light to reach every part of the hangar, Ben was not obliged to sit in the cockpit for his watch.

Believing Roger's creative mind had not totally absorbed the import of a fall down an entire flight of steps, Ben took his painkillers covertly while listening to rain drumming on the roof and soft snores from the man sitting beside him. During those early morning hours he reflected on his own words concerning the aftermath of next Wednesday. He would have reached a pinnacle. What did the climber do after he had fought his way to the summit? Go down again, of course.

Julia was set on helping him on his way with a hefty kick. He had the means of silencing her but Deborah was stirring up suspicion in the presence of Jim Tilbrook. If he began to take too great an interest Ben would have no weapon to use against him. All in all, there were eleven more days in which to live the challenge before John Benjamin Norton sought another identity for the next phase of his chequered life.

They went singly to the canteen for breakfast having discovered the small toilet and changing room in the rear of the hangar would not serve to wash, shave and don fresh clothes. A swift triple agreement brought a change of plan. Once the day shift arrived they would go to their nearby homes for these tasks, leaving one person at a time to watch the *Lance*.

Within an hour of this decision Ben and Roger were summoned to Hugo's office. Fearing the low strafe with live ammunition to end the display had been vetoed by Sir Edwin, they walked silently through the corridors to then wait ten minutes before being admitted. Ben's heart missed a beat when he saw Julia sitting beside her brother who was clearly very angry. She had sworn to keep silent until the display was over. Why had she seen fit to act now?

'Good morning, gentlemen,' said Hugo without inviting them to sit. 'This newspaper—' he waved it in the air— 'contains a highly coloured article about "the courageous pilot who is preparing to fly another prototype of the warplane in which his close Royal Flying Corps friend plunged to his death just a few months ago". It weaves a luridly melodramatic fiction of heroic exploits over enemy lines "while their faithful sweethearts waited as tears dried on their cheeks to learn that their brave menfolk were safely home.".'

Hugo's biting tone provided more. 'You, Captain Norton, are apparently "making this historic flight as a tribute of love and respect to your fallen comrade".' Hugo threw the newspaper on his desk. 'I hope your expression properly shows your disgust at this betrayal of our hospitality, even friendship on the part of my sister. We have, of course, informed Miss Keene that she will no longer be admitted to our homes or business premises, and that we withdraw our permission to use photographs or personal recollections of Captain Peterson in any form of publication, interview or lecture she might embark on in the future. This family will challenge in court any use she attempts to make of information gleaned during her contact with its members and their associates.'

Aware that he was expected to fill a lengthy pause, Ben was lost for words due to the sparkle of enjoyment in Julia's eyes. She really was a heartless creature. Was Hugo aware of her true nature? No doubt she had read to him what could have been an extract from a cheap romance with the very emphasis Hugo had used, delighting in every nuance.

'It's pure invention, sir,' Ben said at last. 'I consistently refused her an interview.'

'Yes, yes, I know that. I'm not suggesting you're behind this,' snapped Hugo. 'I sent for you both because the woman has published the date of the proving flight, and given your name. I have carefully avoided releasing that information for the sole purpose of preventing what is now certain to happen. My secretary has been swamped with telephone calls, and there were already a few sightseers outside the gates when we came through an hour ago. Next Wednesday will bring a horde of brainless people to Marshfield in the hope of some cinematic drama being played out here.'

Another pause waiting to be filled. 'You can't stop them seeing what happens in the sky,' Roger pointed out quietly.

Hugo ignored that. 'Throughout the run up to the vital day there'll be determined voyeurs doing their utmost to climb over the wire, burrow under it, cut through it, to take pictures of anything and everything to impress their friends or sell to magazines and newspapers. That damned woman has lit a fire of romantic patriotism which leads normal people to indulge in antisocial behaviour. As they did at the funeral.'

'As his widow that must have upset you terribly, Julia,' said Ben, taking pleasure in turning her optical sparkle to one of anger.

Hugo pointed in the direction from which Ben's comment had reached him. 'You will be hounded from the moment you exit the gates by reporters and their cameramen. Also by the untutored hoi polloi. The Dancing Bear will be under siege.'

'I'm no longer lodging there. Roger is the only person who knows my address.'

'Was,' came the curt retort. 'You'll be followed there like a comet with a tail and the whole of the county will soon know where to find you.' He slapped the desk with the flat of his hand. 'By God, that stupid woman should be horse-whipped.'

Julia leaned forward in her chair. 'You were all in favour of her proposed biography, Hugo.'

He ignored her, concentrating on the matter in hand. 'I've put in place measures to deal with the situation. Security guards from a top agency will patrol the perimeter day and night. Hangar two will have a man outside and another inside to keep the *Lance* protected from intruders set on getting photographs and souvenirs.'

Ben and Roger exchanged significant glances on hearing that.

'I'll leave you to devise your own defence against press scavengers and silly females who chase after men in the public eye, Captain Norton.'

'Men like Freddie,' Julia said dryly.

'But I want you to hold aloof from everyone but those who're concerned with the proving flight until that day ends. What you do after that is of no concern to me.'

'Oh, I think it will be, Hugo,' Julia murmured, staring at Ben.

He put in quickly, 'Has Sir Edwin approved the mock strafe with live ammo to end the display?'

Hugo relaxed enough to almost smile. 'He's very enthusiastic about the manoeuvre. Keen to witness it on Monday.' He angled his head to address Roger for the first time. 'My father asked me to tell you he wants you to join him and the VIPs on the balcony to watch the display.'

'Sorry, Major, I'll be manning the intercom during Ben's flight. I'll join Sir Edwin and you, in company with the triumphant pilot, soon after he lands.'

'Of course. We didn't have intercom facilities when I did my flying.'

This subdued response invoked one of Ben's spasms of sympathy for this blinded pilot. 'We didn't have aircraft as spectacular as the *Lance*, either, sir. Marshfield has produced one men will be thrilled to fly.'

'Thank you.' Hugo nodded. 'That's all, gentlemen.'

They passed through the outer office and into the long corridor before Roger spoke. 'What did you make of all that? I know she's ingenuous and over eager, but I didn't believe the Keene girl would act so stupidly in spite of what some rag paid her for the information.'

'She didn't,' said Ben thoughtfully. 'Yes, she's immature and impossibly dewy-eyed over Chris Peterson, but she'd have shot herself in the foot by selling out on the Lance family. The biography now can't be written; she needed their cooperation. If she tried to publish an unauthorized version, Sir Edwin would act to prevent her.'

Roger gazed at him as they pushed open the swing doors. 'You're suggesting someone at Marshfield's behind it? All that romantic gush is just what she'd write.'

'Which he'd know very well and simulate. Roger, it's obvious to me who's behind this. Jim Tilbrook.'

'What? Why would he do something so crass?'

'Why did he put bromide in my tea?' Ben stopped and Roger watched him itemize reasons on the fingers of his hand. 'He doesn't agree with the production of warplanes. He has a pathological dislike of men who fly them, particularly in conflict. He's an inveterate womanizer and resents any rivals. He's set on seducing Deborah Keene. She's so dazzled by the image of Peterson and, by connection, me, she'll have no truck with his advances. We now know he's not the saboteur but he's well capable of writing that piece in the language she would use. That gives him the satisfaction of hurting her and the family which is planning to turn to manufacturing something he disagrees with strongly. It also puts pressure on me at a time when I need to concentrate on the next eleven days. He's a vain, vindictive character. Of course he's behind this.'

Roger shook his head, frowning. 'I thought I knew Jim well. Never would have believed him capable of something like this.'

'You're more in tune with the complexities which produce sensational aircraft. I've knocked around the world long enough not to put my trust in people too soon.'

They moved on to pass through the second set of doors. 'Well, whoever is responsible at least did us one favour. With all those security guards patrolling around the clock, we won't have to sleep in the hangar each night. Ray will have no chance of getting to the *Lance*.'

No, my innocent friend, thought Ben. He'll get at the pilot instead.

The heavy rain persisted; the cloud base stayed too low to allow any flying. Ben was not altogether unhappy. There were still ten more days in which to fine-tune his display and, if the truth be told, he was really not up to it right now. Painkillers had helped him through the first half of the day. His body now needed some kind of embrocation to ease the stiffness resulting from that fall, so he decided to leave soon after the lunch break.

'The security team has arrived and men are being deployed all-round the premises, Roger. Everyone at Marshfield knows why they're here, including Povey, so we can safely resume normal routine. I'm going home for a hot bath and a decent night's sleep. You should do the same.'

Roger looked glum. 'An entire day lost, the details of your flight splashed across the pages of a scandal-mongering newspaper, and beefy men with shifty eyes at every corner. It's turning into a circus. I don't like it.'

'Nor me, but you have Tilbrook to blame for publicizing facts intended to be kept secret, and Povey for the bruisers on guard wherever you look.'

Roger frowned. 'You sound so certain about Povey.'

'You were just as certain someone had cut that cable before Chris took off.'

'Yes. Well . . . Look, Chris said the stick was locked. That would have been the obvious cause because I knew there was no design fault. Those three men were the only ones who had had the opportunity to sever the cable.'

'Yet you hesitate to single one of them out. Face it, Roger, the finger points at Povey. If a man has a wife who spends more than he earns he'll look for ways to get more. I've known men to force their wives or sisters to have sex with their friends for money. The women get none of it. It feeds the man's gambling craze, or allows him to buy something he wants. Get wise, my dear friend. No man is what you think he is, believe me.'

Those words stayed with Ben as he walked across to his van. The time was coming when Roger would learn they applied to John Benjamin Norton, too. It was a lowering thought. Roger meant a lot to someone who had never before had the kind of friendship with an older, sincere and knowledgeable man that he had forged with this talented designer. It would be hard to see him disillusioned. To break the link with Roger would be almost as painful as losing Stella, although it would be himself doing the betraying this time.

There were a couple of raincoated men at the gates who could be journalists, but the downpour made visibility difficult and Ben didn't think they would imagine the man of the moment would drive a small delivery van. They'd be looking for the kind of vehicle Freddie would own.

He was right. They took no notice as he drove through the gates, but a hundred yards further on a small drenched figure emerged from an embrasure in the wall and stood in the road forcing him to stop. She dragged open the door and dropped on to the passenger seat, dripping water on the floor. Sorry though he was for the way she had been treated by Tilbrook, he was nevertheless exasperated.

'Why are you still here? The Lance family intend to stop all attempts by you to produce any kind of prose featuring Chris

Peterson, and are even considering taking action against you for the piece you published, giving away facts you were well aware were privileged information.'

'I didn't write it,' she cried. 'I had to tell you that before I left.' It came out jerkily because her teeth were chattering. 'I've been waiting since noon because I'm determined to exonerate myself. I knew I'd recognize your van when it came along, even in this rain.'

Her face was pinched, her close-fitting feathery hat sent runnels of water down her cheeks to plop on the large handbag on her lap. Her pale blue coat was oozing water to add to the puddle on the floor. She looked distressed, exhausted and nothing like the earlier precocious girl.

Ben sighed. 'I know who sent that piece to the editor. It was a vicious thing to do, but the Lances reacted as Tilbrook knew they would. You have to accept that your project is dead and buried. If you were paid a retainer you'll have to return it, I imagine, unless you offset it with a similar sum for expenses.'

'How did you know it was Jim who played that dirty trick on me?'

'I guessed it wouldn't be long before he would demand more than you were prepared to give. Men like him won't accept rejection. Your proposed biography gave him the perfect means of hitting back at you, and also upsetting a few other people.' He looked her over. 'You're soaked to the skin. I'll drive you back to The Dancing Bear.'

'I paid my bill and left after breakfast. I'm going home.'

'Where's home?'

'Dundee.'

'A long journey. Where's your suitcase?'

'The left luggage office at Lewes station.'

Ben considered that, then asked, 'When did you decide to wait for me to leave? I could have put in extra time. Would you have stayed until midnight?'

'I don't know,' she said miserably. 'Everything's such a mess.'

He put the van in gear. 'You can't undertake a long train journey in that condition. Your hat resembles a wet hen sitting on your head and your coat must have a gallon of rainwater lying between the inner and outer layers.'

'Where are we going?'

'First to The Green Man where you can dry out a bit and have a hot meal. Then I'll deliver you to Lewes station to catch a train to London.'

'You're being very kind, Ben.'

'No. I told you I don't give up easily.' He grinned at her. 'I want to make sure you leave the area.'

A few miles along the way Deborah said quietly, 'Nobody commissioned the biography. I lied.'

'Mmm, I thought so.' After another long silence Ben added, 'Keep your childhood dreams of Chris Peterson intact if you must, but leave it at that. There were hundreds of thousands like him, but their exploits died with them. Let them all rest in peace. As I told Julia, dragging up things better left buried in the past is a mistake.'

Deborah turned to him. 'She's really got it in for you.'

'She's made that obvious.'

'D'you know why?'

'Because she has too much money, too much social influence and too much time on her hands to fill. Playing people off against each other, using her acid tongue to unsettle them, prying into their private lives is her way of making her pointless life bearable. She's completely heartless.'

Ben pulled in to the parking area outside The Green Man and switched off the engine. 'We'll have to make a run for the door, but you can't get any wetter than you are already.'

'She's not completely heartless, Ben. She has a thing about you.'

'I've just said I know.'

Deborah made no attempt to leave the van. 'I mean she has a *thing* about you. Hooked on you. Sort of like Jim and me. The more you reject her the more she wants you. When you humiliated her in front of others drinking in The Dancing Bear and walked off to your room, there were tears on her cheeks as she drove away.'

He opened the door and prepared to climb from the van. 'She's hooked on herself, my dear girl. If there were tears they were caused by vexation because I bested her among people she regards as village peasants. Tilbrook made you pay for rejecting

him in the eyes of workmates whom he's led to believe that
women fall eagerly into his arms. Similarly, Julia means to make
me pay for turning the tables on her too often.' He pulled up
his jacket collar ready to brave the deluge. 'She's apparently
holding back until after I've put Marshfield back in the top
league by dazzling investors with my proving flight. Does that
make her not completely heartless in your book? Come on, let's
make a dash for it.'

The lunchtime customers had dwindled to a couple of elderly
men bemoaning the prospect of the inter-village cricket match
having to be postponed if the pitch became waterlogged. The
landlord said his good lady could still offer lamb hotpot with
dumplings, or toad-in-the-hole with bubble and squeak, and
suggested they should eat at the table by the log fire he had lit
to warm the few souls who had braved the weather.

They stayed to also enjoy the summer pudding, then still
lingered for a pot of tea and slices of fruit cake – something she
didn't normally offer but made an exception for a young couple
in love. Well, the 'good lady' had a very romantic nature.

Ben actually enjoyed those two and a half hours. Deborah was
pleasant company when she wasn't acting the part of a questing
journalist probing his past, and she had the good sense to leave
the subject alone until they prepared to set out for Lewes.
Regarding her feather hat which still resembled a drowned
chicken, she laughingly put it on Ben's head.

'Wear it for the proving flight. The feathers will be dry by
then and help to keep you airborne.'

A swift vision of Icarus plunging to earth with feather wings
on the melt, made him snatch it off. His expression sobered her
and she headed for the door, ignoring the landlord and his wife.
Ben said goodbye and promised to come again, then trotted
through lighter rain to where she was already seated in the van.

'I thanked them on your behalf,' he told her pointedly, starting
the engine with an unnecessary roar.

She swung to face him. 'I touched a nerve just now, didn't I?'
Her hand closed over his on the wheel. 'Something to do with
Chris Peterson and why they split you up when you were such a
successful duo? Ben, *why* didn't you join Hugo's squadron with
him? Surely you can tell me now the biography won't be written.'

He jabbed at the clutch and yanked the gear lever hard over to swing out on the road. 'That, Miss Keene, is one of those things better left buried in the past.'

The journey to Lewes rail station was made in silence, Ben castigating himself for forgetting his vow never to trust a woman. All that innocent sweetness she had exuded had been to soften him up and it had nearly worked. He stared ahead as she climbed from the seat beside him, and kept his eyes on the distance as she thanked him for giving her lunch and driving her to the station. That said, she bent to the open door for more intimate words.

'Dear Ben, unless you talk to someone about it, it'll haunt you for the rest of your life. Don't let that happen. Goodbye. Good luck with the proving flight.'

He drove away telling himself he should have swerved around her and left her in the middle of the road outside Marshfield, then gone home to rest, as planned. If she hadn't been wet through, and if he hadn't been feeling more benevolent towards her now she could not publish Peterson's biography he would never have spent time with her. She held no attraction for him, but he had forgotten how enjoyable feminine company could sometimes be and that rediscovery had lulled his usual caution.

The short break in heavy rain ended with thunder and a veritable cloudburst five miles from the coach house. It forced Ben to slow down. He might otherwise not have spotted Ray Povey's car heading for Fossbeck Camden ahead of a small green bus he was himself following. Knowing Povey lived beyond Clanford in the opposite direction Ben felt a jolt of excitement. What was the bastard up to now?

The adverse weather had kept local residents at home, so the bus trundled onward past stopping places devoid of hopeful passengers which allowed Ben to keep track of his quarry without revealing his own presence on that road. Povey must have left Marshfield at the usual knocking-off time, but surely he would have checked if Ben was still on the premises first. Trying something in daylight, even in this early evening gloom, was risky and Ben wanted to catch the man in the act. He had the revolver with him and wouldn't hesitate to use it if it became necessary.

Lost in speculation, Ben was caught unawares when Povey's

car turned into a narrow lane at the approach to Fossbeck Camden. Where the hell was he heading? Apparently not to the coach house. Ben cursed this development. Without the bus as a shield the van would be visible to Povey. However, the next bend led to a public park around which the lane circled before returning to join the main road through the village. On the far side of the green a wide gate gave access to the cricket ground where a few hopeful players were clustered on the veranda of the pavilion in the vain hope of the game going ahead.

Povey had drawn up outside a house on the circle, so Ben stopped where the grass began. His quarry quit his vehicle and moved smartly to where a young woman carrying a baby was standing in the doorway. Ray Povey, the man known as knowledgeable but very bossy and short-tempered, took the baby in one arm then pulled the woman close with the other and kissed her with passion.

The door closed on them, leaving Ben puzzled. A man would not kiss a daughter or a sister that way, nor a friend. The woman was unlikely to be Povey's co-conspirator with a small baby to care for, so who was she? The basic standard of the house surely ruled out any connection with whoever was paying Povey to sabotage the flight.

For half an hour Ben sat watching the house while rain drummed on the roof, but it seemed Povey was there for more than a flying visit. When the dejected cricketers left in a file of cars Ben tagged on behind them knowing what he should do next.

Fossbeck Camden's post office and shop also acted as the village telephone exchange, so it remained open until late evening. Young Henry Jenks was behind the counter, although Ben saw no customers. The boy grinned widely when he entered and revealed he had almost enough now to buy the pogo stick. Dr King's car had broken down so Henry had delivered medicines on his bicycle and received payment.

'I wasn't half wet by the end,' he said with a laugh, 'but 'twas worth it.'

After purchasing some therapeutic ointment to ease his stiffness, Ben asked, with his eye on Mrs Jenks busy in the cubicle containing the basic switchboard, if Henry delivered letters and telegrams to houses at the far end of the village near the cricket ground.

'Course I do, Captain. Went there this morning six o'clock as usual. Delivered four and a small package.'

'And got thoroughly wet,' put in Ben with a smile. 'You must know the names of everyone in Fossbeck Camden.'

He nodded. 'And they knows mine.'

'Can you recall who lives in number twenty-nine Cricket Lane?'

'That's Mr and Mrs Povey, sir. Just had a baby, they have. Two months ago. I took round all the baby cards and presents. Enjoyed doing that. Course, Mr Povey don't see much of his little girl on account he works away a lot. Now, at number twenty-seven there's old Ma Pearson. When I took her bottle of tonic there this afternoon she asked me in and give me tea and cake. Nice lady she is. Never gets any letters, though. I think that's sad.'

While Henry rattled on, Ben was busy adding two and two together to make a hell of a lot more than four.

The alarm clock woke Ben in the early hours. He pulled on a pair of trousers and an old shirt, then made some tea which he took to the chair beside the window that overlooked the manor driveway entrance. His instincts told him Povey would pull in there, as before, to reconcile himself to returning home to Rita, his avaricious wife, and to maintaining the pretence of lengthy overtime. The recent welcome contract for *Snowbird* would have given the man an excellent base for his lie, but how had he got away with it for so long? Henry claimed the baby had arrived two months ago, so the secret liaison had been up and running for at least a year.

During his lengthy deliberations Ben had considered the prospect of Povey sabotaging the *Lance* because Peterson had discovered the man's dual life and resorted to blackmail. But that wasn't Peterson's style, and Povey was more likely to have planned to kill him on a dark night in a lonely place than to commit murder by a means that would threaten his own future with Marshfield.

Such a conclusion also gave strength to the belief that the chief engineer would have sawn the step apart rather than damage the *Lance*. There was no love lost between himself and Povey, but Ben had offered no threat to him yet. Now he so easily could, hence the intention to confront the man if and when he stopped for a relaxing smoke at the foot of the flight of steps.

Ben had not long to wait. Sure enough, Povey's car stopped and was backed into the driveway entrance fifteen minutes later. After a moment or two of apparent deep thought he pulled out a packet of cigarettes and lit one. Ben then descended silently, opened the passenger door and slid on to the seat, bringing a cry of alarmed protest which died away when Ben switched on a torch to identify himself.

'Bloody 'ell, what're you doing here in the middle of the night? Where'd you spring from, you sneaky bastard?'

'I've been waiting for you, you adulterous bastard,' Ben returned levelly. 'This is where you stop each night after leaving your mistress and baby daughter. Has Rita any notion of what you're up to during your long hours of overtime at Marshfield?'

Povey was full of bluster as he first accused Ben of telling filthy lies, then thought better of it and pretended he had suddenly made sense of the accusation.

'Ah, I see what it is. You saw me with my sister and her kiddie who lives on the far side of this village.'

Ben shook his head. 'That was no brotherly greeting you gave her on the doorstep for anyone to witness. But as your neighbours know you as Mr and Mrs Povey I suppose it would seem natural enough to them . . . especially as you work away from home a lot,' he ended with heavy emphasis.

'Christ, you've been sniffing around like a dog after a bitch on heat. What gives you the right to spy on me?'

'The fact that you tried to kill me two nights ago by sawing through the top step.'

Povey studied him agape. 'What? Are you bosky or summat? Kill you? When everyone's relying on you to sell the *Lance* next week and set the workforce up for years to come?' He sounded genuinely puzzled. 'Sawing through the top step? What step? You hallucinating?'

'No, it was real enough, believe me.' Ben released breath on a sigh of frustration. 'Ray, did Chris Peterson know about your family living by the cricket ground?'

That brought a grunt from Povey. 'He was too busy playing away himself to take an interest in anyone else. Not that I blamed him. That shrewish wife of his would drive any man to seek it elsewhere.'

'As you have. Because of your wife's extravagance. Heard she's fond of expensive things. So how d'you manage to also support another partner and a baby?'

Another grunt. 'That's my business . . . as is my family by the cricket ground.'

'I won't argue with that. I've known men with several partners, not all of them women. Warfare changes people, Ray. I'm not interested in anything you do so long as you don't have evil intent. Tell me, though, why you've parked up here for the past three nights.'

After a long silence Povey eventually decided to trust Ben. 'Every time I leave her and that little girl of mine it gets harder. I'm trying to work out the best thing to do about it.'

'Divorce not an option?'

A shake of the head. 'I've tried putting Jim Tilbrook in her way but she's the one woman he don't seem to fancy.'

'Hard luck.'

Povey stubbed out his cigarette, took another from the packet, then offered it to Ben.

'No, thanks. In my time I've smoked some really foul fags, until I told myself I didn't have to; it wasn't compulsory. So I stopped. Anyway, when a man's working around aircraft it's safer to keep anything inflammable well away from it.'

They chatted for a while with more understanding than ever before, then Ben said, 'I wasn't hallucinating just now. Someone at Marshfield is trying to abort the proving flight by putting me, or the *Lance*, out of action. If he succeeds it will almost certainly put paid to hopes of future production of the fighter. That'll not only damage the company, but it will also rob our country of parity with our former enemies who are rattling sabres again. It's vitally important to have the *Lance* approved by the government and the RAF next week, then swiftly on the assembly line.'

'Who'd be crazy enough to want to stop that going ahead?'

'Someone who *is* crazy, or who's working for someone else.

Another aircraft manufacturer. In other words, an industrial saboteur. Any ideas?'

'No. Christ, no!' Povey frowned through the smoke he exhaled. 'What was that again about a sawn-through step?'

Ben pointed through the window at the flight rising beside the car and described what had happened. Knowing journalists would almost certainly discover this address he felt there was no further point in concealing it.

'When I spotted you apparently lurking here I thought you were the person responsible.'

Still frowning, Povey said, 'Could've been anybody. Someone from this village who's not right in the head, or a couple with hopes of living here when they married. It's been empty a long time. What gave you the idea it was connected with the *Lance*; some kind of sabotage?'

'Because that's what caused Chris Peterson's crash. Roger knows it for certain, and I believe him.' Ben saw the other man's scepticism. 'Jim Tilbrook put dope in my tea just as I was set to do a test flight. Oh yes, my friend, he did exactly that. It was a mild dose; just blurred my vision enough to make me glad to feel the wheels touch down again.

'He's also responsible for sending that overblown piece to the editor of a third-rate newspaper, alarming Sir Edwin and Hugo enough to hire security guards to stop trespassers and sightseers. He's a nasty piece of work but his spitefulness doesn't go deep enough to send a man to his death in the prototype of an exciting new warplane, leaving the company he works for to face the consequences. As I said before, something like that's the work of a man who's mentally disturbed, or who's being paid to do it. Any suggestions on who that might be?'

Povey shifted uneasily in his seat. 'There's one or two I'll never see eye to eye with but, like Jim, they're not unbalanced, or criminal in their attitude to the company. Anyway, the Board of Inquiry had it Peterson passed out before the crash. Are you sure about . . .?'

'Yes, and it'll happen again unless we prevent it.' Leaving a pause, Ben asked, 'How d'you get on with Kershaw?'

Povey must have been mentally still with his mistress and their baby for he apparently missed the inference of the question. 'He's not been in the job long enough for me to know much about him. A man who fills a senior post like that who's a personal friend of the bosses I treat a bit wary. His wife's well in with Mrs Peterson, too. You've to be careful that what you say won't be passed around over the dinner table between them.

'Look, I'd better be off,' he added, starting the engine. 'My missus'll likely be awake listening for me to come home. I'll keep my eyes open after what you've just told me, but I can't see anyone stopping that proving flight with all them guards keeping their eyes open, can you?'

Ben prepared to climb from the car. 'Mine are firmly closed concerning a small family living near the cricket ground. I know nothing about them. Goodnight, Ray.'

Once indoors Ben divested himself of the shirt and trousers, applied more embrocation to his body, then got between the sheets again.

The rain had stopped, the night sky was clear and filled with stars, he would be flying within a few hours, and John Kershaw was once more heading the list of suspects.

# ELEVEN

The next three days bore out the Lance family's fears. National newspapers picked up the information revealed in the local rag and reporters flocked to Marshfield hoping for interviews, photographs, anything that would give them the edge over their journalist rivals.

To Ben's relief they repeated the facts, as given, of his close friendship with Chris Peterson without attempting to dig deeper. Instead, they concentrated on his more recent background in the Middle East, but he had been too successful and they failed to unearth personal or business scandal. One more enterprising journalist had discovered the 'love that broke the brave aviator's heart' and printed a colourful account of his brief engagement to Stella who 'deserted him almost at the altar for a former lover'. This angered Ben a lot, but four years had passed and momentous changes in his life had put that episode on his emotional back burner. All he cared deeply about at that moment was flying the *Lance* so spectacularly he would achieve what Chris Peterson had failed to do.

As predicted by Hugo, Ben was pestered when he left Marshfield and chased to the coach house by young hacks bent on getting a scoop. They then virtually camped outside on the chance of photographing any visitors. There were none, so they wrote overblown pieces that described how Captain Norton needed to be alone during his preparation for a flight that would revive the grief for his wartime partner and close friend.

Ben regularly flew twice daily to perfect his planned display. Two old military trucks had been brought to Marshfield so that he could practice his attack on them using blanks. With seven days to go his excitement steadily grew, but he never lost sight of his certainty that John Kershaw hadn't abandoned his attempt to sabotage the launch of the fighter, one way or another. With so much security surrounding Marshfield and, particularly hangar two, the pilot would be the easier option for him.

With five days to go Ben discovered the van wouldn't start. He tried the usual tricks with no success and kicked the front tyre in frustration. Ben knew aircraft like the back of his hand, but he was not in love with motor vehicles. He returned to his flat, rang Jimmy Nunn and arranged for him to come and fix the problem, then called the post office and asked Mrs Jenks to send Henry along to his uncle who ran the taxi service.

During the drive to Marshfield, Albert Jenks talked non-stop while Ben mooned about the bad weather forecast for the morrow, which would probably keep him grounded for at least half the day. He dared not think about the risk of rain and low cloud base on Wednesday. He also decided he must press Hugo to obtain the live ammunition needed for the last two flights before the display itself. That dramatic strafe was the action most likely to impress observers, so it was vital for Hugo to shake himself and get those bullets in right away. Ben needed to be reassured they would be available, but the Lance heir was not a man to be dictated to.

Sure enough, when Ben went to Hugo's office and broached the subject, he was told his job as test pilot was to fly, not to believe he could order directors about. Both were under strain during this run-up to what could make or break Marshfield's long-term future, and they parted tight-lipped at odds with each other.


After letting off steam with Roger, Ben took to the air and was soon calmed by engaging in what he believed to be life's greatest freedom. Roger's voice came to him over the intercom and he replied, but he plunged and climbed through a wide blue expanse where no one could reach him. There was nothing to stop him crossing Pitman Hill and never turning back. Nothing except a day that would prove to be the Everest in his determined climb through life. He would cross Pitman Hill and never turn back after that day.

He landed and taxied back to the fuelling area, leaving the *Lance* there to be serviced for the afternoon flight. As he walked away he saw Kershaw watching his approach from the overgrown area between the hangars. The man looked white and haggard, staring as if in a state of shock.

Ignoring him, Ben headed for Roger's small office for their usual after-flight discussion, but Kershaw's curious behaviour had unsettled him. The aircraft couldn't have been tampered with. She was under guard the whole time, and there had been no sign of trouble during the flight, yet there had been something in Kershaw's attitude that was deeply menacing.

Before his afternoon flight Ben personally checked over the entire machine, despite having been assured there had never been less than six people present. He did not experience the same joy as in the morning. He persistently gently waggled the stick to ensure it wasn't locked, and watched the gauges to check they were recording data correctly. In consequence, Roger sounded concerned when he asked if there was something wrong.

'No, just making this a slow run-through to confirm no further adjustments are needed before Wednesday. I'm coming in now; leaving the strafe until we have the ammo.'

Roger was still concerned when Ben landed and left Felix with the rest of the ground crew to tow the aeroplane into the hangar for the night.

'She's running all right? No hint of malfunction?' he asked anxiously. 'Why weren't you using full power?'

Ben smiled wearily. 'Roger, your baby is behaving beautifully. It's just one of those days we all experience. The van wouldn't start, Hugo was in his most autocratic mood – I guess the strain of waiting must be worse for a pilot who can't see – and Kershaw was watching me as I left the *Lance* this morning and gave the impression he was seeing a dead man walking.'

'What?'

Ben sank on a chair, stretching out his legs with a sigh. 'Wednesday's getting close. If he's going to make a move it'll have to be soon. I'm not sleeping well. He sawed through that step without waking me. While the press gang were camped outside I felt safe from him, but they've tired of that and won't appear again until Wednesday morning. That day can't come quickly enough for me.'

'Nor for me.'

He gave an apologetic smile. 'Sorry, Roger. I only fly her. You created her.'

'But you're the one who makes her live.' He gripped Ben's shoulder. 'Come on, I'm taking you home with me to get a good sleep. And a good meal. I don't suppose you've eaten properly, either.'

It sounded a very good idea, so he nodded. 'We'll pass Jimmy Nunn's place. I'll check with him if he managed to repair the van on site or took it back to the garage on a trailer. If that's the case I'll hire a replacement.' He forced another smile. 'That'll fool the press gang who've been following the other one.'

They left before the major outflow at the end of the working day and Ben relaxed with his head tipped back against the seat. Neither man spoke. Each was lost in his thoughts until they reached Nunn's place. It was quiet; the garage looked shut up for the night.

'Must be some family do on,' guessed Roger. 'It's not like him to finish so early.'

Ben got out to take a look around. 'Can't see my van anywhere. Jimmy must have put it right back at the coach house.'

Just then an overalled youth appeared from behind the work-shop and stopped short on seeing them. Recognizing him as Nunn's slightly retarded nephew who was as good as any young-ster with machinery, Ben strolled across to him.

'Hallo, Norrie. Is your uncle around?'

Full lips jutted. 'In the hostible. All burned up.'

'In hospital?'

'S'right. All burned up.'

Roger joined them. 'What happened, lad?'

'The van burned him up.'

Goose bumps began to form on Ben's scalp. 'Which van, Norrie?'

'One outside all them steps. He gets out the spanner and starts a-turning it. Then there's fire. He's all burned up.'

Ben stared at the burnt wreck of the small van on the concrete yard where he had left it that morning after failing to start it. He had seen aircraft in that condition; wrecks in which the pilot had died or had climbed from like a living torch, so he should be hardened to such a sight. But he stood there suffering from a different kind of shock. If he had raised the bonnet and used a spanner . . .!

Roger was similarly silenced by the implication of that wreck, but he soon put a hand on Ben's arm and led him away to the car. Once they reached Roger's home, he put in a call to the hospital to enquire about Jimmy's condition. Ben waited trance-like on a chair beside the telephone, still finding it difficult to accept that Kershaw had intended him to suffer that ordeal by fire. No wonder the man had been so badly disturbed by evidence that his victim was alive and unharmed this morning.

Roger brought him from his thoughts. 'He'll survive, they said, but he has serious burns to his hands, arms and face.'

Ben put his head in his hands. 'Oh God, that poor devil!'

'Could it have been an accident?' asked the designer who, like Ben, knew aircraft down to the finest detail, but only basics about motor vehicles.

Ben knew it was a rhetorical question and took a few moments to pull himself together before saying, 'That bastard has to be stopped. We must alert the police before he has another try. Time's running out. Just four more days. Christ knows what he'll do in desperation.'

Roger waved away his wife who peered around the kitchen door offering tea. She got the message. 'Ben, it's the same story. We haven't any proof that Kershaw's responsible. Norrie was the only witness to what happened. We can't make a case on that to present to the police. Whatever was done to that van was done during the night because you couldn't get it going first thing. Kershaw will have witnesses galore to his arrival at Marshfield at his usual hour.' He leaned back against the wall, adding quietly, 'All we have is a threat from him to leave his wife alone. You only met her once, but he has a history of instability, drunken-ness according to your chum in South Africa, so maybe he'd go to such extremes of jealousy. There's no way we can prove it was he attacking you to prevent your making that flight on Wednesday. The police would say you were imagining it through stress and nervousness about what happened to Chris.'

Those last words revived Ben's fighting spirit. 'There's one option left. If we can't get the police to lock him up we'll have to put him out of action ourselves.' Seeing his friend's expression, he gave a grim smile. 'Don't worry. I'll do the deed. You just cover for me.'

'What are you talking about? You can't harm the man, you fool. The police would lock you up,' cried Roger, very agitated. 'You have no proof, Ben! A few days ago you were certain it was Povey out to get you.'

'So I went after him and uncovered the truth,' he snapped. 'Now I'm going after Kershaw. Well known tactic in warfare. Attack is the best form of defence. If you're not prepared to cover for me just turn a blind eye and stay comfortingly innocent.'

After a long moment Roger got to his feet and went to the sideboard where he poured whisky and offered Ben one of the half-filled glasses.

'Let me know what you plan to do and I'll play my part as best I can. Just make sure it doesn't rebound on you, my friend. Marshfield needs you to work the miracle on Wednesday. I need you to do it. But I also want someone I care about to reach old age.' He raised the glass. 'Here's to your success in both those endeavours.'

Another restless night, this time full of feverish hatching and dispatching of plans. Those years in Cairo and Alexandria had made Ben adept at contriving ways of countering the business wiles practised in the Middle East, but how to defuse the danger of a man with a burning desire to stop the proving flight as fierce as his own was to make it, eluded him. When the first light of a wet, cloudy Sunday broke through, he finally drifted into a light sleep having decided the easiest and bloodless solution to the problem was through Mirium Kershaw.

Unless the band of rain moved away during the day there was no question of taking the *Lance* up that morning, so they had a leisurely breakfast after which the two men went to the sitting room with newspapers, while Roger's wife washed-up and prepared the lamb and vegetables for lunch. Ben closed the door for privacy, then told Roger his plan.

'With some regret I dismissed the best two means of dealing with Kershaw – shooting him or luring him to a spot where I could imprison him for four days. Both these actions would constitute a crime and I've no wish to serve a jail sentence when this is over.'

'Especially when he's the one deserving penal punishment.'

'Exactly! I've hit on a solution which involves an age-old practice and obviates any risks. Kershaw is highly possessive of his wife. He threatened and manhandled me just because I took her to dinner after she had sold me a painting. She promised a return invitation to their new home in Fossbeck. It's never arrived, which shows she heeds her husband's jealous temperament.'

Roger nodded. 'She stays at the Chelsea flat four days a week, where she could be getting up to all manner of mischief, so how does he cope with that?'

'It also makes me wonder why he took on a job that demands of him less than his professional capabilities, in an area so far from London, and lives alone in a large house out in the sticks for the greater part of the week. It doesn't add up unless he wangled a position at Marshfield for the specific purpose we suspect him of. The man he replaced was badly injured by a runaway pallet remember.'

'Right, you've made your point. What's this non-criminal solution you've come up with?'

Ben hunched forward and lowered his voice, although there was no one to overhear them. 'From the short time I was in her company I deduced she enjoys her days of freedom in London. That's probably due to what she had put up with during his alcoholic depression after the failure of the *Duiker*, and I doubt very much that she's aware of her husband's intent to maim or kill me to prevent the *Lance* being a success.'

'That's rather too cosy a supposition, Ben.'

He shook his head. 'I spent four hours in her company, during which time Peterson's crash was mentioned. Unless she's a superb actress no woman who knew, and had concurred with, the deadly intent to cause such a disaster could have behaved as she did that evening. After all, she had met Chris with Julia at the Chelsea flats; she and Kershaw had entertained the Lances and been invited back by them after they bought that place in Fossbeck. I swear the woman has no idea of his intention to create another public disaster before or on Wednesday.'

'So go on,' Roger urged quietly.

'Mirium will be down here for the weekend at the moment. I'll devise some means of getting Kershaw over to Marshfield, and while he's away I'll talk to her; enlist her help to create a false emergency in London that'll have him chasing up there tomorrow. She only has to keep him there until Thursday.'

'And after Thursday?'

Ben sighed. 'That'll be up to her. In my opinion he needs several months in a private psychiatric clinic. Maybe longer. I'd say her future's rocky unless she acts on what I'll tell her. After Thursday he'll no longer be my concern.'

Roger looked at him speculatively. 'Why's that? He'll surely still be driven to punish you. For succeeding.'

Aware that he had let slip too much, Ben gave a half smile and got to his feet. 'Let's succeed first. To which end I'll go ahead to put the first stage of my plan into action. May I borrow your wife's bicycle to ride over to Fossbeck? Nosy neighbours are less likely to take note of that heading for the Kershaw's house than a taxi.'

The plan fell at the first fence. Mirium answered when Ben telephoned and asked in a man-of-Sussex accent to speak to Mr Kershaw.

'He's in bed feeling very unwell. I can take a message but he's in no state to deal with it, I'm afraid.'

Putting the little trumpet back on its rest, Ben wondered if he should read 'blind drunk' for 'very unwell' or was Kershaw really ill? Thwarted, he decided to cycle to Fossbeck anyway. In either case Kershaw would be in bed upstairs so it would surely be possible to speak to Mirium without his knowing.

At the second fence the plan fell even further. He arrived at the house to find Julia's Lagonda parked there. Within minutes she and Mirium emerged from the stable area on horses and turned on to the bridle path leading up to the Downs. For several seconds Ben was tempted to go in the house to discover Kershaw's true state of health, but wisdom prevailed. He cycled back with just the small comfort of knowing the man was unable to cause him harm today. The same didn't apply to Julia. Was she at this moment passing on what she had discovered about a man calling himself Captain Ben Norton to her friend Mirium Kershaw?

He took the *Lance* up in late afternoon pale sunshine, but concentrated on the low-level manoeuvres that always impressed because the accompanying roar of engines added to the thrill of watching an aeroplane flash past before one's eyes. It also put a surge of excitement in Ben's breast. Those twelve years of flying in the Middle East had never done that.

He climbed from the cockpit reluctantly. He had two more days; tomorrow and Tuesday. Then, in a matter of minutes, it would be over. His Everest would have been conquered and the descent would have to be faced.

Yet another restless and anxious night in Roger's guest room brought the resolution to visit the doctor in Lewes for a few pills to help him sleep during the next two. News from Hugo's office brightened Ben somewhat. The ammunition was on its way and would be available by late morning. The day was sunny and cloudless so Ben went through the entire display twice without the final strafe, and landed brimming with confidence. He had polished it to perfection and the weathermen promised a week of real English summer to come.

All that was left to do today was to get the timing of the attack on the trucks right and the *Lance* would be fulfilling her natural role with the RAF before the year was out, without a doubt.

The entire day passed without a sight of Kershaw, but Roger had wandered through hangar one and spotted him in his office, showing no signs of being under the weather. So had he yesterday had a mammoth hangover, or had Mirium simply lied to get rid of an unwanted caller? What was the true state of that marriage?

The temperature had risen with the passing hours so, after making three attacks on the trucks, Ben climbed from the cockpit drenched with sweat. The dry-throat tension of lining up the guns on the target, and a revival of that mixture of fear and excitement of the war years, left him exhausted and craving sleep. First, however, he and Roger went out with Felix in the tow truck to see the location of the bullet holes on both vehicles.

Not perfect, but he had another day in which to make sure it was. On Wednesday explosives would be placed inside the trucks to make that final strafe as impressive as a real attack would be. If that didn't sell the *Lance* nothing would.

Roger was elated, all thoughts of sabotage forgotten for the moment. But they returned when Ben said he should go back to the coach house.

'I've used the spare change of clothes I kept here in my locker, and I need a long, relaxing bath followed by a long, relaxing sleep. I've been cluttering up your house for too long, Roger.'

'But you're safe there,' he protested.

'No, I make us all vulnerable. We've reached crisis time. Kershaw knows he'll never get close enough to inflict damage on the aircraft so he's got to stop me from flying on Wednesday. If it also means harming you and your wife, so be it. He had no qualms about murdering Chris, had he?'

Roger only stopped arguing when Ben said he would take the little green bus in to Lewes and have dinner at a hotel in which he'd also book a room.

'I'll call a taxi to take me home. Kershaw will see us departing in different directions which should persuade him my sojourn with you is over, but he won't know where I'm staying at night. No one will, not even you. I'll telephone and give you the number to ring in an emergency, but that's all.'

'You're beginning to sound too serious. I don't like it,' mumbled Roger.

'Forty-eight hours from now it'll be over, and you'll be the man of the moment,' chaffed Ben as he raised a hand in farewell and left the hangar. And in seventy-two, he thought, my moment will have passed leaving Julia to do her damndest. I can stop her for now, but I have a feeling she'll not give up.

The burned-out van was still there on the yard to remind him of how close he had come to being the victim. Jimmy Nunn was holding his own in hospital, but it would be a long time before he could return to work and provide for his family. Ben was filled with anger. The Kershaws were well off. If he could just prove who had caused Nunn to be injured Kershaw would be forced to pay compensation. Life was frequently unfair, he reflected as he soaked in the bath until his tension eased.

After packing clothes into a suitcase, Ben took a long look from his window before carrying it and his briefcase down the steps and along to the bus stop at the commencement of Fossbeck Camden. He left the bus when it reached the next village along its route to collect his mail from the shop he used as a poste restante, before catching the next green bus. Reaching Lewes, he alighted outside a large hotel which he entered then departed from by the rear door. Five minutes later he climbed the stone steps of a small guest house and booked a room with a window that overlooked the road. Christ, I'm behaving like an actor in a Hollywood film, he told himself. Kershaw couldn't have followed me from Marshfield all the way here.

Dinner was served early. The food was plain but tasty and reminded him of Mary Bunyan's generosity in cooking meals she knew were his favourites. Like his mother would surely have done if she had lived long enough.

Back in his room Ben recalled his intention of getting sleeping pills from his doctor. Too late now, but he surely would not need them tonight. The room was quiet and comfortable, the bed reasonably well-sprung considering the number of people who had used it over the years. Having given Roger the number of the telephone he was calling from downstairs, he put on pyjamas and sat in bed to deal with his post.

Tucked between some business communications and a large envelope containing information he had sent for he found a letter from South Africa addressed to Jack Norton. The envelope also contained a press cutting. George's message was short and cheery, as usual.

*Thought this might interest you,* he had written.

*Got it from a chum who writes freelance for several scandal rags. As your exploits have even penetrated the vastness of the veld, my chum is now pumping me for the lowdown on you, but my lips are sealed. I told him we don't want to revive memories of those years. Good luck with the* Lance. *What would I give to fly something like that! If you ever tire of it, the offer of a partnership is ever open. Chin, chin. George.*

Ben took up the newspaper cutting and began to read. It was dated March 1929, fifteen months ago. George's chum clearly specialized in pursuing scandal to its bitter end.

It seems the case of the doomed Duiker has not yet played itself out. After the veld hopper hailed by Sturt and Cleeves as 'the aeroplane that can be used like a car' was withdrawn from production following two fatal crashes, there was a long drawn-out court case in which the manufacturers and the two designers, Philip Westberger and John Kershaw, blamed each other. S and C insisted there had been a design flaw; Westberger and Kershaw blamed faulty workmanship. A team of air crash investigators found the probable cause was heavy overuse of an aircraft designed only for light duty. S and C were told to remove their slogan.

The judge in the court case used that ruling to weigh the scales in favour of Westberger and Kershaw because there was no absolute proof of a design flaw. Nor was there of faulty manufacture, of course, so he awarded minimum costs knowing there would remain doubts on both scores. S and C were then sued by the families of those who had died in the crashes. Philip Westberger, an American with several design successes in his homeland, returned there claiming he was devastated by the tragedies. Kershaw, on the other hand, went into hiding overnight and proved to be untraceable.

Today, three years later, I received information from one of my reliable sources that the former designer suffered a total breakdown following the untimely death of his wife so soon after the *Duiker* scandal, and is now living in a rondaval existing on mealies and native-brewed alcohol.

How are the mighty fallen!

With all thought of sleep driven away by rushing adrenalin, Ben read the cutting again. A year ago the journalist had learned Kershaw had gone to the dogs after the death of his wife. So who sold him a painting and told him over dinner in London that her husband had not enlisted during the war because his work in the aviation industry had been too vital to the war effort? Who is the woman calling herself Mirium Kershaw? What was behind Kershaw's violent threat to leave his wife alone or else?

Dressing swiftly, he tucked the revolver in his waistband and left the building. It was early enough for the streets to be busy and for the small green buses still to be running. Mid-June and the sun had gone down to leave a pale yellow haze over the sky. It wouldn't grow dark for at least another hour. There was soft twilight over Fossbeck village and residents were still working in their gardens. The pub was busy inside and at the tables outside.

Good. Less chance of anyone being concerned about a stranger strolling past dressed like a young man on a walking holiday.

A light was on in a downstairs room indicating Kershaw was at home. He applied the heavy knocker to the front door with enough force to suggest the caller was unlikely to go away if refused attention, yet it seemed that Kershaw was going to brazen it out. Ben thumped the knocker with even greater force and was about to do so again when a shadow appeared behind the glass panel and the door opened just a crack.

Ready for this, Ben threw his weight against it and charged inside, almost knocking Kershaw to the floor. That he had been drinking was obvious. His eyes were glassy, his face was red and he was unsteady on his feet. But he came at Ben with fists bunched and an aggressive roar.

'Forget that,' Ben snapped, pulling the revolver from his waist-band. 'I want some answers from you and I'm prepared to make you suffer in order to get them.' He waved the gun. 'Let's go in that room and talk. This is liable to take a long time.'

Kershaw's good looks vanished under a patina of fear. The aggressive man who had thrust Ben against a wall to warn him of physical harm if he had further contact with his wife stared goggle-eyed at the revolver. It was plain he had never been to war; there was no real fight in him right now.

The room was a small study with bookshelves, filing cabinets and a large desk. Telling Kershaw to sit on an upright chair with polished wooden arms, Ben then pulled into place with his foot a similar chair and sat on it facing the other man, still holding him at gunpoint. Kershaw's surrender took Ben aback. He'd come ready for a fight, but this was turning into a walkover which didn't satisfy his desire to attack the man physically. Words would have to suffice.

Drawing the press cutting from his pocket he held it out. 'Read it.'

'What?'

'Read it!'

Kershaw took it with a hand that shook and looked at it long enough to take in the content, but Ben wasn't sure he had. He was in a blue funk.

'Who is that woman you claim to be your wife?'

Kershaw continued to stare at the cutting. 'Oh God! Oh God!'

Ben's anger was growing out of control. 'Who is that woman I took to dinner who calls herself Mirium Kershaw? She spoke about her husband whose work for the aircraft industry was too valuable for him to put on a uniform like the rest of us during the war. But your wife died just over a year ago, didn't she? So tell me who it is who runs an antiques business in Knightsbridge, who owns an expensive flat in Chelsea and who shares this large property with you at weekends.'

'What?' Kershaw's glassy gaze suggested he hadn't heard a word of that demand.

Ben pressed the revolver against the man's chest, saying harshly, 'I'll get the information I want, believe me. I'll begin with a kneecap and go on from there until you realize I mean what I say. Who is Mirium, you bastard?'

Kershaw's eyes slowly filled with tears. 'She died in my arms. I killed her.'

Ben was shaken. He studied the other man, conscious of his audible distress and the ponderous ticking of a pendulum wall clock. 'You killed her?'

Swallowing his sobs with difficulty Kershaw falteringly began a tangled story. 'The *Duiker* tragedy left me without a job and little hope of working with aircraft again. I . . . I didn't know what to do. We went on the road for . . . for six months. It's easy out there to leave civilization behind. Mirium . . . she became ill. I sold the car and bought a shack at the back of beyond, growing enough food to keep us alive, like the Bantus do. But she was . . . never well. Hated the loneliness. Forever urging me back to the city. But I couldn't face pointing fingers and innuendo again.' He made a piteous appeal to Ben. 'People died in the *Duiker*. Maybe I . . . I could never be certain if I'd overlooked something. If . . . What if more people had been killed? Sturt and Cleeves recalled all of them. Suppose they'd found evidence of errors in the design?' His voice broke. 'You must understand. I couldn't go back and face that.'

'So you killed your wife?'

Violent nodding. 'Yes, yes.'

Ben drew in a long breath. He had come to hold Kershaw to ransom until Thursday, but he was being overwhelmed by what he was uncovering. Was this man a schizophrenic? A killer one minute, a quivering penitent the next.

'She didn't tell me how ill she was, why she tried so hard to persuade me to move back to Port Elizabeth. I would have gone,' he moaned. 'Of course I would.'

Then Ben realized the real manner of Mirium's death which had apparently pushed Kershaw over the edge, as claimed in the press cutting. Total breakdown. Laying the revolver on his knee, he returned to his original question.

'Who is the woman posing as your wife?'

'What?'

Ben snatched up the gun again. 'Don't play that innocent game with me. You've tried to put me out of action twice, I won't hesitate to do the same to you. And I'll succeed. Who is the redhead living with you?'

When Kershaw hesitated too long, Ben stood and stamped down hard enough on the man's foot to bruise it badly or even break small bones. 'Who is she?'

Face screwed up in pain, Kershaw gasped, 'My sister, Mary.'

Of course! The same red-gold hair, similar facial bone structure. The resemblance had struck Ben on meeting her. He suddenly had a fair idea of what he was about to be told. By force, if necessary. He was ready to stamp on the other foot, break a finger or two, even dislocate a shoulder, but he was not unwise enough to put a bullet in the bastard. Certainly not before he had made the proving flight.

Kershaw didn't have that reassurance, so he spilled out the story while gazing hypnotically at the weapon in Ben's hand.

On the death of the real Mirium he had roamed the veld until an ancient Bantu claiming 'healing powers' took him in. When the old man moved on one night five months later, Kershaw had almost emerged from his black despair and felt ready to go back to Port Elizabeth. He found his sister had moved into his house after a fractured love affair, and the siblings settled into a tentative shared life until a letter addressed to Mrs M Kershaw from a London solicitor arrived. That letter changed everything.

When her mother was drowned in a boating accident, Mirium had become her father's next of kin. On his death from influenza she had gained several large properties along with considerable wealth. Mrs Kershaw was invited to visit Pugh and Gilmore to discuss her wishes regarding her inheritance.

Kershaw had known little about his wife's family apart from their decision to send her to her aunt in South Africa, where she wouldn't curb their passion for sailing the high seas without responsibilities. Mirium had been happier with her aunt and virtually put her parents from her mind for twenty years. Kershaw was sad she couldn't enjoy the compensation for their rejection but his sister saw an exciting opportunity.

'It was her idea. It was all Mary's idea,' he kept saying during the telling of criminal deception.

The last time anyone in England had seen Mirium was as a child. The bank in Port Elizabeth still held all the legal documents including Mirium's birth and marriage certificates. Mary Kershaw knew many facts about Mirium's early years with her aunt and John could add others. Why shouldn't he have what his wife had inherited? If she was alive she would share it with him, wouldn't she? Why not share it instead with his sister? If he didn't, it would all go to the British Government, or the King, wouldn't it? Why should it? This was the chance of a lifetime for them both.

'She kept saying that; kept saying it was mine by right,' Kershaw said doggedly.

'You came to this country as Mr and Mrs Kershaw, claimed it all and no one suspected the fraud?'

'Not until you started poking around. She told me about your visit to the antiques store; all those searching questions over dinner. Then you snooped around this village to find where we lived. That's when Mary began to worry.'

A surprising suspicion began to form in Ben's mind. 'So she told you to threaten me with violence if I tried to see her again?'

'That was after you dropped the comment about my having a licence so I could test the *Duiker*,' Kershaw said. 'Nobody at Marshfield knows about that. It wasn't reported globally, so it was obvious you had been digging further into our affairs. Mary said you had become dangerous and had to be stopped before you found out the rest.'

Waving the revolver suggestively Ben asked, 'What did she mean by the word "stopped"?'

Kershaw licked his lips nervously. 'Look, we couldn't let you destroy our new life over here. Not after what we'd been through.'

'So you obeyed her command like a good boy,' Ben said with a sneer. 'What a good thing Mirium can't see what you've become. After being the cause of her death with your egocentric self-pitying, you're now wallowing in the riches she would have had as an apology from her parents who had given her away like an unwanted puppy. You're despicable!'

In his anger Ben put the revolver at half-cock, which set Kershaw pleading for his life. 'It wasn't me. It was Mary's idea. She said Mirium would want me to have it.'

'You set about trying to "stop" me by sawing through that step, but you made a mess of it like everything else in your life.' Ben's voice grew louder and harsher. 'I was lucky then, but your second attempt left a poor innocent chap in hospital with serious burns, and his family with no money coming in. I'll make sure you pay dearly for that after I've done what I need to on Wednesday.'

'It was Mary's idea,' Kershaw whined again. 'When I refused to do it she threatened to cut off my allowance and turn me out of this house. She owns everything. All the property, all the money, all the investments are in her name. I have to do as she says or I'll have no home – nothing!'

Feeling nauseous after this pathetic attempt at justification, Ben got to his feet again. 'Give her this message from me. She's going to lose more than her ill-gotten gains by the end of the week. If anything should happen to me before then, my solicitor will hand Sir Edwin Lance a letter from me outlining what you've just told me about your criminal activity. He will also send one to Deborah Keene who'll surely be delighted to write your biography instead of that of a man she hero-worships.'

Finally losing control Ben stepped forward and pistol-whipped Kershaw on his temple. 'That's for Chris Peterson's murder.'

Clutching his head where blood now coursed down his cheek, Kershaw panted, 'Peterson's murder? What're you on about? He was killed in that crash.'

Standing over him ready to inflict further pain, Ben said, 'You cut the elevator tab cable to prevent him pulling out of that dive. Did sister Mary force you to "stop" him, too?'

'What? She had a thing about the man. Ready to have a fling with him any time he asked. You're crazy,' he accused trying to sink back in the chair, still clutching his head with a blood-covered hand.

'Are you asking me to believe you didn't sabotage the *Lance* when Chris gave his display, and you're not bent on doing it to prevent me from making the one I'm set to give on Wednesday? Because you can't allow another designer to succeed where you failed. Because you're a spineless loser who can't face up to life.'

'Sabotage?' Kershaw echoed through his pain. 'Everyone knows he blacked out during that dive. It's the official verdict. Accidental death.'

'But I know it wasn't. So does Roger. And so do you, you ruthless sod.'

Kershaw struggled from the chair and headed unsteadily for the telephone, but Ben got there first and smashed it with the revolver to leave the other man gazing wildly around seeking help.

'You're on your own, Kershaw,' Ben snapped. 'As was I when you cut through that step. If I'd broken my neck in falling would you also have called that accidental death?'

Backed against the wall where his outspread hands were making bloody marks on the wallpaper, he shook his head rapidly. 'Not death. Stop him, Mary said. She said give him a warning to go away and leave us alone. That's what it was. Just a warning.'

'And the exploding van; was that just a warning?'

'You wouldn't go. She said you must. That's all she wanted.'

'And all you wanted was to stop the *Lance* from becoming Marshfield's greatest success by putting me out of the picture.'

'No!' he cried wildly. 'You just won't listen.' He suddenly slid down the wall to double over on the floor. 'Oh God! Oh God! It's all going wrong again. It'll never end. I'll never stop paying for letting her die out there alone.'

Ben left him curled into a tight ball, sobbing for his dead wife. He needed medical help, but someone else would have to see to that. A person who hadn't been the target of his avaricious sister's attempts to harm him.

He caught the next green bus back to Lewes deep in thought. He didn't know Mary Kershaw well enough to be certain she wouldn't have a last desperate attempt to silence him, but of one thing he was now certain and it would keep him awake tonight. Kershaw was not the saboteur. Which put Tilbrook back on the list as the front runner.

# TWELVE

After a satisfying breakfast taken before other guests had left their rooms, Ben went by taxi to Marshfield and was relieved to see a security guard at his station outside hangar two. He approached the beefy man beside the huge right-hand door which was still closed, work hardly having started yet.

'Everything quiet last night?' he asked.

'I only began my watch at seven, sir, but when I took over from Alan he said there'd been nothing but a bosky lad wandering around just after midnight. Must've climbed the wire without being spotted. Claimed he did it for a dare. His details were taken before he was escorted out through the main gate.' He nodded. 'Tonight'll be the busy time. Chaps wanting to sneak a close look at the aeroplane, and silly girls wanting to sneak a close look at you.'

'If your colleagues are as vigilant as they were last night a lot of them'll succeed,' Ben said sharply before pushing open the small door giving access to the hangar, deciding he must sleep here tonight. If Hugo's so-called superior security force could miss seeing a drunken boy entering at night for a dare, they'd certainly be fooled by a sober, adult male bent on a criminal act.

Roger arrived half an hour later, by which time the main hangar doors had been opened and the *Lance* towed out to be fuelled up. Having decided on two flights in the morning and two in the afternoon Ben was already in his flying suit ready to take off once Roger was manning the intercom.

'Good lord, Ben, you're eager today,' he said, removing his jacket and rolling up his sleeves. 'You don't look well rested. You should have stayed with us.'

'I want to go up now, and again at noon. Then twice more this afternoon. It's my last day. Tomorrow will be win or fail time.'

Roger shook his head. 'Tomorrow will be all we want it to be. Get up in the air, man, and remind yourself of that.'

As usual, communing with azure eternity lightened Ben's spirits and drove away the anxieties of life on the ground. The intercom was silent. The aerial display had been perfected; there was no need for conversation unless there was an emergency. Ben landed and taxied to the end of the runway before turning ready for the next takeoff two hours later. *Coming down to earth again*, he told himself, knowing he must make Roger aware of what he had learned last night.

When he walked in to the hangar tea had been made and poured in readiness. Beside the trestle table holding the mugs stood Jim Tilbrook.

'Hail the conquering hero!' mocked the Irishman, 'but he appears to have last-minute doubts. What's the problem, Ben? Stage fright? Or do you enjoy firing guns so much you rise at the crack of dawn to have an extra go?'

'Problem with your hearing, Jim?' asked Ben, very pointedly ignoring the Dancing Bear mug and taking up one at random. 'I didn't fire the guns. I'll be doing so this afternoon, so keep well out of range in case I mistake the target.' He sipped his tea. 'Shouldn't the production manager be keeping an eye on production of *Snowbird* with skis . . . or are you drinking your tea here for some specific purpose?'

Tilbrook's eyes narrowed. 'Once you've done your brief flight tomorrow you'll be no more than the company test pilot flying any machine you're told to. Routine, unglamorous work. No more zooming around firing guns and pretending you're a war hero. You won't be such a cocky bastard then.'

Ben gave the hint of a smile. 'Perfect opportunity for you to write an overblown piece à la Deborah Keene about a cocky bastard's fall from grace to send to the rag you used before. Should earn you the same amount they gave you last time.'

'Maybe there'll be no need for that,' Tilbrook riposted, turning away. 'Worldwide newspapers might be full of sensational news, like last time, by tomorrow evening.'

'Jim! You've gone too far,' Roger protested heatedly.

'Sure, but it's a mistake you're making,' came an over-the-shoulder deliberately Irish last word. 'Your friend might so impress the VIPs he'll be offered a knighthood. Sir Ben would make the headlines, wouldn't he?'

There was an awkward silence around the trestle table after
Tilbrook left, the ground crew concentrating on scoffing buns
and eyeing each other expressively. Felix spoke up.

'He's the only man at Marshfield who isn't excited about
tomorrow, Captain. We all know you'll do it; get the *Lance* on
our production line by Christmas. We know it for certain.'

Ben smiled at the young mechanic. 'So do Mr Hall and myself,
Felix. Between us all we'll ensure the *Lance* makes headlines so
high Marshfield will be flooded with orders.'

Everyone cheered up and went out to the aircraft looking for
any spot of oil or dirt to clean from the gleaming silver fuselage
and wings. Roger frowned at Ben.

'You shouldn't rise to his taunts. That's why he does it.'

'I don't want him in this hangar, or anywhere near the *Lance*
for the next few days. And I don't want him anywhere near me.
He's the one, Roger, and he's devious. That just now was another
of his warnings, so I let him know I was on to him.'

After a pause, Roger took him by the arm. 'Let's go in the
office and sit down. The lads won't disturb us there.' Once
settled he frowned at Ben again. 'It's not necessary to make
four flights today. You can't improve on perfection. I want you
to rest instead. You've not been sleeping; you look haggard.
That exchange displayed your edginess, your anxiety about
tomorrow.' He brushed a hand over his brow. 'It's my fault. I
shouldn't have told you my belief that Peterson's flight was
sabotaged. At the weekend you had Povey as the villain, then
it was Kershaw. Now you're saying Tilbrook's out to wreck the
proving flight.'

'He's the only one left on your list of three, Roger,' Ben said
quietly, and related what he had discovered about the Kershaws.
'He admitted to sawing through that step and causing the van to
burst into flames in order to stop me from uncovering their
fraudulent marriage, but he didn't sabotage Chris's flight. Didn't
understand what I was talking about, even at gunpoint.'

Roger looked horrified. 'You meant to shoot him?'

'And face a murder charge and the gallows? Of course not!
But I clocked him with my revolver and reduced him to a
gibbering weakling with threats to bring their criminal deception
to an end at the end of the week. I left him cowering on the

floor riddled with guilt over his selfish treatment of his sick wife. The real one.'

'Oh God, what a hellish business this has become,' cried Roger. 'I wish I hadn't heard Chris say he couldn't move the stick. You wouldn't have pried into their lives and put your own in danger.' He gave a heavy sigh. 'Is there a jinx on the *Lance*?'

'A moment ago you were insisting that tomorrow will be all we want it to be,' Ben reminded him. 'Who's getting edgy now? And if we're talking about looking haggard, have you looked in a mirror lately?'

Before Roger could reply to that the door opened and Julia announced that her brother wished to speak to them both, at once. They had not noticed the Lances arrive and Ben now wondered if they had overheard anything they had said. The office wasn't soundproof.

Hugo was clearly in his most autocratic mood. He began by demanding the reason for such an early flight and why the pilot hadn't fired the guns at the conclusion of it. Was there a fault with the guns? Had there been an aircraft malfunction? Were they having doubts about tomorrow? If they failed to justify their assurance of being ready to display before prospective investors he would . . .

Ben stopped Hugo's diatribe because Roger seemed unable to. 'If you'd pause long enough to allow us to answer, Major, we can justify our claim to be ready to display before anyone, even royalty. I made the early flight because I intend to go up several times today, then have an early night. Tomorrow will be a heavy day for us all, but the greatest weight of responsibility will be mine. Roger and I have worked hard towards getting his sensational fighter the recognition she deserves in spite of the earlier disaster, so we both need a quiet relaxing evening followed by uninterrupted sleep.

'As for the guns, I didn't fire them because the men who affix the targets on the trucks had not had time to do it. You'll hear gunfire at the end of my second run at eleven, and again at fifteen hundred. There's no fault with the guns or the aircraft, and we have no doubts whatsoever about complete success tomorrow.' He took a deep breath. 'Does that answer all you wanted to say? If so, we have things to do, Major.'

Those grey eyes could not register emotions, but Julia's sparkled with something Ben had difficulty in identifying but reminded him of Deborah Keene claiming the woman 'had a thing' about him.

Hugo said, 'I'll put your incivility down to the stress of the moment, Captain Norton, but I must remind you that if you fail to achieve tomorrow what we are paying you to do, your reputation will suffer, as will Mr Hall's, but Marshfield will take the brunt of the failure and may never fully recover. Bear that in mind while you do those things you say I may be keeping you from doing. I'll return in time for your next flight.' With that he clasped Julia's arm to walk from the hangar.

'You took a chance there,' murmured Roger.

'I could have been even more uncivil by suggesting he gives Tilbrook his marching orders if he wants his company to survive.'

'Yes, well . . . If you were serious about leaving early for a relaxing evening and a sound sleep it's the most useful thing you've said today. Go to your secret hotel and do just that. No nocturnal outings with a revolver.'

'Oh, I'm sleeping here tonight. The guards failed to prevent a tipsy boy climbing over the fence last night. Tilbrook will be far more crafty when he . . .'

'Ben, you are not sleeping here tonight. You'll do as you stated, even if I have to take you home and lock you in my spare room until morning. I'll have a word with Felix and the others. They'll not be averse to bedding down here to keep watch with the security man. They've probably planned on that, anyway.'

During his second flight Ben's elation restored his optimism. He fired at the target erected on the side of the trucks and imagined how impressed the VIPs would be when explosive charges placed in the vehicle were set off by the *Lance*'s fire power. His optimism rose further when they went to inspect the targets and found his aim had been spot on. So much for the jitters!

Hugo and Julia walked away without speaking to him, but when Ben made his third and last flight at mid-afternoon Sir Edwin was with them and, to Ben's surprise, Freddie. The Lance family mood was generally enthusiastic and complimentary as they ran through the timetable for the following day. Drinks on arrival for guests. Gathering on the balcony for the aerial display. Introductions to pilot and designer during champagne and buffet lunch, after which they would all go to the hangar for a close inspection of the *Lance* during which both pilot and designer must be on hand to answer questions. In the evening the family would entertain to dinner the most influential guests. The pilot and designer should hold themselves ready to come to Clanford House if called for discussion after the meal.

Ben and Roger had heard it all before but they nodded attentively, as necessary. They were both surprised when Sir Edwin shook them by the hand and offered congratulations on producing such an impressive flight display.

'Completing your aerobatics with the low-level strafe was a brilliant notion, Captain Norton,' he added with a warm smile. 'After my initial doubts on your ability to carry this off I have to admit you are an outstanding pilot. When things settle down and we have a definite idea of how productive tomorrow proves to be, I'll have a chat with you about an idea I have for the future. You're the right man for the job.'

Ben caught Julia's eye. I won't be here for the future, she knows that all too well.

Freddie stayed when the others left, and chatted in friendly fashion for ten minutes or so before shaking hands and wishing both Ben and Roger every success next morning. Ben couldn't help wishing Freddie's social life was not as pointless as Julia's. Unlike his sister, the young racing driver could be a worthwhile person if he broke away from his society friends and allowed his inborn abilities free rein.

Forcing himself to depart from the silver aeroplane in which he would live the greatest twenty minutes of his thirty-two years tomorrow, Ben told Roger he had decided to return to the coach house.

'It's the nearest I have to a home of my own and there'll be a group of journalists outside overnight ready to get pictures of me setting off in the morning, I'm sure. Perfect security guards. If I ask them to prevent anyone from disturbing my sleep that should keep Tilbrook at bay during the night hours.' He did not add that it might be the last night he spent there so he needed to prepare for a swift departure with those of his worldly goods he could carry.

Roger insisted on driving Ben home. He was silent during the short journey. The prospect of leaving this man he had grown close to, despite his vow never to do so with anyone, made him immeasurably sad. All he could do was ensure the *Lance* so captured the interest of men who would invest heavily in the production of the fighter, that Roger would get the acclaim he deserved.

A few spectators had arrived to take up places alongside the wire fence to be certain of the best view, although as all the activity would be in the air it didn't matter where people stood to watch. Ben noticed the security guards were talking to the early birds. He hoped they wouldn't forget to patrol the rest of the stretch of wire as well.

When they reached the coach house they found the wreck of the van had been removed from the yard, leaving just a black smudge on the concrete. Ben supposed the widow up at the manor house must have arranged for it to be shifted. Two or three men with cameras stood talking on the spot where Ben had landed from the fall. They grew aware of the car slowing to a halt and pressed forward to take pictures.

'Get a full night's rest,' said Roger. 'Tell these chaps to wait until morning for you to say anything worth printing. That'll ensure they stay put until then.'

'Oh, there'll be a dozen or more along later.'

'Good. While you were shedding your flying suit I did some checking. Kershaw didn't make an appearance today. I suspect you scared him so much he's gone to the Chelsea flat to join his pseudo wife. Nothing to worry about in that direction. As for Tilbrook, I gave Ray Povey a fiver to go to The Dancing Bear tonight and ensure his colleague imbibed twice as much as usual, with several whisky chasers in addition.' Roger grinned. 'I hinted that it would be in Ray's best interest to make Tilbrook unfit for anything but his bed.'

Ben stared in astonishment. 'You old dog! You have talents I never suspected. Thanks.'

'No, my dear fellow, it's in *my* best interests to relieve you of any worries, real or imagined.' He grinned again. 'You can rid yourself of them after noon tomorrow.'

These words caused another pang of regret, but Ben forced himself to say, 'I'm not thinking of anything beyond that.'

'The road'll be busy from the crack of dawn and I want you there with plenty of time to spare, so I'll pick you up at seven. We'll have breakfast in the canteen.'

'Righto.' Ben climbed from the car.

'I think the Lances should have arranged to send a chauffeur-driven car for you. It wasn't necessary for Chris because he was staying at Clanford House.'

Ben bent to look at Roger through the open door. 'Ah, I haven't done the deed yet. I might merit a car and chauffeur by the time the champagne has stopped flowing. Goodnight, Roger. We'll meet in the morning on the brink of fame.'

Taking the other man's advice to discourage eager journalists, Ben climbed the stairs studying each one before stepping on it and entered what had been his home for such a short while. Two envelopes lay on the floor, which surprised him because he had not given this address to anyone. One was blank but sealed. The other bore his rank and name, along with the full address typewritten on it. There was a hint of officialdom about it so he opened it first after pouring himself a whisky.

The communication – he couldn't dub it a letter – was headed FOSSBECK CAMDEN POLICE STATION and signed by Constable A Frith. In police wordage Ben was informed that a vehicle rented in his name had caused severe injury to Mr James Nunn of Fossbeck, who had been summoned to examine said vehicle to identify why it could not be driven away. Captain B Norton had not been present at the time. Mr J Nunn had given evidence from his hospital bed that it was his opinion that the vehicle had been tampered with in such a way that when he raised the bonnet and attempted to remove a small component an explosion occurred. This was a serious criminal offence which was under investigation by Constable Frith, who asked Captain Norton to report to the station to answer some questions at his earliest opportunity.

Inside the blank envelope was an invoice for the removal of

a fire-damaged transport vehicle from Fossbeck Manor coach house to Fossbeck Camden police station for examination.

Ben took up the telephone receiver and spoke into the little trumpet shape to Henry's mother, asking her to connect him with the police station. It was no more than a room in Frith's house, but it served the village and various isolated dwellings on the outskirts. Mrs Frith said against the noise of small children squabbling that her husband was on his rounds. Could she take a message? Ben simply gave her Kershaw's name and address, adding that the man who had caused Jimmy Nunn's injuries lived there.

Knowing it would be pointless getting into bed before midnight, Ben cooked himself a meal, relaxed in the bath until the water grew too cool, then dressed in pyjamas and sat in his chair with a whisky to read the newspaper one of the journalists had thrust in his hand as he climbed the steps on arrival. He scanned the words but his brain didn't register their meaning because it was focusing on other things.

The printed pages were lowered to his lap as Ben's thoughts of the past held him captive. His father's harshness and derision of scholastic achievements. His rudeness to the young teacher who came to talk to him about the certainty of a scholarship for his son to college and then to university. That night he had rolled a few essentials into a bundle secured by a leather belt and left home to become a soldier. He had never been back; never seen his father again.

The war. The gaining of pilot's wings. The lad who had become the brother he had never had. Betrayal and heartbreak. Yes, it was as cruel as that because their friendship had been so close. Egypt. Lies, sweat and toil. New identity, new attitude, new determination to get where he wanted to be by any means, and never to trust a man again. Stella. Deep, passionate love. Betrayal and heartbreak again; determination never to trust another woman. More sweat and toil bringing mercantile and financial success. The *Lance*. The ultimate professional and personal goal; the perfect opportunity to collect an outstanding debt.

The sound of jeering rivalry outside in the yard brought Ben back to the present. He went to pour another whisky. The outstanding debt would remain unsettled, but he would have tomorrow. It would dim the past. The future was unknown, but tomorrow . . . ah, tomorrow he would be a high flyer and, unlike Icarus, he would descend triumphant.

At 7 a.m. Ben had virtually to fight his way down to reach Roger's car. The crowd of newsmen had grown much larger; the entire yard, driveway and road were filled with cars. Cameras flashed blindingly and voices shouted questions which were lost in the general hubbub and so never answered.

As he pushed through the clamouring throng, Ben was thumped on the back, clapped on the shoulder and deafened with good luck messages, all of which lit the spark of excitement within him that apprehension had kept at bay for most of the night. Roger's car was like a comet with a tail as they drove to Marshfield, but the tail was detached at the gate to wait until eleven thirty when the press enclosure could be accessed.

From then on Ben alternated between excitement and apprehension as the time crept towards noon. Felix and the rest of the ground crew had spent the night in the hangar. Each man assured Ben nobody had approached the aeroplane. The official security guards reiterated that with some huffiness because their efficiency had been undermined.

Ray Povey confirmed that he had seen Jim Tilbrook back to his lodging late last night highly inebriated, and the man had not yet arrived at Marshfield. Ben was not entirely happy about that. He wanted Tilbrook on the premises where he could be kept under observation every minute leading up to takeoff. While he was out of sight he could be up to something dangerous.

Not long after eleven, VIP cars began arriving outside the main building where secretaries waited to take them to join the Lance family for champagne and effusive conversation before gathering on the balcony for the aerial display. At eleven thirty the press enclosure filled to capacity and some enterprising young women who had stolen in with the journalists had to be rounded up and escorted out through the main gate, to much reaction from spectators lined up beside the wire fence.

Ben had been given two flying suits with Marshfield Aviation embroidered on the back and on the right breast. He was instructed to wear one for pre-flight pictures and the display, then, in case oil or dirt marred it, he was to change into the other one in which to mingle with the VIPs. He was more concerned with the *Lance* than his appearance and still wore his old overalls while checking the aircraft thoroughly, particularly the elevator trim tab cable. Once he was fully satisfied, he told everyone save Roger to gather at the rear of the hangar.

The *Lance* had been fuelled up early that morning and towed back in to the hangar, out of sight. Ben wanted to begin his display by emerging into the sunlight like a silver bird and straight into the air. This meant there'd be no photographs before the flight. Hugo had not been told about this change of plan, but Ben was in charge today and planned to remain that way until the sun went down. And that didn't happen until late in the evening in mid-June.

Five minutes before noon he changed into the new flying suit and discovered his hands were shaking. Tilbrook could not have sabotaged the *Lance*, nor could he have drugged the food or tea. How else could he stop the flight from going ahead or disable the pilot?

Roger came up and gripped his shoulder. 'Time to climb in and start her up.'

Their eyes met. 'I'll fly my heart out for you.'

'I know, son.'

Those three words banished apprehension. Sitting in the cockpit and strapping himself in, Ben was already mentally in that other world way above the earth where he was whoever he wanted to be for as long as he stayed up there. He switched on. The propeller began to circle. Roger beckoned forward Felix and his friend Billy, ready to pull the chocks away when Ben nodded.

On the stroke of twelve, thousands of spectators gasped in delighted surprise when the *Lance* appeared like a shining capsule, on the move ready to rise up and head into the cloud-less blue overhead. Their delight increased as the fighter raced and climbed, dived and turned, spiralled or sped past mere feet from the ground. More hearts than the pilot's beat faster on each dive until the *Lance* pulled out of it safely, memories of the former tragedy still vivid.

After twenty minutes of head turning and neck twisting, the fighter disappeared over Pitman Hill. Everyone guessed that was it and Ben Norton would come in to land, but there was a final unexpected thrill. Returning over the hill, bathed in sunlight, the warplane raced low along the length of the airfield producing the sound of gun firing. Next minute, the two old vehicles at the end of the runway exploded with a great roar. Three minutes later the aircraft returned quietly from behind the hangars and dropped gracefully to the ground.

After taxiing to the entrance of hangar two, Ben sat on in the cockpit with the propeller turning, unwilling to bring the flight of his life to an end. His sense of elation was so great tears rolled down his cheeks. He truly had flown his heart out, but it had been done to put Flight Sergeant Jack 'Farmer' Norton finally up where he deserved to be.

He grew aware of someone thumping on the fuselage and looked down on a face smiling broadly even though the cheeks were wet. As if in slow motion Ben reached out to switch off the idling engine and, still lethargic, slid back the hood. At first he was only half aware of a curious noise, but when he climbed out and dropped to the ground he identified it as cheering. Roger seized his hand and shook it fiercely, unable to speak, as the ground crew surrounded them still cheering. They lifted Ben and carried him shoulder high in to the hangar where Felix was pouring beer into the mugs on the table.

During that brief celebration the *Lance* stood unguarded, but it would have been impossible for anyone to approach it without being seen. Ben quaffed beer, further intoxicated by the realization that nothing had stopped him from displaying the country's greatest aerial challenge to warplanes being produced in other areas of the world. Roger was equally overwhelmed by relief amid the jubilant men surrounding them. This was too immense for them to take in after weeks of suspicion, anxiety and sleeplessness.

It was still so when, wearing the second flying suit, Ben walked with Roger to the main office and up the stairs to where the Lances were entertaining the financiers, politicians and senior RAF officers who must surely have been impressed by what they had witnessed.

In that large room, champagne was flowing and tables laden with finger buffet delicacies were being raided several times over in hearty conviviality by guests who had been fired with the enthusiasm of all men who love flying machines. Sir Edwin spotted their arrival and raised his voice to command attention. Into the eventual hush he introduced Mr Roger Hall, designer of the *Lance*, and Captain Ben Norton who had just given a scintillating display of the aircraft's full capabilities. There was polite applause and quiet congratulatory comments.

Glasses of champagne were offered to them and Sir Edwin shook them by the hand, as did Freddie. Then Major Hugo Lance, who had long ago dealt Jack Norton an unforgivable and unforgettable public insult, approached him.

'I've never cursed my blindness as much as I did when you took to the skies this morning. To be robbed of what hundreds of spectators could see was hard going, but I heard your display, and their spontaneous response to it told me you had produced a matchless performance. From initial comments to myself and to my father, it would suggest what you've done is to sell the *Lance* despite all the bad publicity after the crash. Thank you on behalf of Marshfield Aviation, and for justifying my determination to manufacture this superior fighter.' He offered his hand and smiled. 'We've had our ups and downs, Ben, but please accept my sincere congratulations on pulling from the hat a twenty-two carat rabbit.'

Score settled! Pity the Major was unaware of it.

For the next hour Ben and Roger were introduced to those guests who were the most influential, and engaged in such intense conversation with them it was impossible to eat anything or even drink the champagne clutched in their hands. However, they were both intoxicated enough by success, and canapés could wait while vital contacts were being cemented.

Sir Edwin eventually set in motion the next phase and everyone made their way to where the *Lance* still stood. Close inspection of the aeroplane, more questioning of the designer and the pilot. Members of the press had been allowed to gather in hangar two from where they could take their pictures, some posed and others at random.

By this time Ben's senses were spinning beneath the barrage of questions and from the wafting alcoholic breath exuded by men of wealth and influence prone to stand too close to him. He suddenly longed to be alone, perhaps walking along the South Downs, hugging to himself those heights of living before the eventual descent. Someone touched his arm; shook it to attract his attention. He glanced round to see Felix, looking curiously shocked.

'Captain, I need to tell you something.'

'I'll come as soon as I'm free,' he responded wearily.

'No, it's very important, sir. I must speak to you,' the lad insisted.

Ben frowned and excused himself to three financiers trying to learn from him in ten minutes how to fly a warplane. Taking a few steps away from the milling guests he asked what Felix needed to say.

'Oh, Captain Norton, it's terrible. Whatever went wrong?'

Ben found it difficult to concentrate. 'What are you talking about? Spit it out.'

The distressed young fitter said, 'We went out to fetch the targets, sir, and there was a man's body in one of the trucks. It's gruesome to look at. Been broken up by the blast. But we could see plainly that it was Mr Kershaw, sir. You killed him this afternoon.'

# THIRTEEN

Once again a proving flight of Marshfield Aviation's *Lance* fighter had resulted in a man's death, this time the company's production manager. Headlines over the following days recorded facts and pure speculations equally. The Lance family remained incommunicado in Clanford House while fresh sensationalism rocked the company's standing and threatened its future.

Following evidence swiftly volunteered by Jim Tilbrook of enmity between the victim and Ben Norton, resulting in a violent confrontation concerning Kershaw's wife outside the hangars, the detective brought from Scotland Yard to deal with this high-profile case homed in on the man who had caused the trucks to explode, killing the person inside. Hundreds of spectators had seen him firing live ammunition into the vehicles.

A statement from a village postmistress who recalled a man with eyes of slightly different colour, claiming to be South African and asking for directions to the Kershaw home, together with the local constable's wife's report of a telephone call from Captain Norton naming the victim as the person responsible for causing Jimmy Nunn's injuries, confirmed Ben's vindictiveness towards the dead man.

Ben's explanation for his actions simply exacerbated his guilt in DI Moore's eyes, and the detective put him virtually under house arrest on suspicion of murder. He regarded as pure fabrication the story of Kershaw's sister posing as his wife in order to gain money and property left in a will. Ben's own admission of visiting Kershaw's house to charge the man with serious fraud strengthened Moore's case against him.

The sticking point was how Kershaw could have been put in the truck and secured there. The two experts who had sited the explosives an hour before the flight said the vehicles had been empty at that point, and Ben had been in company with a number of people from the moment he had arrived at Marshfield before breakfast until he had climbed into the *Lance*. Moore said he must have paid someone to do it for him.

Ben's persistent demands that Moore should investigate the Kershaws' fraudulent appropriation of the real Mirium's inheritance were each met with the comment that the victim's wife was so demented by grief her doctor refused to allow her to be questioned.

'She's not his wife!' Ben cried for the fourth time during another interrogation on Sunday morning. 'She was the controlling force in that partnership, threatening to stop his allowance and turn him out of the house if he defied her. He was totally subservient to her; tried to kill or badly injure me twice because she ordered him to stop me from probing into their lives.'

'And why did you, sir?'

'Because I received the cutting from South Africa.' He glared at the implacable man. 'We've been over and over that and still you refuse to follow it up. Why?'

'I'm asking the questions, sir.'

'And I'm giving you the answers you don't like, aren't I?' He lost his temper then. 'When I left Kershaw last Sunday he was in a psychological frenzy of self-blame for his wife's death. If that woman had told him to lie in that truck and thereby scourge himself of his guilt, he would have obeyed. I've come to see that's what must have happened. He had every opportunity to do it, and it explains the whole thing.'

'To you, maybe, but not to a trained mind like mine. There are a number of holes in that theory.'

'Then, for God's sake concentrate on filling them in and stop trying to make a villain of me,' he raged. 'Yes, I fired the guns, but I didn't put that pathetic bastard in the truck. You bloody know I couldn't have. Interrogate Mary Kershaw, who seems to have both you and her doctor well and truly eating out of her hand, too. Can't your trained mind see that?'

Later that day Ben listlessly munched a sandwich in the large flat he had believed would be his home for the next few years, until Julia had begun tracing his past with the help of her influential friends, making it too difficult for him to continue living there. She had not been in evidence on Wednesday; it had been an all-male affair. She was probably incarcerated with the rest of the family riding out the latest disaster to hit them. The faint hope that she might consider being the prime suspect for murder might be enough to destroy the myth of Captain Ben Norton, without dragging up the past, soon faded. She was more likely to be encouraging her friend 'Mirium' Kershaw in her feigned grief in order to prolong Ben's ordeal.

Gloomily gazing at Icarus and sharing with him a fellow feeling, Ben heard a knock on his door. Moore again with more questions! He stayed in his chair until Roger shouted through the letter box that he had come bearing gifts. The man's friend-ship at this present time made the prospect of leaving him in the lurch increase the sense of betrayal that bothered Ben during wakeful hours in the night.

'Sitting in semi-darkness living off sandwiches isn't good for you,' Roger said, switching on the small lamp as he entered. 'I've brought a pork pie, tomatoes, a cucumber, a jar of pickles and a large Dundee cake. Get out some plates, and your two tumblers for the whisky I also have with me. While we eat I'll give you some interesting news.'

Not for the first time Ben thought how different his life would have been with a man like Roger for a father. His appetite returned and he began on the pie, asking through a mouthful of pork and pickles about the interesting news.

Roger waved his fork bearing a large pickled onion. 'There's been no official statement but everyone's talking about it. You know how village gossip soon mounts. It's my guess Constable Frith's mother has spread it around. She lives with them, and the police station is simply their front room so it's easy for her to overhear what he says on the telephone.'

'So what's everyone talking about?' Ben urged impatiently.

'Kershaw's sister has vanished, along with enough money and assets to allow her to live well for a considerable period.'

Anger rushed through Ben. 'I told Moore umpteen times she couldn't be trusted. That doctor's as big a fool as our Scotland Yard man "with a trained mind". When was her absence discovered?'

'This afternoon. The doctor's not really a fool, Ben. He saw the Kershaw woman on Wednesday evening when she'd been told about her "husband's" death and thrown a very believable fit of grief. He was called, gave her a bromide and told Moore's sergeant she wasn't to be disturbed until he considered she was able to cope with questioning. Next day, his father had a boating accident which left him critically ill, so Dr Dean and his mother spent the past three nights in Brighton at his bedside.

'The neighbours believed Mary Kershaw was still in a distraught state so thought nothing of the drawn curtains and silence in the house until one woman decided it was time she offered palpable sympathy and knocked on the door. When no one appeared after heavy banging she went for Constable Frith, fearing the bereaved woman had done away with herself. He forced an entry and found all her clothes gone and the rooms stripped of valuables. She'd obviously made her getaway in the dead of night.'

'And that bloody fool Moore has been refusing to disturb her!'

'He's made up for it now. As soon as this was discovered he contacted the Yard and had a couple of lads sent to the antiques shop premises.'

'And?' demanded Ben, his pulse quickening further.

'She'd cleared out the storeroom and taken a number of items from the showroom judging from all the empty spaces. They forced entry to the Chelsea flat in the hope of finding the stuff there, but they were too late. Traces of sawdust and other packaging were found on the carpet but she had got well away with it by that time.'

Ben's mind was buzzing with excitement. 'She must have left Fossbeck on Wednesday night, then organized everything from the Chelsea flat. I'd guess she's shipped the valuables abroad under a false name, and probably sailed with them. When the bank opens tomorrow the police will discover she's emptied the strong box and the cash account.'

'Most likely,' Roger agreed. 'Some lady!'

'Some cold-hearted, greedy bitch! She won't get away with it. The first time she attempts to sell an antique they'll be on to her, even if she waits a few years to do it.'

'Trouble is, Ben, nobody's sure of what was originally in those empty spaces, so by the time the authorities have established without doubt that she's not Mirium Kershaw and there's not another will which names Mary as the beneficiary, the valuables will be safely stashed in a place very hard to find.'

Ben slumped in his chair. 'The real Mirium must be turning in her grave. She had a rough deal from life one way and another.'

'So had Kershaw,' Roger mused quietly. 'It would have been a devastating blow when the *Duiker* crashed killing those on board. Twice. In spite of the court's verdict he would have been haunted by the dread of being responsible for the loss of those lives. Had his design been flawed? I know what such doubt can do; I know what press condemnation can do to a man with such doubt. But I can't imagine how anyone could handle that and the knowledge that his weakness had led to his wife hiding the severity of her illness for his sake and dying prematurely, because of it.'

Ben's far wider experience of life governed his next words. 'He handled it by pretending his sister was his wife and enjoying the, fruits of that criminal act. He handled it by causing me to fall twenty feet on to a concrete yard. He handled it by fixing my van's electrics so that I'd be severely burned and unable to spoil his life of luxury paid for by the devotion of the dying Mirium.' He gave Roger a straight look. 'The man was lily-livered. Don't waste sympathy on someone like him.'

Roger responded thoughtfully. 'You have a pretty low opinion of your fellow men, my friend.'

Ben chose not to comment further on that. 'Now I know that woman's skipped it, I've got the complete picture. A week ago I left Kershaw jibbering like an idiot, terrified by my knowledge of what he'd done. He would have then gone to Chelsea and poured out his fear to Mary. Once she realized her good life was in jeopardy she began planning her own getaway and how to rid herself of him. On the night before my flight she and Kershaw returned to the Fossbeck house where she worked on her brother's psychiatric state to convince him he must surrender his own life to assuage the guilt of killing Mirium; and what better way than to do it so that the man who intended to take away all his darling wife had so wanted him to have would be held to blame and punished.'

Roger slowly lowered his knife and fork. 'That's a wild theory, Ben.'

'You think Moore's theory that I paid someone to secure Kershaw in that truck so I could kill him with an armed aircraft is less wild?'

The older man sighed. 'I don't know what to think. The whole business is too bizarre to understand.'

'My pretty low opinion of my fellow men allows me to,' he said quietly. 'I can no more prove my belief of what happened than Moore can prove his, but Mary's action will send him in a new direction which should take the spotlight off me and, by association, off Marshfield and the *Lance*.'

'Mmm, ironically, Ben, Kershaw's death has kept the *Lance* in global headlines far longer than without the scandal element, which is actually a good thing. Each time they speculate further they always describe your spectacular flight that ended with a realistic attack on supposed enemy vehicles. That's excellent publicity for the aircraft.'

'No such thing as an ill wind,' Ben said dryly.

Tardily recognizing the darkness of Ben's mood, Roger topped up his friend's glass. 'You'll get through this, lad, and so will Marshfield. Last time, the press damned the fighter and the designer; had me down as a killer. Four months later all the superlatives are being used about the *Lance* and the pilot. I'll drink to both, then start on this fruit cake.' He raised his glass. 'Here's to my creation and to the pilot who has given his all in forming the perfect combination. Long may it last.'

Ben was too choked to respond.

On Monday morning Ben woke late after a fitful night's sleep and made tea. The heatwave was over. Grey skies and drizzly rain added further gloom to his outlook, and the day stretched emptily ahead. Nothing to do; nowhere to go. Moore had stipulated he must not leave the village, but he'd no wish to. On Thursday and Friday the coach house had been under siege by those he dubbed the press gang, as ready to condemn as they had been to praise. No one there now, but when the news about Mary Kershaw's midnight flit broke they'd be back in force, wanting an interview.

Drinking his tea, Ben stared at the latest pile of letters Roger had brought from Marshfield last night. Fan mail, he called it.

Boys and young men wanting him to help them become pilots; girls and gullible older women wanting to meet him secretly. In the act of sweeping them into the waste basket Ben noticed an envelope bearing a German stamp and pulled it out in curiosity. It contained a polite request for an interview in connection with a book about aerial warfare 1914–18 that Dieter Kramm was engaged in writing.

> I wish to include a profile of Oberleutnant Gustav Blomfeld, one of my nation's great pilots of that conflict. I have read in newspapers that you flew with Captain Christopher Peterson who is credited with shooting our hero from the sky. Information has come into my possession that has some question on this. As Captain Peterson is not now able to answer this question I would appreciate a meeting with you to make everything clear. I will be happy to attend any place at any time. I shall be in England for when you make the brave flight of the *Lance*.
>
> I give you the telephone number of my hotel in Lewes. Please to contact me there when I will explain more for you.

Ben read and reread words that chilled him. What information could have emerged to cast doubt on something that had happened fourteen years ago and consequently entered the history books? Who was Dieter Kramm? A scandalmonger? A writer well-respected in his field? A zealous young German of the growing breed, strutting around wearing armbands and boasting of a pure race?

Reading the letter once more Ben knew there really was such a thing as an ill wind. It was about to blow through Sussex and do nobody any good.

This seemed to be borne out when the telephone rang and Sir Edwin's secretary announced that Ben was required at Marshfield. A car would be sent to collect him at ten o'clock, which would give him just enough time for a brief breakfast before dressing suitably to face Lance's contempt. An inner voice told him to send the car away with a message along the lines of 'go to hell', but he had never refused to face the inevitable and there were a few things he'd be happy to get off his chest to that family in return.

At Marshfield, work in hangar one was continuing as usual. That lucrative contract for the modified *Snowbird* would keep the workforce busy well into the following year. Inside hangar two the silver *Lance* stood alone like a Christmas toy the recipient had lost interest in. The sight added to Ben's sense of a loss as painful as the other two he had suffered. Yet it wasn't the aircraft that had betrayed him. Fate had done the deed, at the very pinnacle of their triumph.

Walking the long corridor to Sir Edwin's office, Ben now lost all inclination to wrangle with this group of unlikeable people. They had also suffered a loss. An obscene killing had put paid to their hope of success for a second time. He just wanted to terminate his contract and put the whole episode behind him.

The well-proportioned office was full of people. Hugo, Julia, Freddie and Roger sat around the impressive desk, on which was an ice bucket containing several bottles of champagne, and six glasses. Ben pulled up short on seeing the smile of greeting on Sir Edwin's face.

'Ah, Captain Norton! Thank you for coming to join us to hear some splendid news after what has been a most unpleasant few days. Please take a seat.' He waved a hand at the empty chair beside Roger. 'Now you're here I can reveal that first thing this morning I received notice that approval has been given to release funds enough to cover the purchase of five *Lance* fighters, with the probability of five more at a later date.'

Against the vocal excitement, he added, 'The Ministry feels that the death of Mr Kershaw was a separate issue which should in no way detract from the superb potential of the warplane desperately needed by the Royal Air Force.' He nodded at Freddie to start filling the glasses. 'The Directors of Marshfield Aviation congratulate Mr Hall who designed the *Lance*, and the pilot who displayed the aircraft with such flair it won us a double contract against all odds.' Ben and Roger sat in stunned disbelief until four glasses were raised in a toast. The truth then sank in and they got to their feet gripping each other's hand so tightly it compensated for their inability to speak. They had done it. *They had done it*!

\* \* \*

Although a great deal of champagne was drunk that morning, that it was also a business meeting was not forgotten. An additional workshop would have to be erected and fully fitted with the machinery necessary to make modern warplanes. Additional experienced men must be employed to work on aircraft more complex than any they had built before. The engineers, fitters and maintenance crew already familiar with the *Lance* would be promoted to train others in as short a time as possible. And so it went on, with enthusiasm from everyone except Julia and Ben. He was watching her watching him. She was unlikely to do anything here and now, but when had she planned to make her move?

Eventually, Sir Edwin drew Ben aside from the group around the desk to speak to him privately, but Julia's eyes were still on him. 'Now, sir, I have a proposition to put to you,' the courteous knight said quietly, 'but first I must know how things stand between you and that somewhat uncouth police officer who has been making your life unpleasant without the slightest justification.'

This was the first indication that any member of the Lance family had had the least concern over the serious charge made against him. Amazing what difference a lucrative order for the fighter he had displayed so impressively had made! Ben shrugged. 'I left my flat and the village to come here today, but nobody chased after me blowing whistles so I'm hoping he's instead set on making life unpleasant for the Kershaw woman, who isn't his . . .' He paused, deciding to leave press reportage to inform this family who Mary was. 'I can't deny I was guilty of causing the man's death by firing at the trucks, but I had no idea he was there.'

Sir Edwin nodded. 'Exactly! Not the slightest justification. If he continues to refuse to see sense I'll get the company's legal man on it: Charles Manning's a canny fellow. He'll sort things for us.' He smiled with rare warmth. 'Let's get down to business. You will, of course, test all five *Lances* as they're completed, but I also want you to fly our superb warplane at air shows not only in this country but all over Europe. Aviation is the future. Every major nation is striving to produce the fastest, biggest, most commercial flying machines to gain world monopoly in the air. We have to show them we're a company to be reckoned with.' His smile broadened. 'If you fly the *Lance* before thousands at air shows the way you did last Wednesday, we'll have our competitors seriously worried.'

He gave a quiet, triumphant chuckle before putting his hand on Ben's shoulder to guide him back to where lists were still being made by Roger and Freddie, at Hugo's suggestions. 'Time for a spot of lunch, gentlemen.' He turned to include Julia. 'Come along, my dear.'

Her eyes narrowed. 'I have another engagement, Father. The company there will be better suited to my taste. They amuse me.' She walked from the office without another word, her parent and brothers seemingly so used to her rudeness it passed over their heads.

It was late afternoon when the car returned Ben to the coach house. More alcohol had been drunk at lunch; more expansive plans had been outlined. Ben's non-participation had apparently also passed over the heads of his hosts. In truth, he was in a state of confusion and uncertainty. Sir Edwin had dangled a hugely enticing carrot before him when he had believed it to be cut and run time.

He wanted that carrot very much, but it was being offered by a set of people ruled by rigid standards. They could effortlessly erase John Kershaw from their lives as if he had never socialized with them and held a senior position in their company, so what would they do on learning they had offered to welcome into their charmed circle a country yokel who had been considered unfit for the title 'an officer and a gentleman' by one of their number fourteen years ago? A high flyer who had lied and postulated before the now blinded man, knowing he would not recognize how he was being duped and humiliated. And as for the rest they did not know . . .

Too tense to sit, Ben gazed from his window listing his options. He could emulate Mary Kershaw and disappear overnight. He could decline Sir Edwin's offer and sever connections with Marshfield Aviation. He could dangle at the end of Julia's string until she decided to speak.

If he did a moonlight flit it would suggest his guilt to DI

Moore, who would set up a police search for him. If he took the second option he would still not be free to leave until the case of Kershaw's death was solved, and how would he live in the meantime? In both instances Roger would suffer a painful breach of faith and friendship, which Julia's subsequent revelations would intensify.

At that point he deleted braving it out until she told what she had learned about John Benjamin Norton. If he wanted that carrot, if he wanted to fly the *Lance* in numerous displays before enthralled crowds as Marshfield's official test pilot, if he wanted to stay on the glittering pinnacle he had reached on Wednesday for a year, maybe two, before coming down to earth, he had the means to silence Julia. The big unknown was how many people she had broached in order to uncover the truth about him. Could they also be silenced?

Then there was the wild card, Dieter Kramm, and the information he claimed to have come across about that unforgettable morning in 1916. As the sun began its downward path Ben was driven to surrender to those memories.

They set out on one of the early morning raids that had earned them the sobriquet The Skylarks, to strafe enemy aircraft on the ground then return for breakfast. Flying wingtip to wingtip with the rising sun behind them they were surprised to see four *Fokker*s approaching, unaware of their presence due to the solar glare that blinded them. Sitting ducks! They grinned across at each other and exchanged the usual hand signals of their attack plans.

These brought immediate success, the victim zig-zagging helplessly towards his distant home territory with the tail plane hanging loose, the wings full of holes and a wheel strut severed. After that they engaged in a deadly aerial melee until a second Hun left the arena belching smoke. With numbers now even, Ben and Chris selected their individual prey with significant nods.

Veering from the *Fokker*'s heavy fire, Ben's sharp gaze spotted an image painted on the fuselage and realized with the familiar fear and excitement that he was engaging in battle with Gustav Blomfeld, son of a farmer, whose wizardry in the air had put him up with the German aerial giants despite his humble background. This renowned pilot's history had long ago prompted a fellow feeling in Ben, so meeting him in a one to one contest of skill and daring demanded also an element of respect for his adversary's reputation. No schoolboy novice, this! It was soon surprisingly clear that Blomfeld was returning that respect during the lengthy tussle that followed. Their aircraft suffered heavy damage though each stayed aloft.

It suddenly became evident that Blomfeld's gun had jammed and he looked set to make a run for home. Banking sharply, Ben closed on him and fired a long burst across the *Fokker*'s nose. When the German reacted, he jabbed his gauntleted finger vigorously towards the ground a number of times until Blomfeld nodded acquiescence and began his descent to French soil where he would be taken prisoner.

Ben circled until the aircraft touched down in a field beside a canal, just four miles from a military post from where an armed escort would soon arrive to pick up their famous captive. Blomfeld climbed wearily from the cockpit and pulled off his helmet. Looking up, he gave a salute of gratitude for sparing his life, which Ben returned without hesitation . . . If that gun had not malfunctioned he might very well have lost the battle. His own life had been spared this morning.

Suddenly, a great rush of air rocked his aircraft as another dived past so close it almost clipped his wing. A stutter of gunfire, then Blomfeld's body twitched and fell beneath a hail of bullets. Seconds later more gunfire. The *Fokker* burst into flames which engulfed the dead pilot and reduced his body to an obscene black effigy. Then Chris was flying alongside again, laughing and giving a triumphant thumbs-up.

Ben moved from the window to pour the remaining whisky from the bottle Roger had brought last night, but the spirit failed to ease his memory of that vicious act and what had followed. Shaking with rage, he had turned for home where he could express his horror and disgust at what his friend had done as soon as they were on the ground. He had had no opportunity. Climbing from the cockpit Chris had announced loudly to anyone within earshot that he had shot down and killed the ace, Gustav Blomfeld.

Cheering men had surrounded him and carried him shoulder high to the officers' mess to celebrate in the usual robust fashion.

Ben had remained in his seat unable to accept what was happening. The man he loved as a brother, would defend with his life in battle, had deliberately killed an unarmed enemy who had surrendered, then had attacked the aeroplane sitting in a field to suggest it had been shot down by him. And he had just boasted of that lie before severing the bond between them by departing without a backward glance.

Chris Peterson's exaggerated fiction became fact in headlines for a dispirited British public to read. The latest RFC hero was nominated for promotion and a Military Cross. A week later, Major Hugo Lance invited Lieutenant Peterson to become a member of the elite squadron he commanded. When Flight Sergeant Jack Norton was pointed out as Peterson's partner in a series of daring raids, cold grey eyes flicked a glance at him before refocusing on the man of the moment. Major Lance only dealt with commissioned officers.

The former friends had encountered each other on the base on a night just before Christmas when no one else had been in sight. Chris had laughed off Ben's heated charge of military murder with a countercharge of weakness in having to leave a tougher man to finish the job off for him. Ben had lost control and seized him by the throat. Luckily, the red mist of vengeance had cleared before it was too late. Chris had then departed to Hugo's peerless squadron and they had never set eyes on each other again.

Ben had kept silent through loyalty to the corps and his country, but he followed Peterson's charmed life through society magazines and gossip columns, waiting for his moment to wipe the slate clean. He had been deprived of that satisfaction, and more had been added to it over the past four months. Had the time now come to smash the bloody thing and concentrate on a future without ghosts from the past?

When night closed in, Ben was still in the grip of restless indecision, hovering on the brink of a beckoning future yet questioning the cost of grasping it, when a loud banging on the door startled him. Almost midnight. Who would come calling at this hour?

Two men, both strangers, but Ben guessed the chubby one in police uniform was Constable Frith. The other, dressed in a dark suit, was surely a detective. Ben frowned. They could not have come to arrest him for Kershaw's murder. DI Moore would delight in doing that himself.

'Good evening, sir. I'm Detective Sergeant Travis from Scotland Yard, and this is Constable Frith of the local force. May we come in?'

'If you give me some idea of why you're here, I'll consider your request,' Ben returned crisply. 'Otherwise you can stay out on that step John Kershaw sawed through to cause me to fall on to that concrete yard and possibly die.'

Travis took that calmly and continued in neutral tones. 'My Inspector has sent us to inform you of some new evidence regarding the death of Mr Kershaw.' He said again, 'May we come in?'

Ben stood away from the door and they were soon side-by-side well into the flat. He didn't invite them to sit and took up a position facing them, where he got to the point immediately.

'So what's this new evidence? As DI Moore hasn't come himself, I'll venture a guess that it doesn't incriminate me in any way and he now has bigger fish to fry.'

The large detective was unfazed by Ben's attack. 'In pursuance of his duty, when questioning the local populace, Constable Frith spoke to a gentleman who had watched the air display you gave, sir. He fell ill that same night, so was not aware of developments regarding the unfortunate death until he had recovered somewhat and heard the gossip.'

'Get to the point!' Ben snapped.

'The gentleman witnessed Mr Kershaw walking out to the trucks holding a small sack, and thought he had stationed himself in the vehicle for professional reasons. The witness recognized the deceased as a member of staff at Marshfield Aviation, you see. Of course, he was unaware of how your display was planned to end, so he thought nothing more of it until yesterday when he was feeling better and learned of the tragedy. He immediately told Constable Frith, who took down his statement.'

Thank God for village gossip! 'So there was no question of Kershaw being forced into that truck at gunpoint by somebody I had paid to do it?'

'We had to consider every possibility, sir.'

'It wasn't!'

'There's more, Captain Norton,' Frith said. 'Several reports have come in which change things to your advantage.'

'Change the emphasis,' the detective amended, scowling at the man he treated as a bumbling village bobby. 'The Pathologist was able to report that the victim had swallowed enough slow-acting barbiturates to cause death, and shards of glass in the wrecked trucks suggested he drank from at least two whisky bottles before the vehicle exploded.'

Ben smiled sourly. 'I told DI Moore that Kershaw was in a manic state of self-blame over his wife's death, and his sister would have used that for her own ends.'

Travis continued blithely. 'Until we make contact with Mrs Kershaw, who will be able to describe her husband's behaviour last Wednesday, we must ask you to keep us informed of your movements, sir, but DI Moore says you are free to travel anywhere within the British Isles.'

Losing his temper, Ben said, 'Have it your own way, but to ask Mrs Kershaw about her husband's behaviour you'll have to contact the Archangel Gabriel.' He walked to open the front door. 'Goodnight.'

Another hour passed while Ben considered his situation. Moore had lost interest in him, so that problem was out of the equation. Until Mary Kershaw was apprehended and had revealed what had passed between herself and her brother, the truth about his death would remain unsolved. Had Mary driven him to end his life, or had Kershaw seen it as a second act of sabotage? Prevented from disabling the *Lance*, and having twice failed to put the pilot out of action, had his deranged mind seen only one means of destroying the aircraft's success? It very nearly had, along with the future of the man who had blasted the trucks with bullets.

Reviewing his options anew, it seemed he was left with just one. He must silence Julia, along with anyone she had used to gain information about him.

Henry Jenks' uncle drove the village taxi to the entrance of Clanford House. 'Did you want to get out here, Captain?'

The Lagonda was inside one of the garages, but that didn't mean Julia was at home. Ben had telephoned to ask if she was at Marshfield and had been told Mrs Peterson had not arrived with Sir Edwin and the Major that morning.

'Please wait while I check if anyone's there.' Ben handed over enough to settle the fare so far. 'If not, you can take me on to Marshfield.'

The young maid opened the door after he had tugged the bell pull twice, and goggled at him as she had at his previous visit with Roger. The mistress was at home but did not wish to be disturbed, he was told.

'She'll want to see me.' He signalled the taxi to leave, then stepped past the girl in to the large entrance hall. 'Tell her my business is urgent.'

He had expected to be made to wait long enough to anger him, but Julia came down the staircase almost immediately, dressed for riding.

'So the mountain decided to come to Mohammed,' she commented coolly. 'Let's talk in here.'

She led the way to a sitting room furnished in green and gold. The sun breaking through after a light shower highlighted elegant ornaments placed to advantage on beautifully polished furniture. Lance personal wealth very obvious.

Ben fired the opening shot. 'Pity you can no longer go riding with your friend Mary Kershaw now she's absconded with her illicit treasures.'

She failed to rise to that. 'Why have you come, Ben?'

He was surprised by her use of his first name. 'I've had a letter from a German author who's compiling a book on aerial warfare 1914–18 in which he plans to include a profile of Gustav Blomfeld. He wants to talk to me and to you about some information he's been given regarding his countryman's death at your husband's hands. I'm in the unenviable position of having witnessed it. My response to him will be governed by what you say to me now. You have no idea how much will depend on that.'

'I believe I have.' She had paled slightly and sank on to the nearest chair. 'You actually witnessed it?'

'Chris and I were on one of our early morning raids.' Ben perched on the arm of a matching chair. 'Whatever you have discovered about me from your friends in high places, whatever threat you think to hold over me, I can counter in equal measure, believe me.'

She gazed at him trancelike. 'Please tell me what you know.'

Unprepared for her yielding attitude he hesitated, so she continued.

'What I found out about you is that you were never in Hugo's squadron, and there was no Benjamin or Benedict Norton on the list of commissioned officers in the RFC during those years. That's all. I've hinted and threatened you merely in an effort to force you to reveal your reason for claiming to know Chris but adamant about speaking of the war. I knew instinctively that you were hiding something connected to him; something you were determined Deborah Keene wouldn't uncover and use in her biography. I couldn't coax it from you with the usual feminine tricks, so I tried threats of exposure. That's all they were. Threats without substance.' She then added urgently, 'Who are you, and why is this German author keen to speak to you about Blomfeld's death?'

Still fazed by her surprisingly sincere manner, and by the news that she had discovered nothing about Jack Norton, Flight Sergeant, Ben said, 'I'm Marshfield's test pilot and shareholder who stands by my belief that the past is better left where it belongs, Julia.'

She got up, taking an envelope from her pocket. Ben also stood so they were eye to eye, intrigued by her behaviour.

'At the end of the war several former members of Hugo's renowned squadron came here to see him. One of them was Captain Christopher Peterson MC. He was tall, good-looking, full of charm, unmarried and a national hero. I fell in love with all that, knowing nothing of the man himself. Father and Hugo saw the commercial value of marriage with a pilot idolized by the British public, so it became a whirlwind romance with national and international publicity.

'The dream lasted three months. Overnighting in a country inn he climbed into the bed of the landlord's daughter instead of mine. When I realized this was to be the pattern of our union, his womanizing stopped hurting and I found lovers of my own. I also made arrangements to prevent Chris from accessing Lance money. Father paid him well enough, but it clipped his wings to rely on his wage to fund his amours.' She walked to look through a window, still holding the envelope, and spoke in a faraway manner Ben had never heard from her before.

'Last year Hugo met the niece of an old squadron friend and a hesitant relationship began. She was a lot younger than he, but her brother had also been blinded during the war so she knew how to cope. Hugo had all the natural reservations about disablement, but she swept his defences aside and they discussed a tacit engagement with marriage after the *Lance* had been publicly launched.'

She swung round to face Ben, her eyes now glassy. 'Two weeks before that event we learned she was pregnant by Chris. They had been conducting an affair without any of us being aware of it.'

Ben frowned. Chris and Hugo had been wartime colleagues, brothers-in-law and business partners. What betrayal of a blind man!

'We understand Jessie's family turned against her. Hugo was devastated. Chris wanted a divorce; I said no. He had never wanted a child with me. I didn't see why a little bastard should take his name. Those two weeks were hell, the only thing holding us together being the launch of the *Lance*. That success would earn Chris a large sum and personal distinction that would make it easy for him to find employment with another company. He knew his life and career with Marshfield would be over after the proving flight.

'He grew morose and uncommunicative, shut himself away in his study or bedroom when he was in the house. I imagined he was planning his new life – with or without Jessie.'

'Without her? He felt no responsibility for the child?'

'I don't know,' she replied heavily. 'He had never before taken a sexual conquest seriously. He was too selfish.'

'But surely the tension between you all was remarked on by everyone at Marshfield.'

'Probably, but they would have attributed it to the importance of the coming proving flight. The *Lance*'s success.'

Into the short silence Ben said, 'But someone was determined to destroy that triumph, and succeeded.'

'Yes.'

She offered the envelope that had her name written on it. Further intrigued, Ben knew he was being invited to read the letter inside and drew out a single page.

> *I loved Jessie deeply. I loved flying. But something has come*
> *at me out of the sun and finally clipped my wings.*
> *Forgive me.*
> *Chris*

The icy chill of realization coursed through Ben. He had seen it happen. He had watched Chris fly deliberately to his death four months ago. Looking up swiftly, he said, 'You knew all along why the *Lance* crashed!'

'It was propped up on my dressing table when I returned here as a widow that day,' she acknowledged quietly. 'You are the only other person who has read it, Ben.'

'Why?' he asked, still badly shaken by this revelation. 'Why me?'

She sank back on the chair she had left. 'Because on the day before the proving flight Chris had received a letter from Dieter Kramm asking for an interview regarding the death of Gustav Blomfeld. I've told you all this in absolute confidence, trusting you never to repeat it. It would create a scandal, break Hugo's heroic spirit and cause great harm to the family and the company. In return, I want you to tell me why a letter from this German should drive Chris to commit suicide in such a way.' She took a deep breath. 'Please Ben, I need to know.'

So he told her.

# FOURTEEN

B en brought the *Lance* in to land at Marshfield with the sensation of coming home which had been growing stronger with every return to base. After three days of the kind of high-powered living he found so fulfilling, he was today very happy to be coming down to earth.

His display at the air show had been one of its highlights. It had prompted men from Australian and New Zealand forces to arrange a date on which to visit Marshfield for an in-depth demonstration of the *Lance*'s abilities, with a view to consider persuading their governments to release funds to add the fighters to their own fleets.

Taxiing to the small hangar reserved for him, which had been erected after general production of the warplane had begun before Christmas, Ben climbed down to greet Felix and his team. Smiles all round, followed by the enthusiastic discussion over a mug of tea they always had on his return. They were delighted by his news of Anzac interest in the *Lance*.

'It's not a cert; not yet,' Ben warned, 'but they looked to be the kind of men who don't easily take no for an answer.'

'Like you, sir,' joked Felix.

'Oh, I've had to on a couple of occasions,' Ben told him, a slight cloud passing over his exuberance as he put the Dancing Bear mug on the table. 'I'd better get up to the Major's office and give him a swift run down of these past three days before he has time to realize you all heard the news first.'

Backed by their chuckles, he went to the changing area and had a quick wash after stripping off the flying suit, then he pulled on grey flannels and a thick white pullover, with a silk scarf at the neck. He gave his reflection a fey smile.

'You look the part, like a natural, young Jack Norton.'

When he reached Hugo's suite of offices the secretary told him there was a visitor with the Major. 'In fact, he came to see you, Captain Norton. I'll buzz through and say you're back and in my office.'

'Who is it, Jenny?'

'A German gentleman. The Captain's here, sir,' she added for Hugo's ears. 'Yes, I'll tell him.' She smiled at Ben. 'You're to go in.'

Hugo had hospitably offered tea – there was a tray bearing two cups and saucers on his desk – but he looked strained and the atmosphere seemed less than cordial. Dieter Kramm fixed Ben with the same expression he had worn eight months ago when he had arrived uninvited at the coach house, annoyed that Ben had failed to telephone his hotel to arrange an interview.

'Good afternoon, sir,' Ben said to Hugo, wondering what was going on here. 'Another visit to England, Herr Kramm?'

'It is always very pleasant to come in the time of spring, Captain. The blossoms on trees, the yellow flowers everywhere, the so green grass of this small country. But I also bring gifts.' He waved a hand at a small package on Hugo's desk.

'Herr Kramm has gone to the trouble of personally presenting us with copies of his book which, he told me, makes reference to Gustav Blomfeld's death in action,' Hugo said tonelessly. 'He has apparently recorded in print a statement made by a French bargee which casts doubt on Lieutenant Peterson's account of what happened.' He fixed Ben with his sightless grey stare. 'He says he spoke to both you and Julia on the subject before publication. Is that so?'

God damn the man! 'Briefly, yes. I told him we were at the time battling against twice our number so I was too busy to watch what was going on elsewhere. And, as you're aware, Chris never spoke to his wife about the war, so Julia couldn't comment on the incident.'

'And the Leutnant Peterson cannot dispute the evidence of the Frenchman,' Kramm put in.

'Hardly evidence when it's given fourteen years after the event, Major, which must cast doubt on his accurate recollection of that day,' Ben put in smoothly. 'Herr Kramm was too young to fight in the war or he would know, as we do, that things are never clear-cut in the heat of battle, especially in the air when the sky is the battleground. However, it's very generous of him to bring us copies of his work, in which there'll surely be more than one account by German pilots that would differ from those given by pilots in books published over here.'

Ben gave Kramm a tight smile. 'Nobody can question the courage of men willing to give their lives for their country, no matter how many authors seek to increase sales by introducing controversial ramblings of elderly French peasants after their heroes have died.' He walked to open the office door. 'Good day, Herr Kramm. Enjoy the daffodils and the very green grass of this small country on the way back to yours.'

Hugo heard the door shut and spoke sharply. 'Why wasn't I told about this? I was caught on the wrong foot in my ignorance.'

Ben sat in the chair Kramm had vacated and adopted a casual tone. 'He turned up last June wanting interviews. I was under house arrest, Julia was in retreat with you all at Clanford House. Not the right time to throw his Teutonic weight around, but he turned up demanding comments from us both on a yarn some Gallic bargee had come up with, almost certainly after being offered payment.'

'And that yarn was?'

Knowing Hugo would not let the matter rest, Ben extemporized. 'The old boy reckons he saw Blomfeld land beside the canal under his own steam. A stand of trees then blocked his view, but he heard gunfire and an explosion, smoke spiralling above those trees, suggesting that he was not actually shot down, as Chris claimed.'

Hugo flushed with anger. 'You were there with him, I'm now told.'

'You were told on the day you invited Chris to join your elite squadron, Major Lance, but the information failed to interest you then.'

It silenced the other man for some seconds, but his inborn impulse to command soon returned. 'I'm fully interested now, Captain Norton,' he snapped, 'and I ask you if there's any truth in this suggestion.'

Staying true to the pact he had made with Julia, Ben said, 'I was too busy fighting my own battle to be in a position to answer you on that. In a war every army has its heroes. I believe in letting them rest in peace.'

He then began his verbal report on the success of the past few days with the possibility of a contract with Anzac air forces. At the end of this he left the office in greater accord with Hugo, having further established his senior position at Marshfield Aviation.

Roger looked up from his drawing board and greeted Ben warmly. 'Hail the returning hero! I've already heard the news about a visit from Antipodean airmen.'

Ben laughed. 'How fast gossip travels in this place! Well, I've done my job. The rest is up to you when they want the finer details.' He leaned towards the drawing board. 'How's the *Snowbird* conversion to floats coming along?'

Waving his arm at the drawings pinned there, Roger countered with, 'I've done my job, the rest is up to you, lad. How good are you at landing on water?'

Studying Roger's work keenly, Ben said, 'Only time I tried, the Camel sank beneath me and I had to swim for it. I'd better beg a few lessons with the Navy before I try it again.'

They discussed the conversion designs for some time, then Roger confessed he had ideas for a *Lance Mark 2*, which kept them deep in discussion for another half-hour. Only then did Roger mention the inquest into the death of John Kershaw, which had been held while Ben had been away.

'The absence of a suicide note but evidence that he had swallowed enough barbiturates to lead to death when combined with whisky, guided them to a verdict of death while his mind was disturbed. It was attended by Detective Inspector Moore, Constable Frith and the solicitor involved in the search for Mary Kershaw.'

'That could take years. Until they find her, the house at Fossbeck and the Chelsea flat can't be sold.'

'Yes, but who'd get the money if they were?'

'I'd do my damndest to get a whack for Jimmy Nunn's family.'

At that point the imperious blare of a motor horn sounded outside the office block. Glancing from the window Ben saw the Lagonda drawn up by the main entrance and guessed why he was wanted.

'I think I'm being summoned, Roger. I'll see you tomorrow, on the dot.'

Even as he slid on to the cool leather seat Julia burst into agitated speech. 'Hugo just blasted my ear about the visit of that Kramm creature, who told him of our meetings last year which I'd kept quiet about. My dear brother claims because he's blind we treat him like a child by keeping things from him.'

'That was your decision, not mine,' Ben pointed out. 'Before I got there, Kramm had informed him of what he'd included in his profile of Gustav Blomfeld. I kept to our bargain and repeated that I'd seen nothing of the encounter between Chris and the German ace, but the damage had been done.'

'Damn the bastard! Can we stop distribution of his book?'

'And indicate our concern over the bargee's claim; arouse a whole nation's interest in what actually happened that day?' He put his hand over hers resting on the wheel. 'This has occurred throughout the ages. Some professor, some historian, some ardent young student rewrites history, putting imagined words into long dead mouths to support their beliefs. Kramm's book might cause a flurry of response from German diehards, but it'll soon die down. As the book is printed in their language there'll be few readers in this country, but any collectors of accounts about warrior heroes who decide to buy it will treat with British scorn the years-old memories of an ancient French bargee which were doubtless revived by a handful of banknotes.'

She was silent for a moment or two, gazing with sadness at him. 'But it's true, isn't it? Chris riddled with bullets a man who had honourably surrendered.'

'Yes.'

'How can you be so relaxed about it?'

He read it as an accusation. 'My dear girl, you've known the truth for only eight months. I've been haunted for fourteen years by what I witnessed, how much he had relished it, how easily he relinquished our close bond. You healed my wound on showing me his letter. By deliberately flying into the ground he had finally faced up to his guilt and atoned. It's time to leave the tragedy where it belongs. In the past.'

Giving a small sigh, she started the car. 'If you say so.'

As it purred its way to the main car park where his own sporty model had stood for three days, he registered her spangled tunic with black velvet trousers and coat.

'Where are you off to tonight?'

'Dinner at Fossbeck Manor Hotel.'

'With your usual madcap crowd?'

'No. With you.' She cast him a warm glance. 'If we're going to relegate our pact of silence to the past we can take our complicity in a new, more rewarding direction, can't we? I'll drive you to the coach house and wait while you change into clothes more suitable for Fossbeck Manor.'

Ben considered what she had hinted at. Did he really want a closer relationship with her? Then he shook his head. 'You can drive yourself to Clanford House and change into clothes more suitable for The Dancing Bear and meet me there at seven thirty. I'm not a champagne cocktail kind of man. You already know that.'

Bringing the Lagonda to a halt, she gave a Mona Lisa smile. 'I look forward to learning a lot more about you, Ben.'

Within limits, he thought, sliding from the luxury vehicle. Certainly not why he had served time in a Cairo prison. That was another issue very definitely best left in the past.